More to Give

AN ANCHOR ⚓ ISLAND NOVEL

ALSO BY TERRI OSBURN

More to Give

AN ANCHOR ⚓ ISLAND NOVEL

TERRI OSBURN

Montlake
Romance

Text copyright © 2014 Terri Osburn
All rights reserved.

Published by Montlake Romance, Seattle

www.apub.com

Amazon, the Amazon logo, and Montlake Romance are trademarks of Amazon.com, Inc., or its affiliates.

ISBN-13: 9781477826041
ISBN-10: 1477826041

Cover design by Georgia Morrissey

Library of Congress Control Number: 2014909728

Printed in the United States of America

For Mom

CHAPTER 1

The last time Callie Henderson had laid eyes on Sam Edwards, he'd been naked and nodding off on the pillow beside her. The pillow that a mere week earlier had belonged to Callie's husband, who'd died in a fiery crash while on a lovers' tryst with another woman.

A woman who just happened to be Callie's best friend. And Sam's wife.

Now, six years later, Callie stood outside his office door, struggling not to toss her breakfast. Closing her eyes, she took a deep breath for courage, and tapped three times on the solid wood door marked HOTEL MANAGER. Three steady knocks. Full of confidence and determination.

Fake it till you make it, Callie, she thought. *You can do this.*

A muffled baritone answered from the other side. "Come in."

Moving on pure adrenaline, Callie turned the stainless-steel knob and stepped through. She wasn't sure what to expect, but Sam's failure to glance away from whatever he was reading felt dismissive, and they hadn't even begun this encounter yet.

Clearing her throat, Callie traveled the four steps it took to reach Sam's desk. She kept the greeting formal. She was here for an interview, after all. "Mr. Edwards."

If he recognized her voice, Sam gave no indication. "Have a seat, Ms. Henderson."

Not so much as an eye roll in her direction. Callie reminded herself this was a job interview and not a long-overdue reunion. She tamped down the ridiculous notion that she was being insulted.

And then Sam did look her way. His brows drew together as he stared at her, as if piecing together a puzzle. Callie held her breath. She could see the moment when recognition dawned. His eyes went wide before he looked back down at the résumé on his desk.

"Calliope Henderson?" he asked.

As Callie wasn't sure what, exactly, he was asking, she lifted one brow and nodded in the affirmative. He could be asking if she was indeed the potential project leader for the renovation of the Sunset Harbor Inn, or he could be wondering why her last name wasn't Wellman, as it had been the last time they'd seen each other.

Until she knew for sure, Callie remained obtuse.

Sam leaned back in his chair, crossed his arms, and narrowed his blue-gray eyes. The intensity of his glare sent a flutter of apprehension up Callie's spine, but she held firm. She had done nothing wrong here.

"Your real name is Calliope?"

"That's right," she said, ignoring the temptation to chew on her bottom lip.

The glare continued, accompanied by a twitch in Sam's solid jaw. Callie could hear the ticking of the crystal clock occupying the left corner of Sam's desk. As if a time bomb had been set in motion. Before this interview could blow up in her face, Callie sought to defuse the situation.

"Calliope is my legal name, but I've been Callie all my life." She wasn't about to clear up the last-name issue until he asked.

She didn't have long to wait.

"And Henderson?"

"My maiden name. I returned to it after . . ." She hesitated. Saying the words was still difficult after all these years. "After my marriage ended," she said.

Another silent pause, then Sam leaned forward, shoving her résumé to the side. "I don't like surprises, Callie. Nor do I like being manipulated."

Before defending that statement, Callie asked, "Could I sit down, please?"

Sam nodded, and the moment her bottom hit the seat, Callie knew she'd made a mistake. At five foot five, Callie wasn't the shortest woman, but she'd been built with long legs and not much of a torso. Which meant when she sat down, her eye level was significantly lower than Sam's and gave him the more powerful position.

Then again, he was the hotel owner in control of her future. He possessed the power whether Callie sat or remained standing.

Scooting to the edge of the chair, she straightened her spine. "I'm not sure how submitting my résumé and then accepting your offer of an interview is in any way manipulative. Regarding the surprise, I wasn't sure you'd remember me." Callie managed to maintain eye contact, but barely. "It's been a long time."

The tic in Sam's jaw sped up. "You were my wife's best friend," he said. Callie waited for him to mention their more intimate connection. He didn't. "Of course I remember you."

The weight of their shared history, mostly painful for them both, hung in the air like the dust on a dirt road on a dry summer day. This was exactly what Callie had hoped to avoid. Six years was long enough for two adults to put the mess of betrayal and bad decisions behind them.

It wasn't as if they'd betrayed each other.

"I honestly never meant to deceive you," she said. "It's been more than five years since I went by the name Wellman. The information on that résumé is who I am now—a professional hotel renovator specializing in boutique hotels—which I believe is what you're looking for."

Though he didn't smile or extend a metaphorical olive branch, Sam's shoulders did appear to relax. Slightly.

"You're definitely qualified for the position," he said. "Your credentials are impressive, especially for someone who's been in the business for such a short time." Callie hadn't embarked on her current career until three years ago, having gone back to school for her hospitality and design degrees after Josh had left her with nothing.

"Which is why you're here," Sam continued. The *but* was coming. Callie could hear it in his tone.

"Sam," she said, then caught herself. "Mr. Edwards—"

"But I'm sure you understand why this wouldn't work."

"I don't understand at all," Callie said, panic thrusting her out of the chair. "There's no reason we can't work together." This job was the jewel she needed to take her career to the next level. She'd assisted in four hotel relaunches in the last two years, and in every situation, the manager above her had taken all the credit.

Credit Callie deserved.

If she could be the person at the top, Callie would finally receive the recognition she'd more than earned already. And, more important, without this job, she'd have to move back in with her mother.

Sam shook his head, sliding her résumé into an empty file folder. "I'm sure you'll find another opportunity."

"Sam, please." She leaned on the edge of his desk, uncaring how desperate she might sound. "I can do this. Let me prove it to you."

Sam buttoned his suit coat as he rose from his chair. Callie had forgotten how tall he was. With shoulders wide enough to block the sun beaming through the window behind him, Sam stood nearly a foot over her. "Your abilities are not the problem here."

"Then what is?" she asked, desperation turning to anger. How dare he take this away from her. After she'd come all this way. When she was the perfect person for the job.

The stubborn man had the nerve to head for the door, as if showing her out. "My apologies for the inconvenience."

He could not be serious.

"Sam," Callie said, then fell silent, waiting for him to look at her. Once he did, she let her desperation show. "I *need* this job. Please."

Any hope of leaving Sam's office with her dignity intact had gone out the window the moment he'd dismissed her as a candidate for the position. There was too much on the line to let pride get in the way.

If only he'd give her a chance.

Squeezing the bridge of his nose, Sam lingered near his office door, eyes closed and head down. Callie feared he might be contemplating how to physically throw her out without facing an assault charge.

Then he dropped his arms and strolled back to his desk, unbuttoning his navy jacket as he returned to his seat. "Are you prepared to take lead on a project of this size? I realize you've only ever assisted to this point."

A spark of hope ignited in her chest. "I am completely prepared. I assure you I would not have submitted my résumé if I wasn't positive I could handle the job."

Sam studied Callie with narrowed eyes, then returned her résumé from the folder to the center of his desk blotter. With a pinched expression, he dropped his gaze to the story of her short but substantial professional life. Without another word, he pressed a button on his phone.

"Yes, Mr. Edwards," came a voice through the speaker.

"Yvonne, could you page Owen? I need him to show Ms. Henderson to Peabody Cottage."

"Yes, sir," said the disembodied voice.

With a blank expression, Sam said, "Yvonne at the front desk will take care of you. Come back tomorrow morning, and we'll get your paperwork completed. I assume you've had a long trip."

Callie wanted to hug him, though that would clearly be the worst thing to do in this situation. Still, she could feel the smile splitting her face. Instead of taking the hint and heading for the exit, she remained in place.

"Thank you," she said. "I promise you won't regret this."

Sam looked skeptical and a bit annoyed. "I'll see you tomorrow morning, Ms. Henderson."

⁓

Nothing like having your past show up unexpected and unannounced to ruin a Monday morning. And then, against his better judgment, Sam had welcomed it to stay. What the hell was he thinking?

He was thinking Callie looked desperate, and the stupid white knight in him, which he'd thought had been buried long ago, had ridden to her rescue.

A muscle ticked in his jaw as Sam stared unseeing at the financial reports on his desk. He should have put Callie Wellman—Henderson now, he reminded himself—back on the ferry the minute he'd seen her. If only she wasn't the best person to turn the Sunset Harbor Inn into a premier boutique hotel.

He'd reviewed countless résumés, and none reflected the expertise and experience Callie possessed. Unless her résumé was exaggerated, which he doubted. Callie wasn't the type to embellish.

Back when they'd known each other, she'd been the most honest person Sam knew.

Certainly more honest than his wife had been.

And then there were the glowing references. Sam had investigated every job on which Callie had participated in the last two years. Every supervisor had been happy with her work. And the images he'd found online of the finished products had been the final proof he needed.

Which meant he'd made a solid business decision. His problem with the situation was more a personal one.

Ms. Henderson had changed more than her name over the years. The Callie he remembered would have apologized for wasting his time and trudged to the door with her metaphorical tail tucked between her legs. Sam had never understood how Callie and his wife had become friends in college. They were complete opposites.

Meredith had been strong and willful, ambitious and selfish. She'd treated Callie more like a servant than a friend. Where Meredith was tall and bold, Callie had been petite and quiet. Sometimes Sam wondered if Meredith hadn't kept Callie around to make herself look better, more powerful, next to Callie's natural meekness.

But then there'd been the other reason.

Dragging himself out of the past, Sam contemplated the woman he'd just hired. That hadn't been the meek, unassuming Callie in his office this morning. The golden-blond hair was shorter. Edgier. Her chin had never dropped, and she'd held his eye throughout the encounter. The burgundy suit had been all business. A stark contrast to the baggy jeans and well-worn T-shirts of the woman who'd followed his wife around.

But the eyes were the same. Ice blue framed in long lashes. Even without makeup, Callie had been pretty. Today she'd been gorgeous.

The phone on Sam's desk buzzed, interrupting that inappropriate thought. Pressing the intercom button, he said, "Yes, Yvonne?"

"Ms. Parsons is here for your meeting, sir."

Sliding the reports back into the blue folder he'd pulled them from, Sam instructed Yvonne to send in his visitor.

Willow Parsons, better known as Will around the island, barreled through his door with a large cup in her hand. "Thank God you keep good coffee around this place."

A wealthy heiress from up north who'd arrived on Anchor under unusual, and still somewhat mysterious, circumstances nearly two years before, Will Parsons ran the newest business in town, Destination Anchor: Weddings and More (the "more" being anniversaries, reunions, and any other destination event a tourist could want.) The success of the endeavor would rely heavily on the hospitality offered around the island, while at the same time, the hotels would count on Will to bring clients their way.

All of which meant Sam made time in his schedule whenever Will requested a meeting.

"Good morning to you," Sam said as Will dropped into the chair Callie had occupied, then tossed a backpack onto the seat next to her. "Make yourself comfortable," he added.

"I hope your Monday is going better than mine," Will said. She was wearing her usual outfit—jeans, oversize sweatshirt, clanging bracelets, and combat boots. Sam seemed to be the only business owner on Anchor Island who actually dressed like one, though he'd been happy to learn that Will took the time to polish up when dealing with clients.

"Mine could be better," he said. "What's so bad about yours? Anything I can help with?"

"You already have." Will held her cup higher. "I dropped my coffee getting out of the car and had to stop myself from licking the gravel to get the caffeine fix." Sam wasn't sure how to respond to that. Will squinted. "That's a disturbing visual, isn't it? Sorry about that."

"No problem," he said. "But you might want to see someone about that addiction."

Will waved his words away. "It wouldn't be so bad if Randy hadn't cut me off cold turkey. Expects me to drink decaffeinated." The snort that accompanied those words was less than ladylike. "Says I'm too wound up with the new business and my system needs a break." With wide eyes, she leaned forward. "You know what I need?"

Sam shook his head in the negative, silently agreeing with Will's significant other but opting not to say so aloud.

"Some damn caffeine."

In the short time he'd known her, Willow Parsons had been a laid-back person. Calm. Rational. He wondered where that woman might be this morning.

"So?" she said, "how did the interview go? Is Calliope your girl?" Will's right foot began to bounce. "Hard-ass? All business? Or laid-back and easygoing?"

He debated how to answer. Considering the Callie he'd hired this morning wasn't exactly the Callie he'd known six years ago, Sam wasn't sure what she'd be like to work with. Maybe he should have thought of that *before* he'd given her the job.

"Yes, she seems to be the right person for the position. Her résumé was enough to convince me she's capable of transforming the Sunset into exactly what I want." With a casual shrug, he added, "I'm sure you two will get along fine."

"You think?" Will asked. "You could tell that from one short meeting?"

Tiptoe around this one, big guy.

"It's the impression I got. And she goes by Callie."

9

Will sat back, dropping her shoulders. "That's a pretty name. Where is she staying?"

"In the Peabody Cottage across from the inn. The proximity made sense." Sam folded his hands on his desk. "I'm guessing my new employee is not the only reason you called this meeting."

"Oh," Will said, dropping the bouncing foot to the floor. "Right. Well, it does sort of cross over. How long did you plan for the renovation of the Sunset to take?"

"I'm not sure." Sam had waited to hire and start the renovations until the main tourist season was over, which was why he was hiring Callie at the end of September. "I'm sure we'll reopen in plenty of time for spring."

"That long?" Will asked. "Any way you could make it sooner?"

The twitch in Sam's jaw that had begun during Callie's interview returned. "How much sooner?"

"Christmas."

Less than three months? They didn't even have a solid plan in place. The delivery of new furnishings could take longer than that. But Will wouldn't be asking without a reason.

"Why?" he asked.

Scooping the backpack into her lap, Will removed a file folder before dropping the bag to the floor. "I have interest in a Christmas wedding. Seventy-five guests. They want cozy, upscale but friendly. The mother of the bride used the word 'boutique.' That's what you're going for with the Sunset, right?"

That was exactly what he was going for. An event that size would fill the inn to capacity. A hell of a way to kick off a reopening.

"Are we talking Christmas Day, the week of, or earlier in the month?"

"They're looking at the weekend before. If you don't think you'll be open by then, I think the Starfish will work—"

"We'll be ready." This was too good to pass up. Whatever it took, the Sunset Harbor Inn would be renovated and ready for business by Christmas.

"Are you sure? I can't book them in and find out a month before the wedding the hotel won't be ready."

"I'm sure." Will held Sam's gaze for several seconds, as if determining whether to believe him. He schooled his features to hide his annoyance.

"Good," she said, breaking the silence. Will slid the folder back into her bag and rose from the chair. "I'll need some kind of info to share with the client. Some idea what the finished hotel will look like, as well as details about the accommodations and banquet facilities."

"Once Ms. Henderson and I have a plan in place, I'll have her contact you for a meeting." Sam stood and rounded the desk. "Is next week soon enough?"

"I can probably put the client off until then." Will hesitated near the office door. "Are you sure you can turn the property around that fast?"

Pasting on his most confident business smile, Sam said, "The Sunset Harbor Inn will be renovated and open for business before Christmas. I guarantee it."

CHAPTER 2

The Sunset Harbor Inn was going to take at least six months to renovate. If Sam wanted the place open for business by spring, they would barely make it. And that was likely with several workers putting in long hours.

Callie had brought two suitcases with her, the plan being that her cousin would bring the rest of her belongings in a couple of days if she managed to land the job, and she dropped them in the cottage that would be her home for the foreseeable future. Peabody Cottage was like a dream, with walls of windows and furnishings that looked as if the place had fallen right out of a magazine.

But she didn't take much time to admire it, as she was anxious to see the hotel. After switching from her interview clothes into something more comfortable, Callie headed across the narrow street. From a distance, the building didn't look half bad.

Upon closer inspection, her estimation changed.

The entire exterior surface of the hotel was composed of worn, faded shingles barely covered by chipping paint. Repainting them would be time-consuming, since the old paint would need to be scraped off by hand before anything new could be applied.

Based on the size of the building, the outside alone would take several months. The front had to push a hundred feet long. A covered porch ran down the midsection, and two large gables held down the ends of the building, making it appear as if two wide towers had been built, then connected by a long center addition.

As was common in these low coastal areas, the entire structure hovered two feet off the ground, which required latticework around the bottom to protect the exposed pipes and duct work from anything that might want to nest underneath.

Regardless of its condition, the place had charm. Old rockers dotted the long porch, and two were occupied near the middle, where a couple of older gentlemen looked to be playing a game.

"Hello," Callie said, approaching the men. She hoped to gain some insight into the hotel from current guests before stepping inside to assess the place for herself. "How are you today?"

"We're playing checkers," one of the men said, not bothering to look Callie's way. "It's your turn, Olaf. Don't be taking all day."

"Don't get your waders in a bunch. I'm thinking."

"I knew I smelled something."

"Shut up, Bernie."

Neither man lifted his eyes from the checkerboard during the exchange.

"Are you enjoying your stay at the Sunset Harbor Inn?" Callie asked.

The man called Bernie finally looked her way. "We don't *stay* here," he said, then squinted his pale blue eyes. "Who are you?"

If they didn't stay at the inn, why were they playing checkers on the porch?

"I'm Callie Henderson. I'm here to help with the renovation of the hotel." She stepped closer to the men. "I'm sorry. Did you say you aren't staying here?"

"Why would we stay at the inn when we live on the island?" the one addressed earlier as Olaf asked.

So the two older gentlemen were natives. They should know something about the place.

"My apologies. But if you're natives, then you must know the inn well. What do you think of the place?"

Two heads turned her way, one covered in wiry, salt-and-pepper hair, the other looking nearly bald beneath his tan fishing hat.

Bernie, the owner of the salt-and-pepper hair, did the narrowed-eyes thing again. "We don't think of the place. It's a hotel, like all the others on the island. If you want to know something about it, walk inside and see for yourself. We're trying to play a game here."

Callie had always thought these quaint little island towns were supposed to be filled with friendly, welcoming people. Bernie and Olaf disabused her of that notion. Maybe island life wasn't going to be the idyllic adventure she'd hoped for.

"Right," she said, backing away from the makeshift checker table, which was a weathered brown barrel. "I'll let you two get back to your game."

Neither man bid her farewell, but she thought she heard one of them grunt. Lovely.

Callie halted in front of the entrance. The white door, flanked by two long, narrow windows, looked solid, if in need of new paint. Callie could only hope the inside was in better condition than the outside.

As she stepped into the lobby, hope went out the window.

A dated, wood-paneled counter sat to her left. The top was Formica and straight out of the seventies. A dim lamp glowed from the left end against the wall, while dirty, ancient ceiling light fixtures cast a dingy glow over the area. The walls were beige, which was a good neutral color, but the finish was flat and dull. Rollers would have to be applied here as well.

The one redeeming quality of the lobby was the beautiful staircase directly across from the door. Though faded by the high-volume foot traffic endured by this sort of establishment, the hardwood treads would definitely be a keeper. The solid oak railing, with its simple white spindles, looked promising as well.

Feeling a bit better about things, Callie waited several seconds for a clerk to arrive at the desk. A chime had sounded as she'd entered, due to the bells attached near the top of the door, and she assumed the sound could be heard wherever the current clerk on duty might be hiding.

But no one came. Odd. Maybe the hotel was already closed for the season. Though she'd spotted several cars in the parking lot, meaning something was going on inside. Several more seconds passed in silence before Callie heard a rumble in the distance.

It was coming from the stairs, and it was getting louder. By the time the source of the thunder bounded from the first landing, Callie had braced for impact.

"Oh," said the young man who'd landed on the lobby floor with a thud. "Hello there."

The boy—Callie guessed his age at no greater than eighteen—was tall and thin, with a sweep of dark hair over his forehead and bright green eyes twinkling with youthful exuberance. Whoever he was, this person stood in stark contrast to the cranky old men outside.

Thunderfeet rubbed his hands on the front of his skinny jeans, then awkwardly ambled his way behind the counter in his bright red Vans. "How can I help you?"

"I've been hired to handle the renovation of this facility. Do you always bound through the hotel like that?" she asked. "I was worried a herd of elephants was about to stampede me into the carpet." The carpet that was ugly, dated, and in dire need of replacing.

The young man stuttered as his eyes shifted between the stairwell and Callie. "I heard the bells and thought you were someone else. I was expecting my friend Lot."

Callie blinked. "You have a friend named Lot?"

"It's a nickname," he offered, as pink crawled up his neck to the tips of his ears. "We go to school together. Well"—he stumbled again—"*went* to school together. We both graduated this past spring."

So her age estimate had been correct. "And what is your name?" she asked.

"Jack," he said, stabbing a hand in her direction. "Jack Barrington."

"Nice to meet you, Jack." Callie accepted the handshake with a smile. "Perhaps we could refrain from charging along the stairs going forward?"

As she'd been talked down to by more than one boss while working her way through the hotel ranks, Callie had determined long ago she would never do so when she was in charge. Be firm? Yes. Run a tight ship? Absolutely. Treat employees like crap? Never.

"Yeah. Sure. I can do that." Jack looked ready to do anything Callie requested, if the goofy look on his face was any indication. She'd expected him to point out her office, but he only stared silently.

She raised her eyebrows and received a similar look in response. She'd forgotten young men weren't the best at picking up cues. Something many of them never outgrew.

"I intend to look around the property, but could you direct me to the manager's office?"

"Oh. Yeah." Callie wondered if all of Jack's responses started with these words. "It's right there," he said, pointing to a door to the left of the stairs marked PRIVATE. Quieter feet were definitely going to be a must.

"Thank you," Callie said, taking a step toward the office.

"But it's locked. I have the key behind here somewhere." Jack disappeared behind the counter, and the sound of rustling papers filled the air. "Here it is!" he exclaimed, returning again, a bright orange keychain of what looked like braided leather dangling in the air. A large, tarnished key hung from the gaudy piece of craftwork.

"Good." She took the keychain between two fingers. "Thank you."

Once again, she didn't make it far before Jack stopped her. "I should warn you. Things in there might be a bit . . . messy. Cheryl, the last manager, wasn't real happy about being let go." Jack shrugged, his shoulders nearly touching his ears.

Callie valued organization. Required it. Dread created a knot in her stomach, and she could feel the first flames of heartburn inching up her esophagus. With a deep breath, she closed her eyes and thought positively. She'd have had to set up the office in her own way regardless of the condition in which she found it. It wasn't as if she needed to have it finished within a day. She had plenty of time to whip this hotel into shape.

"I appreciate the warning," Callie said. "I'm sure it'll be fine."

With that, she crossed the small space and unlocked her new office door. This was the first step to her new life. The realm from which she'd lead her first renovation project. With renewed enthusiasm, she pushed the door open and stepped through.

"Holy mother of God," she uttered. Cheryl hadn't been unhappy when she left. She'd been downright pissed.

~

Sam had spent the last twenty-four hours debating how he would inform Callie of the new shortened time frame for the project. Not that he was worried. He was the boss, she his employee. Her job was to complete the tasks assigned.

But less than three months was asking a lot. He knew that. Sam had given so much focus to renovating the Anchor Inn, the larger of the two properties he'd inherited three years ago upon his uncle's passing, that he'd ignored the Sunset Harbor Inn for too long. The smaller hotel had been his uncle's first purchase back in the seventies, and he'd shared his love for the place with his nephew during the summers Sam spent on Anchor Island.

Those visits were the few positive memories Sam had from his childhood, filled with adventure and affection, two things he hadn't received at home. He'd dreamed of the day his uncle would say, "Sammy boy, I'm going to keep you here with me. You don't have to go home ever again."

But that day never came, and the island wasn't the same without Uncle Morty. Anchor had been the setting for the memories, but Morty had been the one who made them. Without him, this remote speck of dirt felt more like a weight around Sam's neck, keeping him from chasing bigger game. Putting his mark on larger, more prestigious properties.

But for now that weight couldn't be dropped, so Sam shook off the bitter irritation and focused on what lay ahead.

Like convincing Callie Henderson to turn a ramshackle seaside inn into a contemporary but cozy boutique hotel before Christmas.

Correction—*inform*, not convince.

Sam was staring out the window behind his desk, watching two seagulls fight over something on the sand, when Callie stepped into his office.

"Good morning," she said, stopping inside the door. "Yvonne said I should come in."

"Yes," Sam said, returning to his desk but waiting for Callie to take a seat before settling into his own. "I take it your paperwork is complete?"

Callie nodded. "Yes."

"Good. Fine." Sam cleared his throat, then took a sip of his black coffee. "After our meeting yesterday, I spoke with the new wedding coordinator on the island."

"The island has a wedding coordinator? That's excellent." Callie crossed her legs and leaned forward, causing her navy blue skirt to ride high on her thigh. "I hope we have a solid relationship with her. Weddings are the perfect business for a boutique hotel."

"Yes," Sam said, tugging on his suddenly too-tight tie. "I'm glad you say that. She has a potential event for the Sunset Harbor Inn, and I told her we would take the business."

Callie sat back. "Good. A wedding would be a great way to kick off the new opening next year."

Sam winced, then mentally slapped himself for the reaction. "Actually, it isn't next year."

Head tilted to one side, she asked, "The year after? That's pretty far out to book an event. Oh, I took the liberty of examining my new office yesterday. I hope you don't mind."

He'd have preferred she waited for him to show her around but took her enthusiasm as a good sign. Since he hadn't been to the inn in several months, he was anxious to hear her assessment.

"Not a problem. I hope everything was to your expectations."

Callie hemmed a bit. "Well . . . not exactly. I don't believe your former manager left on a positive note."

Cheryl hadn't done anything to give Sam the impression she'd been unhappy. She'd thanked him for the opportunity, admitted she was ready to move on to something else, and bade him farewell. As she didn't live on the island, but rather over on Hatteras, he hadn't encountered her since.

"What gives you that impression?"

Ice-blue eyes narrowed. "Based on the condition in which I found her office. Plus, it's the impression I got from Jack."

"Jack?" Sam asked, trying to place the name.

"Your front desk clerk? I expected you to be familiar with the staff."

Another area in which he'd been lax when it came to the Sunset. An error he would not repeat. "Cheryl handled the hiring. What exactly did Jack tell you?"

With one brow lifted, Callie said, "Let's say Cheryl wasn't as amicable about terminating her position as she might have seemed. When I walked into the office yesterday, it looked as if it had been ransacked by angry marauders. I managed to collect things into somewhat manageable piles, but it could take me weeks to get things organized."

They didn't have weeks to focus on an office when they needed to renovate the entire hotel before the holidays.

"I'll send Yvonne over to assist you, but we need to get started on the plans and set things in motion. The wedding I mentioned earlier is not next year or the year after, it's this Christmas."

Several emotions danced across Callie's features as his words sank in. Sam recognized doubt, confusion, and disbelief. He hadn't expected to see anger.

"Are you saying the Sunset Harbor Inn has to be completely renovated into a top-of-the-line boutique hotel in less than twelve weeks? Have you set foot inside the building lately?" She was up now, pacing in front of his desk. "The entire exterior needs repair and a new coat of paint. That alone would take longer than you're requesting."

"Ms. Henderson—"

"For heaven's sake, call me Callie."

He didn't like the informality, but, as they did have a history, it was ridiculous to maintain the charade. "Fine. Callie—"

"I don't think you understand what you're asking. The inside isn't much better than the outside. The carpet is old, stained, and smells in some areas. Every room has to be redone. And a boutique hotel does not have cookie-cutter, uniform rooms. Each will need its own theme and design. Don't even get me started on furnishings."

She stopped abruptly, bracing her hands on the front of his desk. "This can't be done."

Sam held his temper. Regardless of their past, she was still his employee, and he'd hired her to do a job. A job she now claimed was impossible.

Granted, the timeline was being altered, but *nothing* was impossible.

"Are you finished?" he asked. "Perhaps you could sit back down and continue this conversation rationally." Sam used a tone that communicated this was an order, not a suggestion.

"Fine." Callie regained her seat. "I apologize, but surely you understand that what you're asking is too much. We'll have to let the wedding coordinator know that the Sunset Harbor Inn simply is not an option for this Christmas."

"Last I checked, Ms. Henderson"—Sam reverted to formality to make a point—"I am the owner of the establishment in question. And I say it will be ready by Christmas. If you're not the person to make that happen, I'm sure I can find someone who will."

Nothing like letting arrogance and ego bite him in the ass. Sam had no other qualified candidates and doubted anyone else would accept this challenge. If Callie walked, he was screwed.

But she didn't know that.

Callie gritted her teeth, holding his gaze as if determining whether he was serious. Exactly how desperate was she? Not that he wanted to use that desperation against her, but he would if necessary.

"This is going to cost you," she said. "Everything will have to be a rush order. Overtime labor. My own overtime." She lifted her chin. "And I won't have time to wait for your approval on every decision. I'll need a high level of autonomy to get things done."

The idea of giving up any level of control went against Sam's nature. But this was his fault for having given up so much already where the struggling inn was concerned. He'd delegated and let the hotel wither, if Callie's summation of the place was any indication. If he expected her to pull off the renovation in the time he was asking, then Sam had to compromise.

"Done."

He took the glimpse of surprise on her face as a small victory. She'd assumed he couldn't be flexible. She'd been wrong.

A new determination filled her eyes. The look hit him in the chest. Hard.

Then she smiled, and that hit him even lower.

"The Sunset Harbor Inn will be a five-star boutique hotel in time for your Christmas wedding," she said. "I guarantee it."

CHAPTER 3

How in the blue blazes am I going to pull this off?

Callie had asked herself this very question no fewer than six times since leaving Sam's office. At least with him being such an unreasonable, egotistical jerk, she'd have no worries about their intimate past getting in the way of their working together. Handsome went only so far. Sam might be one of the most attractive men Callie had ever met, but his personality negated any effect those blue-gray eyes and that sculpted jawline might have.

The broad shoulders were another matter altogether. Damn if she hadn't always been a sucker for a good set of shoulders.

She'd looked forward to this job. To six months of taking her time with it, digging into the details, and making the Sunset Harbor Inn the masterpiece upon which she would build her career as a project leader. Now she'd barely have enough time to put new paint on the walls.

Callie put a halt to the negative thoughts before they could take hold. She could do this, and she would. So six months was now three. Fine. They'd just need a sound plan.

The first order of business was to survey the inn from top to bottom to create a running inventory of what could be salvaged. Though most of what she'd seen the day before qualified as dated, there had to be something closer to antique quality on the property. And some of the dated furnishings—dressers and nightstands—could be brought up to boutique standards with a simple makeover.

In fact, Callie wondered if there weren't some sort of craftsmen on the island who could handle restoration and refurbishment. A thorough exploration of Anchor Village and the resources available went on her mental to-do list.

And then Callie remembered the one thing she'd forgotten to do the night before.

Call her mother.

Taking a deep breath, Callie closed her eyes, mentally preparing herself for the call. Best to get it over with. Her mother was what one might consider . . . difficult. She'd never given Callie a compliment, let alone the benefit of the doubt in any situation, including when Callie's husband had cheated with another woman.

And not any woman, but the one woman he must have known would hurt Callie the most.

According to Evelyn Henderson, Josh would never have strayed if Callie had kept him happy. So much for maternal support.

Standing on the front porch of the Sunset Harbor Inn, Callie touched her mother's name on her cell phone screen, pressed the cold metal to her ear, and waited.

Nothing.

Pulling the phone from her ear, she glanced at the screen. No signal. Walking to the other end of the porch didn't help. Callie even leaned over the railing, holding the phone high above her head.

Still no bars.

"You're wasting your time," said an unfriendly voice from behind her. Callie had ignored Bernie and Olaf today, since neither had been much help during their first encounter, and neither had acknowledged her presence when she'd walked past them seconds before.

"Excuse me?" she asked, not sure which of them had spoken. Or if the comment was even meant for her.

"No cell service," Olaf said, offering a smile that revealed two missing front teeth. The expression looked like a snarl, but there was friendliness in his eyes.

And then she realized what he'd said.

"There is no cell service here, around the hotel?"

Bernie shook his head, never taking his eyes off the checkerboard. "No service on the island. And don't get yer knickers in a twist. You won't die. The landlines work."

"But surely there's somewhere—"

"Nope," Olaf said. "None." The gap-toothed grin widened, as if he found joy in sharing this sort of news. Maybe watching visitors deal with this information was a form of entertainment for the locals.

Fine. She could live with no cell service. Her cottage had come with Wi-Fi, so she wouldn't be completely disconnected from the world.

"I appreciate your letting me know," she said, stepping closer to the two men. The smell of fish hit her full-on, sending her a step back. "How often do you gentlemen come here to play?"

"Every day," Bernie said, still not bothering to glance her way. "What's it to ya?"

Callie tried to be polite. "As you might know, the Sunset Harbor Inn is being renovated. We're going to be closed for business for a few months. I'm afraid you'll have to play your game someplace else."

This gained Bernie's full attention. "Says who?"

"Says me," Callie answered, before realizing she was mimicking the older man. "I mean, I say so. There is too much to be done, especially on this front facade, to have to work around a game of checkers."

"Who's doing the work?" Olaf asked.

Callie blinked. "Well, I don't know yet. We haven't gotten that far."

"Then we'll help with the work and play checkers here on our lunch break." Olaf said these words as if there need be no further discussion.

"I don't think that's a good—" Callie started.

"All worked out." Leaning over the board once more, Olaf moved one of his black checkers. "King me!"

In lieu of arguing with the men, Callie decided to let Sam handle his locals and proceeded inside to make the call from her office. It would be long distance, but surely Sam couldn't hold it against her when using her own cell wasn't an option.

As soon as she entered the inn foyer, Callie heard some sort of muffled music coming from the front desk area, but there was no one behind it. She stepped closer, thinking maybe someone had left a radio on somewhere, and found the source of the noise.

Jack was practically horizontal in his chair, wearing a pair of earbuds. His ears should have been bleeding, considering how well she could hear the music. Her trusty desk clerk had his eyes closed and was playing a mean air guitar as he jerked his head from side to side, sending the dark sweep of hair flipping back and forth over his forehead.

She tried clearing her throat, but that was a waste of time. Callie rang the small bell on the counter, something she intended to do away with immediately, but the rock star continued his performance. Walking around the counter, Callie waited for an opening, then tapped Jack on the forehead with one finger.

Green tennis shoes hit the floor as Jack leaped to his feet so quickly, he knocked Callie backward while sending the desk chair slamming against the wall behind him. The dying plant in the window teetered but thankfully did not fall.

Callie did not fall either, but only because Jack's reflexes were quick enough to catch her by the forearms. The pair froze, both in shock. Jack looked as if he wanted to let go but seemed aware that if he did so Callie would hit the floor.

And, of course, that was the moment Sam Edwards walked through the door.

~

Sam wasn't sure what to make of the scene he found behind the counter of the Sunset Harbor Inn. Callie hovered at a severe angle as a goofy-looking teenage boy clung to her forearms. A boy who looked scared enough to piss himself when he caught sight of Sam, causing him to let go, and nearly dropping Callie to the floor.

She was quick enough to step back and regain her balance, saving herself from the fall. The pair looked from Sam to each other and then back again in awkward silence. Then they spoke over each other.

"I walked in and—"

"She poked me and—"

Neither finished their sentence, and at that point, Sam didn't care what the hell had been going on. In fact, he preferred *not* to know.

"Ms. Henderson, I'm here to make a full inspection of the inn and discuss the overall direction we want to go in. If you can peel yourself away from whatever it is you're doing there, I think we should get started."

He may have agreed to be flexible and allow Callie some decision-making leeway, but he wasn't about to turn the entire project over and remain mute.

"Yes," Callie said, pressing her skirt back into place and straightening her jacket. "Of course. Let me grab a legal pad from my office, and we'll get started."

Within minutes, Sam was so angry with himself he couldn't see straight. The inn was an embarrassment. Faded paint, dated furnishings. It was clean, thank God, but glaringly neglected. How had he let this happen?

When he'd taken over the hotels, he'd silently, if reluctantly, promised Uncle Morty that he would make him proud. But there was nothing to be proud of here.

"The columns are going to be an issue," Callie said, bringing Sam back to the conversation regarding the dining area. "But I doubt we have any choice other than to leave them."

"We don't," Sam said. He'd learned as a child that the six pillars scattered throughout the center of the dining room were all load bearing.

The room was currently sectioned off into small areas, some with couches, while others included dining tables and chairs. A large fireplace occupied the wall to the right of the entrance and faced a cozy seating arrangement that included a coffee table covered in magazines. None of them looked current.

"We'll need all new furnishings in this room," Sam noted. "The area rugs have to go, as do the light fixtures."

Callie took notes as he spoke. "I think we can salvage some of the furniture," she said. "This will predominantly be a dining hall, but I like the option to switch things out and give it this homey, bed-and-breakfast feel when possible."

Sam looked again at the chairs before the fireplace. Dark, carved wood. Faded upholstery circa 1982, covered in maroon flowers. The color might have been almost white once upon a time but had yellowed with age and use.

"There is no saving this furniture."

Callie argued. "I think there is. Touch-ups to the wood. New upholstery. All some of this needs is updating. Considering the time restraints we're under, salvaging as much as possible is the best way to go."

He had to agree, the more they kept, the lower the overall cost. Sam was willing to do whatever it took to turn this inn around, but there was still a bottom line to consider.

Good to know Callie didn't intend to spend him out of business. And that she was willing to hold her ground when she believed she was right.

"I want approval on the upholstery."

"Noted," she said. "I'll get samples as soon as possible."

"Good. Then we move on," Sam said. "What's next?"

Callie looked up from her notepad, glanced around as if not understanding the question, then turned a subtle shade of pink. After a quick bite of her bottom lip, which did strange things to Sam's breathing, she said, "The bedrooms."

CHAPTER 4

*T*his should not be awkward, or so Callie kept telling herself. They were in an unoccupied hotel room to evaluate the space for remodeling purposes. The presence of a giant bed in the middle of the room should not have had any effect on her ability to focus on the task at hand.

But it did.

If Sam was similarly afflicted, he covered it well.

"All the rooms but two are this same size," he said, crossing to the window to the left of the bed, which put some distance between them. *Thank the heavens.* "Did you have a plan for what we can do in here?"

The answers that flew to mind were not professional ones. Callie used the legal pad as a fan while she concentrated on finding the right answers.

"New draperies and bedding. Each room will be unique, so we'll need several sets of every color and pattern. New paint and area rugs over newly installed hardwood floors. Industrial grade to withstand the level of traffic a hotel endures, of course."

There. Back on track. All business.

"We'll need new mattresses," Sam said. "I'll give you the name of the company we used for the Anchor. So far the guests have been happy, so I trust we made the right choice."

"Mattresses," Callie said, keeping her eyes on the yellow lined paper and not the man with whom she had once shared her own mattress.

"Okay," she said, stepping toward the door. "I think that does it. I can get started on this—"

"Why are you here?" Sam asked, taking Callie completely off guard.

She stared blankly. "Excuse me?"

Sam crossed his arms, pulling the suit jacket tight over his broad shoulders. "You weren't surprised when you walked into my office yesterday, so you knew I was the person you were coming to interview with."

She'd forgotten how direct Sam could be.

With a brief hesitation, she considered her answer, but in the end, Callie told the truth. "I need this job. I knew any operation run by you would be top quality. I've worked hard since earning my degree four years ago, and have assisted in several hotel transformations, but I've struggled to find anyone who would let me lead a project." Standing tall, she added, "When I found the ad for this position online, I applied immediately, hoping our previous connection wouldn't be a problem."

Once her full confession was out, silence filled the air around them. Tiny dust particles danced in the beam of sunlight behind Sam's head as his eyes narrowed, boring into her as if he could see the words she hadn't said. Then his stance loosened.

"Fair enough," he said. "Looks like your gamble paid off. Hopefully for both of us."

The breath Callie hadn't realized she'd been holding whooshed out. "I really appreciate this chance, Sam. I won't let you down."

"I wouldn't have hired you if I didn't believe that." Sam glanced around the room. "Back to the task at hand. You said each room will be unique. That's forty-two rooms. What do you plan to do to make them all different?"

"Right," she stammered, jarred again by the sudden change of subject. "In the past, I've created a sort of color block for the layout. A four-block of rooms in blues, the next in reds, and so on. That helps the painters keep things straight and gives the hotel a flow and consistency, even while nothing is exactly the same."

Sam nodded. "A sound strategy. And the style?"

"Clean lines and simplicity with touches that make the rooms feel cozy and welcoming." Callie warmed to her subject now that she was discussing the part she loved most about these renovations—the actual decorating. "Nothing too frilly or cluttered. Elegant but accessible. We want guests to explore the local attractions but feel at home enough in the room that when they make a return trip to Anchor, we're the first place that comes to mind."

Sam smiled, and Callie realized it was the first time he'd done so in her presence since she'd walked into his office the day before. Maybe even longer. His full lips stretched over straight white teeth, and tiny laugh lines appeared around his eyes.

He looked younger when he smiled. Though Callie knew Sam was only thirty-six, he looked much older than she'd expected him to. Older and sad. Though she hadn't put that emotion to it before, since he covered so much with formality. But there was definitely sadness in his eyes.

"We're clearly on the same page, Ms. Henderson," Sam said, joining her once again at the door.

"Please," she said, "call me Callie. Every time you say *Ms. Henderson*, I want to look behind me for my mother."

Sam's smile turned into a grin. "I met her once, didn't I?"

"Yes." Callie cringed. "She shook your hand and said if only she was twenty years younger, you two could have some fun."

His deep chuckle set butterflies loose in Callie's midsection. "Interesting lady."

"That's one word for it." But Callie didn't experience the usual annoyance she felt when thinking about her mother. Standing this close to Sam, sharing a moment from the past, she felt lots of things, but none of them was annoyance.

Several amicable seconds passed, and then Sam's eyes dropped the few inches to Callie's lips. She stopped breathing. Stopped thinking. Waited.

Then a door slammed down the hall and Sam stepped back.

"I think we have a good plan of attack here," he said. "I'd like to see a full proposal by Friday."

Callie nodded, hugging the notepad to her chest. It wasn't much, but she needed something to hold on to.

"I'll have it for you first thing in the morning." Desperate for space and fresh air, she stepped into the hall and led the way to the lobby. Callie could feel more than hear Sam following behind her. She picked up the pace. "You offered to send Yvonne over to help with the office," she said, stopping near the front desk. "When can I expect her?"

The storm-gray eyes were serious again. The grin vanished. Whatever had just happened down the hall must have been a figment of Callie's imagination.

"I'll send her over this afternoon."

She'd thought he would leave immediately, but Sam lingered near the entrance. "I forgot to ask, is everything good with the cottage? Seemed the right place to put you, considering its proximity to the inn."

Callie hadn't expected Sam to be concerned about her comfort, but she certainly had no complaints about the cottage. "It's wonderful. Perfect, in fact. I think I'll be quite happy there."

A glimpse of the smile returned. "Good," he said. Another brief hesitation, and then, "I'll see you Friday morning at nine."

Callie nodded, then watched Sam walk to his car. The words she'd last spoken played on a loop in her mind. There was definitely a chance she could be happy here. Though she did hope the rest of the islanders were friendlier than the checker players outside had been. Still, Callie preferred to think positive. As her cousin Henri liked to say, you never know what might happen if you keep an open mind.

And an open heart.

≈

Sam walked into the Anchor Inn still contemplating his encounter with Callie. She'd always been honest, but brave was not something he would have called her six years before. It had taken incredible courage for her to walk into his office, not sure what he would say or do when he realized who she was.

What astounded him more, though, was the fact that she had yet to bring up the last time they'd seen each other. Hadn't asked him why he'd left without so much as a note the morning after they'd been together. Truth be told, after six years, Sam still didn't have an answer, even for himself. That part of his life was a blur of anger, confusion, and hurt. He could express the anger, but Callie had given him a way to express the hurt. Or at least put a bandage over it for one night.

The next morning, he'd simply needed to get away. To start over. He'd never meant to fall into bed with Callie that night. Sam had needed a friend. Someone who would understand what he was going through. Callie had seemed like the only person on the planet who might know how he'd felt.

And she had. She'd said all the right things. Given him exactly what he'd needed. Maybe what they'd both needed. The memory, which had come back like an assault the moment he'd stood next to her in that bedroom, revived the feelings he'd long ago buried.

"Mr. Edwards?" Yvonne said, jerking Sam out of his reverie.

Sam stopped before walking into a chair. He glanced to his left to find Yvonne watching him with concern in her yellow-gold eyes.

"Sorry," he said, stepping up to the counter. "My mind was someplace else." Somewhere he'd spent six years avoiding. "Are you going to lunch soon?" he asked.

Yvonne checked the clock on the wall behind her. "I planned to leave in about ten minutes. Did you need me to stay and handle something?"

"No, I need you to spend the afternoon helping Ms. Henderson organize the Sunset Harbor office."

Yvonne nodded. "Not a problem. I'll have Rachel cover the desk while I'm gone. Do you know if Ms. Henderson needs any sort of office supplies? File folders and the like?"

Sam didn't know anything. He hadn't even bothered to look in the office to assess the damage for himself.

"I'm afraid not. Give her a call and see what she needs. Take her anything she asks for."

"Yes, sir," Yvonne responded, though still eying him as if he might plow into a wall.

With a quick tap on the counter, Sam nodded, then headed for his office. His suit jacket hit the coat stand in the corner and his tie was loose before his ass hit the leather seat. In less than forty-eight hours, Callie Wellman—Henderson now—had surprised, debated, cajoled, and aroused him. He shuddered to think what the hell she might do next.

~

Callie had moved to her third pile of invoices, customer receipts, and unopened mail when Yvonne knocked on her office door. Resisting the urge to hug her would-be savior, she offered the woman a seat instead.

"I brought everything you asked for except the graph paper," Yvonne said, setting a stack of printer paper, file folders, pens, highlighters, and labels on the only corner of the desk Callie had been able to clear. "We didn't have any in the supply room. But I called in an order and we should have it tomorrow."

Somewhere in her upper twenties by Callie's guess, Yvonne was quite beautiful, with a runway-ready body and a distinct air of confidence, as if she felt completely prepared to take on the world and win.

What Callie wouldn't give for that trait. Or that body.

"Is there an office supply store on the island?" Callie asked, noting again that she needed to take a day to explore her new surroundings.

"Not on Anchor, no. But there's a store farther up the Outer Banks willing to deliver down here if we order enough." Yvonne shrugged. "I put all of this on the order as well, since we'll need it again eventually."

"Thank you so much." Callie indicated the stacks on the desk. "I'm not sure where to begin. The place looked as if this Cheryl person purposely threw every piece of paper into the air before she left."

Yvonne looked as horrified about the mess as Callie had been when she'd first entered the office. "I had no idea she was this pissed off," she said, shaking her head.

Yvonne's combination of mocha-colored skin and amber eyes made her look like a one-of-a-kind work of art. Callie had never seen eyes that color before. They were mesmerizing.

"How about I start with the piles," Yvonne offered, "and you assess the file drawers? Did she leave anything in them at all?"

Callie opened the desk drawer to her left. Papers were wedged in every which way, many folded or mangled completely. "She did." Callie sighed. "Your plan sounds as good as any. Stack by year, then by expense. Was payroll handled out of this office as well?"

Yvonne shook her head. "No. All payroll for both hotels is handled from the Anchor."

"Thank God." The task ahead felt overwhelming, but at least she wasn't in this alone. "Let's get started. Once we get this mess organized, I can make sure everything is in the system before we archive. Keep your fingers crossed the database doesn't look nearly as bad as this office."

As the two of them went to work, Callie was tempted to ask why a woman like Yvonne was on Anchor Island, instead of gracing runways in Milan. She also wondered how Sam managed to resist his office manager's exotic beauty.

Or maybe he didn't.

Callie gave her full attention to the messy file drawer and ignored the knot of jealousy that last thought had created.

∾

By five o'clock, Callie and Yvonne had transformed the office into something almost workable. They'd put four banker boxes full of older documents in a storage closet, filed documents dated with the current year into the file drawers, and Yvonne had even swept the floor. The desk was bigger than it had looked hidden beneath the mess, and Callie had several ideas of how to make the space her own. With a feeling of accomplishment, she strolled across the street to her new abode.

The cottage was larger than the word implied, with an open floor plan, whitewashed paneling, and shiny hardwood floors. The kitchen was a wide galley style, with new appliances that retained a retro look. Dark, narrow beams ran along the high ceiling in the living room at what looked to be three-foot intervals and gleamed in the light brought in from the wall of windows along the back side. French doors led out to an expansive deck that provided a gorgeous view of the ocean.

Callie looked forward to watching the sunrise with a mug of hot tea in hand and fresh salt air blowing through her hair. She didn't know how long this dream home would be hers, but she intended to enjoy every moment of her stay. Sam might expect her to rent her own place in town once the renovations were done, which was only fair.

That was, if he kept her on afterward. The position had been for someone to turn the place around, not become its caretaker beyond that. It was highly possible that once her initial job was finished, Callie would have to seek employment elsewhere. And for some reason she couldn't fathom, the thought made her sad. She hadn't even seen most of the village yet. There was no reason to feel so attached already.

Pushing thoughts of the future aside, she kicked off her shoes, leaned back on the soft blue suede armchair, and crossed her ankles on the matching blue ottoman. Tense muscles loosened as the chair enveloped her, as if giving her a warm, welcoming hug and promising to never let her go. And then the phone rang and Callie realized she'd never called her mother.

She looked at the caller ID on the handset.

How did she get this number?

"Mother?" she answered.

"So you *do* remember I exist. Did you forget how to use a phone? Calliope Mabel, I have been worried sick."

What was it with moms and the first-plus-middle-name thing?

"I've been a little busy, Mother," Callie said, ignoring the guilt in her chest that her mother nurtured more than she'd ever nurtured her daughter. "I meant to call this morning, but there's no cell service here on the island."

Evelyn's voice turned doubtful. "I suppose you expect me to believe that."

"It's true, Mother." Callie sighed.

"I'll check for myself once I get there."

Callie jerked up in her seat. "What do you mean, when you get here?"

"I'm coming with Henri to bring your belongings," Evelyn said. "I assume, since you haven't called to say you're on your way home, and I was informed by the friendly woman at that Anchor Inn place that you were living in some cottage with this number, that you got the job."

"Yes, I did. But why are you coming with Henri? There's no need for you to travel all this way." Callie tried applying logic. "You don't like traveling long distances by car, remember?"

"You're my daughter, and I need to make sure you're somewhere safe. Please tell me this cottage has running water and electricity."

Callie took a deep breath, squeezing her eyes tight as she pinched the bridge of her nose. "Mother, I'm thirty years old. I don't need you to make sure I'm safe. I'm fine, I promise." Flopping back in her seat, she added, "The cottage is large and clean and fully equipped with all the required utilities. I'm practically living in luxury."

"We're leaving first thing tomorrow morning," Evelyn said, barreling through her daughter's arguments. "I've ordered Henri to pick me up by seven. I estimate we'll be there between four and five in the afternoon."

Callie didn't bother to argue further. Once Evelyn Henderson made up her mind, there was no getting around her. She was like a giant boulder, rolling where and when she wanted, and to hell with anything in her path.

"Fine," she said, sinking deeper into the comfy chair. "I'll email Henri directions to the cottage." Callie considered calling her cousin to suggest she conveniently forget Evelyn, but Henri might actually do it, and that would lead to more guilt.

And her mother would still find a way to land on her doorstep within the day. She'd probably fly in. By broom.

"I assume you've made sure this cottage allows pets," Evelyn said. Her questions always came out as statements. A trait that had been annoying to Callie as a child, but maddening as an adult. "Or maybe you've forgotten about Cecil already."

She had not forgotten about Cecil, though she might have failed to mention him to Sam.

"Cecil will be fine," she said, jotting down a note to ask Sam about the cottage's pet policy. "He'll have a lovely view." Callie glanced through the wall of windows to her right. The ocean stretched as far as the eye could see.

"Good. I need to go feed him and pack his things," Evelyn said. "We'll call when we reach the island."

"Unless you stop and find a landline, you're not going to be able to call."

Evelyn snorted, though she'd never admit to doing something so unladylike. "We'll see."

The line went dead. Callie pressed the END button on the handset and sank even deeper into the chair, until she was nearly horizontal. Twenty-four hours of peace before Hurricane Evelyn arrived. Enough time to buy provisions. Now to figure out where to get wine.

CHAPTER 5

Sam wasn't sure what had compelled him to drive over to the Sunset Harbor Inn on Wednesday afternoon. As he pulled into the parking lot, he reminded the questioning part of his brain that he didn't need a reason to visit his own hotel. A hotel that was about to undergo a full-on renovation. A renovation that had to be finished in less than three months.

Hitting that deadline would require his full attention, and Callie would have it whenever she needed it. He'd agreed to turn over *some* of the decision making, but on such a tight schedule, he couldn't afford for Callie to make a major purchase that didn't fit his vision, only to find out after it was too late to choose an alternative.

Or so he rationalized.

As he stepped out of his Murano, something caught Sam's eye from across the street. There was an older-model green pickup parked in the cottage driveway, and two women unloading boxes and suitcases. One of them was Callie, but all Sam could make out of the other was a shock of white-blond hair and dark clothing.

Curiosity carried him the short distance to the cottage; he told himself the entire way that he was not being nosy. They might need him to help carry something. Big, muscly man to the rescue and all that.

Sam had never fancied himself a Neanderthal, but even he recognized the caveman idiocy in that thought.

As he reached the tailgate of the truck, the platinum-haired stranger stepped off the porch. "Hello," she said with a smile, curiosity glowing in her chestnut eyes. "I'm guessing you're not a well-dressed bandit looking to steal my cousin's meager belongings from the back of my truck."

"No," Sam said, extending a hand. "I'm Sam Edwards. If Callie is the owner of these boxes, then I'm your cousin's new boss."

"That Sam, huh?" The eyes turned knowing, and he opted not to comment further as they shook hands. "I'm Henri," she said. His thoughts must have shown on his face, since she added, "Cal's mom and mine are sisters. They like old-fashioned names. Henri is short for Henrietta."

Sam nodded. "Pretty name."

"Old name," Henri said with a laugh. "I assume you're here to see Cal. Grab that box." She pointed to a large one in the corner of the truck bed. With a wink she said, "I'll get the door."

He'd wanted to play caveman. Now was his chance.

The box was heavier than Sam expected and sent a jolt of pain shooting up his back as he lifted it. He dropped it back down and caught sight of Henri's raised brow. "Slipped," he said.

"Sure," she said, crossing her arms and patiently waiting for him to move things along.

Sam lifted with his knees, holding in the groan as much as possible, and followed Henri into the cottage. Thankfully, he didn't have far to go before he set the box atop another, but the moment he stood up, something green flew at his head.

"What the—"

"Cecil!" Callie yelled. "Come back here!"

The green menace flew at Sam again, this time scraping a claw along his hair as he passed. If he hadn't known any better, Sam would have thought the bird was trying to kill him.

"No men allowed," cawed a voice that sounded computer generated. "No men allowed," echoed again as the bird headed straight for Sam's face.

He ducked in time to avoid a direct hit but felt a puff of wind from the deadly beast's wings dance across his right ear.

"Mother, how could you teach him that?" asked Callie as she charged after the bird while waving a cracker in the air.

"Why are you blaming me?" asked an older, well-dressed blonde sitting on the couch, filing a fingernail as if there weren't a maniacal fowl on the loose. "He's your bird."

Callie ignored the woman as she cornered the flapping dive-bomber in the corner, speaking in soothing tones, presumably to calm the beast. Whatever she said seemed to work as the creature settled enough for her to get her hands around him.

"I've got you now, buddy," she said. "Everything's all right."

"'S'all right," the bird chimed. "'S'all right."

Sam knew a talking bird wasn't all that unusual, but he'd never actually seen one in person before. At least not outside a variety show or circus. Callie held the bird perched on her right hand now as she crossed the large living room toward him.

Sam tensed for a new attack.

Wings spread as if ready to take flight but relaxed when Callie stuck the cracker under the bird's pointed beak. It didn't take a genius to know a peck from that beak would hurt like hell.

"Cecil, this is Mr. Sam. He's given us this wonderful place to live." Callie ran a hand along the parrot's back as she spoke, keeping her eyes on the pet. "Say hello to Mr. Sam."

Cecil munched on his cracker, which he now held in one talon, and nodded his head up and down. "Hello, Mr. Sam."

"Hello, Mr. Sam," echoed a far sexier, more feminine voice. "It's so nice to see you again." Evelyn Henderson extended a hand, palm down, as if expecting Sam to kiss it. He shook it instead.

"Nice to see you, too," he said, struggling not to step back as the older woman invaded his space. He strove to be polite without offering encouragement.

Evelyn Henderson didn't need encouragement. Sliding her hand around his elbow as if they were entering a ballroom some hundred years ago, Callie's mother led Sam to the sofa, sat down, then pulled him down to sit beside her. She had a strong grip for a woman pushing retirement age.

"Since I doubt she's done it herself, I'd like to thank you for giving my daughter this opportunity. And myself even more reason to visit this quaint little island of yours." She was leaning into him now, her linen-clad leg pressed firmly against his own.

Sam looked to Callie for rescue and caught her rolling her eyes. "Mother, I haven't needed you to speak for me in more than fifteen years, and I'm sure Sam would appreciate it if you'd give him a little space to breathe there."

Evelyn shot an unfriendly look in her daughter's direction. "I'm showing the man proper gratitude for taking pity and giving my daughter a job. There's nothing wrong with that."

Callie closed her eyes, and Sam could almost see her counting to ten. Gripped with a strong urge to defend his new employee, Sam extricated himself from the older woman's grip and returned to his feet.

"I can assure you, Ms. Henderson, there was no pity involved. Callie is the most qualified person for this position, with a proven track record to recommend her. It is more her taking pity on me by accepting my offer instead of pursuing a more prominent position elsewhere."

A weighted silence settled over the room, broken seconds later by the less-than-tactful bird. "*He told her*. Need another cracker."

Callie carried Cecil to a large white cage in front of the wall of windows that led to the deck, then dropped in several crackers before closing him in. The color on her face was heightened when she turned back Sam's way.

"You have no idea what that means to me," she said. "Could we step into the kitchen for a moment?"

With that flush on her cheeks and look of hero worship in her eyes, Sam would have followed Callie anywhere she wanted to take him. Without a word, he stepped in line behind her, leaving the huffing mother and smiling cousin alone in the living room.

As soon as Callie reached the retro stove he'd searched for a week online to find, she turned and let out a whoosh of air. With one hand on her hip, she lifted her ice-blue eyes to his and rewarded him with a smile that made Sam feel woozy.

"I wasn't kidding. Thank you for saying that. Especially to my mother. I doubt she believes you, but I couldn't care less at the moment. Did you mean what you said?"

There he was again, his latent white knight rearing his damn noble head. Valiant or not, Sam saw no reason to lie.

"I did mean it. Granted, I've never visited any of the facilities you list on your résumé, but I did my homework. The before-and-after images I could find online were impressive, to say the least. And your references didn't so much recommend you as rave about your talents." The more he spoke, the more animated Callie's features grew. He found himself enjoying putting that look of joy on her face.

"You could find work anywhere you wanted," he said. "You can't tell me you doubt that."

Callie shook her head, but the smile never faltered. "I could *assist* anywhere I wanted, but I've interviewed at nearly every transitioning hotel east of the Mississippi, and no one is willing to let me take lead." Her eyes beamed at him. "Except you."

Sam spoke without thinking. "Then they're all idiots."

Her burst of laughter filled the galley kitchen. "That's what Henri says. Only she threw a four-letter word in for added punch."

He couldn't help but smile along with her. Callie being professional was sexy. Callie relaxed and happy threatened to short-circuit his brain—though he was feeling the effects much lower.

For maybe the first time in his adult life, Sam didn't know what to do next. He knew what he wanted to do, but that was a line he had no intention of crossing. Instead, he stared at the black-and-white floor tiles as their laughter faded into a comfortable silence.

"I wanted . . . ," he started.

"I guess . . . ," she said at the same time. "I'm sorry. What were you going to say?"

Sam cleared his throat to extricate the frog that had taken up residence there. "I wanted to let you know why I stopped by. This project is important, and I do understand I'm asking a lot. I'll be available whenever you need me. Day or night."

Why in the hell had he said that?

"Anyway," he added before Callie could reply, "I'd better be going."

"Sure." Callie's brows were drawn, and she looked both confused and a bit dazed. He was feeling both himself, which was all the more reason to cut and run. "You should probably go out the back door to avoid my mother," she said.

"Good idea. I'll see you Friday morning to discuss the proposal for the inn. If you need anything before then, contact Yvonne and she'll take care of it."

Callie nodded as he crossed the kitchen to the side door. He was stepping over the threshold when her words stopped him.

"I know I keep saying it, but I really do appreciate this chance, Sam."

"You're welcome," he said, then felt the urge to clear something up. "I didn't offer you this job because of our connection. I thought I was hiring a highly qualified stranger before you walked into my office. You got the job because of those qualifications and nothing more."

She rewarded him with a half smile before Sam closed the door between them. He considered stepping into the cold surf in search of his sanity but opted instead for a lukewarm shower and a glass of scotch at home.

Christmas could not come soon enough.

～

Callie wasn't sure how long she remained there in the kitchen, leaning on the counter edge, staring at the checkered floor. What exactly had just happened? One minute she'd been thanking Sam for seeing her true value and giving her the opportunity she needed to create the future she longed for. The next they'd been laughing together and the whole world had fallen away.

She'd never considered how intimate shared laughter could be, but something had changed. Sam wasn't the buttoned-up hotelier. She wasn't his eager-to-prove-herself employee.

They'd been . . . friends. Friends with a spark of something they'd spent one night six years ago exploring. Callie had wondered a few times if they would have gone further had Sam not disappeared, but she'd convinced herself his leaving had saved them both from an awkward morning-after exchange.

Or maybe only delayed it. Though they were both dancing around the topic, the awkwardness was there every time they were together. If their professional relationship was going to work, they were going to have to drag the elephant out of the shadows and do something with it.

But what did one do with a six-year-old invisible elephant carrying the weight of two broken hearts and a lifetime supply of insecurity? Even though that insecurity was all her own.

"You okay in here?" Henri asked, ducking into the kitchen. "Aunt Evelyn is over her fit and suggested we go out to dinner. I assume she was including the man you came in here with. Where did he go?"

Callie nodded toward the door where Sam had exited. "He left. He came to give me a message about the hotel renovation."

"Is that why you look like you've been run over by a bulldozer?" Henri wasn't the type to avoid the obvious. She was more a face-things-head-on kind of person. "I can see why you fell into bed with him all those years ago."

And Henri had a good memory.

"We fell into bed with each other. It was a rough time for both of us."

"After what your shitty spouses did, you both deserved a night of consolation."

Callie snorted. "Consolation sex. My therapist used to get pissed when I called it that. She deemed it an 'understanding through intimacy.' Didn't make much sense to me, since I didn't understand anything about what happened back then, least of all between Sam and me."

"How do you feel about him now?" Henri asked, leaning her hip on the edge of the counter. "Are you mad at him for leaving?"

"My anger was always reserved for Josh, though a good dose of it was toward myself." Callie turned to swipe a mug from the cupboard behind her. "I ignored what was right in front of me, believing that if I tried hard enough, I could make Josh happy."

Henri stepped forward, taking the mug from Callie's cold fingers. "You and I both know nothing that happened back then was your fault. Josh didn't have an affair with Meredith because you weren't enough. He's the one who wasn't enough."

"Maybe *you* should be a therapist," Callie said, feeling better, as she always did when Henri was around. "Knowing that and believing it are two different things."

"You still didn't answer my first question." Henri poured coffee into the mug that Callie had pulled from the cupboard. "How do you feel about Sam now?"

"I don't know," she answered honestly. "I mean, there's an attraction."

This time Henri snorted. "You'd have to be dead or gay not to be attracted to that. I'm gay and I still felt a little quiver when he showed up in the driveway."

Henri always could make her laugh, no matter what was going on. "I'm sure he'd be flattered to hear that. I was going to use that mug for tea, but I guess I'll get another one."

"I spent nine hours traveling alone with your mother today," Henri said. "You're lucky this isn't rum instead of coffee."

"Fair enough," Callie said, closing the cupboard she'd opened. "There's a bar and grill in the village. I bet they have amazing seafood."

"Sounds good to me." Henri took another swig of coffee and scrunched up her face. "I forgot Aunt Evelyn made this. Does she carry tar in that Kate Spade purse of hers?"

"I think it's ground coal."

Henri poured the coffee into the sink. "I would not be surprised. Now, let's go find me some alcohol. You're buying."

Following her cousin back toward the living room, Callie said, "It's the least I can do."

CHAPTER 6

The jukebox was playing Bob Marley and the Wailers as Callie, her mom, and Henri walked through the entrance of Dempsey's Bar & Grill. A combination of gleaming dark wood, soaring wood beams, and picture windows, the place was both fancier and more interesting than Callie had expected. There was also quite a crowd for so late in the season.

If this was the crowd in late September, she couldn't help but wonder what the place would look like in the heart of July.

"Give me two seconds, ladies, and I'll be right with you," said a young, dark-haired waitress as she breezed by, carrying a tray full of drinks as if it weighed no more than a feather.

Standing beside Callie, Henri watched the pretty girl walk away in her denim shorts, which showed a significant amount of leg. "I like this place already."

Callie leaned close enough to whisper, "You know my mother will have a conniption if she has to witness you hitting on a woman. I'm not sure I could endure one of her fits tonight."

"Relax," Henri said, watching a tall, blonde waitress stroll through the middle of the room. "I'm sightseeing. Isn't that what you're supposed to do on vacation?"

Callie glanced her way with one brow raised.

"I'll behave," Henri promised. "Scout's honor."

"You were never a Girl Scout."

"No, but I like their cookies."

"Hi there," said the brunette as she stepped up to the podium before them. "Sorry for the wait. Welcome to Dempsey's. Are we looking for a booth or a table tonight?"

"A booth," Callie and Henri said in unison.

The waitress smiled, grabbed three menus, along with three sets of silverware wrapped in white napkins, and headed for the wall of windows to the far right. "Here you go," she said, dropping the menus and silverware onto a table in the center of the wall. "Daisy will be your server, and she'll be with you in just a minute."

"Thank you," said Callie, climbing in to allow her mother to sit on the end.

"Enjoy your meal," the waitress said, then disappeared into the crowd.

The group focused their attention on the menus in front of them. Evelyn flipped the pages with the tips of her fingers as if she might catch a germ. She looked uncomfortable and unhappy, but then, Callie's mother always looked that way. Unless she was at her country club, and even then she was usually glaring disapprovingly at another woman who had the nerve not to match her shoes with her handbag.

Callie had given up trying to please her mother long ago, which made ignoring her distaste for their choice of restaurant a matter of habit.

"At least they have a large selection," Evelyn said, a thin line of tolerance in her voice. "I would assume the seafood is fresh. Now let's hope someone in that kitchen knows how to cook it."

"I doubt this crowd is here because the food sucks, Aunt Evelyn."

"Using vulgar language makes you sound vulgar, Henrietta. How many times do I have to tell you that?"

"Maybe a couple hundred more and it'll sink in, Aunty."

Callie cringed. The only thing her mother hated more than Henri's language was being called Aunty. Instead of arguing, Evelyn gave Henri what she called the cut. She huffed, kept her eyes down, and pretended her irritating niece was no longer there.

By all accounts, Evelyn Henderson had been born in the wrong century. She'd also been born into the wrong family, considering she was a sharecropper's daughter and not the child of a powerful politician. So she'd simply married one to change her circumstances.

Unfortunately, Callie's father had died of a heart attack less than a year after his daughter's birth, leaving Evelyn as a single mother with grand aspirations and no way to reach them except to groom her child to be the first female president. Needless to say, Callie had turned out to be a disappointment in all areas.

Evelyn had remarried twice before Callie's twenty-first birthday and stood stoic in black as she watched each husband get lowered six feet into the ground. Unwilling to take another chance, the professional widow had avoided a walk down the aisle for the last ten years. Callie almost wished her mother would find another husband so she'd have something else to focus on besides her disappointing offspring.

"I think I'll have a burger," Callie said.

"You should stick with a salad, dear," replied her mother. "Your jeans are looking tighter than usual."

The cousins exchanged a look, and Callie sighed, counting the hours until Saturday morning, when this little visit would come to a blessed end.

She could not wait.

~

Sam had found that the shower and aged liquor weren't enough to get him through the evening and turned to physical exertion. Not the kind he'd have preferred, as he reminded himself for what must have been the tenth time that he was not crossing that line with Callie.

Again.

Instead, he'd made the trek to Island Fitness for a good workout. He vowed to continue doing sit-ups until the image of Callie occupying his bed was burned from his system. He'd counted past one hundred when Randy Navarro joined him at the weight bench.

"You going for a record?" Randy asked, sporting an enormous grin that matched the rest of him.

Roughly the size of a large building, the gym owner matched Sam in height but had him beat in every other area. Arms the size of Sam's thighs. Shoulders broad enough to block out the fluorescent lights shining down from the ceiling.

Sam removed his legs from the barbell, dropped his feet to the floor, and sat up on the bench, accepting the towel Randy offered. "Going for a clear head is all."

Sweat dripped from a lock of dark hair dangling over Randy's brow. "Anything I can help with?"

Unless the man could exorcise demons or conjure up a time machine, there was little he could do. "Afraid not, but thanks for the offer."

Of all the people he'd met on Anchor Island, Randy Navarro was probably the closest Sam had to a friend. The men worked on a committee together to increase tourism on the island, and it hadn't taken long for Sam to realize that not liking the big man was simply impossible.

Whereas his size could seem intimidating, the personality was all friendly concern and generosity. Which were likely the reasons he'd landed the mysterious heiress from the north.

That and the biceps.

"Will came to see me yesterday. She seemed a bit . . . wired."

"Let me guess," Randy said. "She was drinking coffee."

"Yvonne gave her some when she arrived at the hotel." There was no reason to take credit for providing Will with the caffeine fix. Especially if her large and protective fiancé didn't want her to have it.

Randy shook his head as he wiped the sweat away with his own towel. "Will is good at looking calm on the outside, but she's more high-strung than you'd think. I thought cutting out the caffeine would help calm her nerves." The men crossed the workout area to reach the locker room. Randy let Sam enter first. "Which is looking like a miscalculation on my part."

"Once she gets her legs under her with this business, I'm sure things will level out."

"About that," Randy said, dropping onto the edge of a bench that ran between two rows of lockers. "She mentioned this wedding coming up at your place before Christmas."

"That's right. We talked about it yesterday."

"Well . . ." Randy rubbed the back of his neck. "She's worried the place won't be done in time. I told her that if you said it would be done, it'll be done, but are you sure? If she can't deliver on a deal this early, that's going to look really bad for a new business."

Sam didn't like being questioned, though he understood Randy's motivations. Will was important to him, and that meant Randy would do whatever he had to do to make sure she succeeded.

"The Sunset Harbor Inn will be renovated and ready for business in time for the wedding. I've already given Will my word on that, and I'll give it to you as well." Randy seemed to exhale and Sam added, "I wouldn't question your business integrity. I'd appreciate the same in return."

Randy's nostrils flared as his brown eyes darkened. Sam was no slouch, but he knew this man could likely stomp him into dust if he wanted. That didn't mean Sam would back down or tolerate having his word doubted.

Several tense seconds passed, before Randy nodded. "Point taken." He tossed the towel over his shoulder. "But don't hesitate to let me know if I can help in any way."

So, Randy was willing to accept his word but still do whatever was necessary to make sure Will wasn't disappointed. Fair enough.

"Will do," Sam said, strolling past the larger man to reach his locker.

"There's no limit to what I'd do for Will," Randy said. "I'm sure you understand."

The words reminded Sam of the limits of what he'd been willing to do for Meredith.

With a nod, he pulled a shaving kit from his locker and headed for the showers.

～

The daunting task of turning the run-down, ramshackle Sunset Harbor Inn into a stylish and modern boutique hotel in record time couldn't compete with the struggle of having to live with Callie's mother, even if for only a few days.

Callie could not get to work early enough when the alternative was running into Evelyn Henderson at the coffeemaker. The evening before had been filled with sighs, backward insults, and a temper tantrum her mother would term her way of expressing her sensitive and stepped-on feelings. If only Henri didn't so enjoy poking the older woman at every opportunity. You'd think having to ride back to Charleston with her would be reason enough for her cousin to embrace peace on the Aunty front.

But Henri had always been the agitator in the family. All Callie had ever wanted was to be invisible, which was why she'd been so silent she could have been mistaken for a mute during her teenage years. As a small child, she'd done everything possible to gain her mother's approval. By puberty, she'd come to the realization that she was wasting her time.

No matter now. Callie was a grown woman taking charge of her own life. So she'd traded seeking maternal approval for chasing professional validation. At least the newer pursuit was a possibility.

Callie was thirty minutes into entering the furniture inventory into a spreadsheet when someone knocked on her office door. Upon opening it, she found a stunning brunette on the other side. The woman was tall and lean, with an athletic build and long, wavy hair draped around her shoulders.

Were all the women on Anchor Island former runway models? If so, Callie's self-esteem would be mush by the holidays.

"Can I help you?" she said, noticing Jack had once again left his post.

"Are you Calliope Henderson?" the woman asked, a hint of New England in her voice.

Callie nodded. "Yes, I am."

A slender hand was extended, bangle bracelets chiming like the bells over the hotel entrance. "I'm Will Parsons. I run the wedding-coordinator business on the island. I hope I'm not bothering you."

So this was the woman responsible for making Callie's life more difficult. Though to be fair, Sam had been the one who'd agreed to the holiday wedding.

"No. Not a problem. Please," Callie said. "Come in."

"I tried to call ahead," Will said, accepting the chair Callie offered, "but couldn't get an answer at the front desk."

Callie sighed. She really didn't have time to train a new front-desk clerk. "I apologize for that. Can I get you something to drink? Coffee? Tea?"

She had no idea if they had either prepared, since she'd brought her own tea from the cottage, but Callie offered out of habit and hoped she could find something.

"I'm good, thanks." Will settled into the small chair in front of Callie's desk, making her long legs more apparent as her knees nearly touched her ears. But she gracefully leaned to one side, crossing her denim-covered legs and bouncing one combat boot.

Black boots, tight jeans, and gold jewelry. The elements should have clashed, but Ms. Parsons made the combination work.

Callie regained her own seat, moving the laptop off to the side so she could see her visitor without obstruction. "I was excited to hear the island has a wedding-coordination business," she said.

"I haven't been in business for long," Will admitted. "I set up shop halfway through the summer, so I'm still working on getting the word out and establishing Destination Anchor as a serious entity."

"I hear you're already bringing business our way. That's a good sign."

Will leaned an elbow on her knee and tapped her chin with one slender finger. "That's what I'm here to talk about. I told Sam I could wait until next week to get a sense of what the end result will be after the renovation, but I'm afraid my client is less patient than I am."

The tapping intensified, as did the rate at which the combat boot bounced. If Callie didn't know better, she'd think Ms. Parsons was nervous about something.

"Are you sure I can't get you anything?" she asked again. *Like maybe a mixed drink or some antacid?*

Will shook her head, but the tapping continued.

"Ms. Parsons—"

"Please, call me Will."

"Right. Will. I'm afraid we don't have a finished plan, as I've only begun the proposal for Mr. Edwards's review today. But I can tell you that the inn will be elegant yet cozy, with quality furnishings and linens. The colors will be soothing but refreshing, in a way that I'm sure your wedding party will find quite appealing."

"And it'll be done?" Will asked. "By Christmas?"

Though Callie had aired her own doubts the day before, she'd given Sam her word the hotel would be ready for business in time for the wedding. And so it would be. But the question did explain her visitor's frayed nerves. As a new business, she couldn't make a promise to a client without complete faith that she could back it up.

Callie understood Will's dilemma.

"Yes," she said, happy to put the coordinator's fears to rest. "I admit there is much work to be done in a very short window, but rest assured that the Sunset Harbor Inn will be ready when the time comes."

They might require a Christmas miracle to make that happen, but Callie had pulled off miracles before. Not of this size, but there was always a way.

Will nearly collapsed under the weight of the breath she exhaled. "Ms. Henderson—"

"Call me Callie."

"That really is a pretty name," Will said, taking her by surprise. "I don't mean to question your ability to do your job, but this hotel . . ." The words trailed off as Will glanced around the room.

"Yes, this hotel," Callie said, leaning forward to set her elbows on the desk. "As I said, there is much to be done, but I've tackled similar projects in the past. With a thorough plan in place, it'll all come together. There's nothing to worry about."

Henri didn't call her Pollyanna for nothing. Whatever it was going to take to whip this hotel into shape, Callie would do it with a smile on her face and a positive attitude.

Will slowly relaxed into her chair, one muscle at a time. The tapping ebbed as a smile spread across her narrow face. "Sam assured me of the same thing, but I could tell he was speaking from ego. Few men can resist a challenge, but they rarely consider the reality of the situation."

Callie couldn't argue with that, but she also needed to back up her boss. "Mr. Edwards knows what he's doing. He once turned an all-but-condemned old factory into a premier hotel in the heart of Charleston—something everyone said he'd never pull off."

The wiry brunette sat up straight. "You knew Sam before he came to Anchor?"

Why did she have to be so damned honest? Not that she'd intended to lie to people, but Callie also wasn't prepared to explain how she and Sam were connected. "It was a long time ago," she said, rising from her chair.

"So he's from Charleston?" Will asked, blue eyes bright with interest.

"That area, yes." Strolling around the desk, Callie struggled to remain polite while giving a clear indication that their meeting was over. "I really do need to get back to this proposal if I'm going to have it done by Friday. The sooner we have a plan in place, the sooner we can start the work."

"Yes," Will said, gathering her bag from the floor beside her chair. "Of course." Upon reaching the door, the taller woman turned.

"I really don't mean to be nosy. I'm not big on talking about *my* past, either. But Sam is the only person on this island that no one knows anything about. I guess I've been here long enough to have caught the curiosity bug of the natives."

"I'm afraid any details about Mr. Edwards's past will have to come from him," Callie said, offering a smile to lessen the edge of her words. "I really am looking forward to working with you. Weddings are my favorite events to hold, and I can't wait to see the inaugural event here at the Sunset Harbor Inn."

Will returned the smile and offered her business card. "If you're interested in getting to know the island, give me a call. I have some friends I'd like you to meet."

The words sounded sincere, and Callie appreciated the chance to make a few friends on Anchor, even if her stay was temporary.

"That would be nice. Thank you."

CHAPTER 7

Sam entered the Anchor Inn at eight thirty Friday morning to find Callie sitting in the lobby, reviewing some paperwork in her lap. He appreciated punctuality in his employees, but a half hour early seemed a bit extreme.

As did the reaction of his body upon seeing her.

"Is there a reason you're here so early?" Sam asked, the words harsher than necessary.

She glanced up, her mouth forming an O in surprise. Then she flashed a tentative smile, as if maybe she'd felt a similar jolt to her system upon seeing him. An idiotic imagining on his part.

"My mother is an early riser."

She didn't elaborate, indicating this statement should be an adequate explanation. Sam considered her words for several seconds before the truth set in.

"I see."

"I know you're not available until nine. It's no problem," she said, lifting the papers from her lap. "I'm fine out here."

"Is that the proposal?" he asked.

"It is."

"Is it ready?"

Her brows lowered. "Of course it is."

"Then follow me."

Sam led Callie through the lobby with the goal of making this a quick meeting and sending her on her way.

"Did you include financial specs?" Sam asked, pushing his office door open and motioning for Callie to enter first.

"I've created a full budget, but I'm sure the numbers will change, as I've no idea what resources are readily available here on the island and what we'll need to source out."

Sam took his place behind the desk as Callie stopped in front of it. He remained standing until she took the hint and lowered into her chair.

"As we're doing this during a slower time of the year, finding manual labor on the island shouldn't be a problem." Sam pressed the ON button of his laptop as he took a seat. "Regarding the furniture you suggested we keep, there are craftsmen on the island who can likely handle refurbishment."

Callie removed a pen from behind her ear, opened her folder, and made a note. The movement drew his attention to the way her gold-streaked hair shimmered in the morning sun. "Excellent," she said, snapping him back to the moment. "I was hoping that would be the case. The more we can handle on-island, the better. For both cost and scheduling."

"Agreed," he said, not completely sure of what she'd said.

"Here's your copy for review." Callie slid the stapled sheets of paper his way. "If you'd rather read it all the way through before discussing, I can come back later today."

Sam flipped through the paperwork, noting she'd included everything from color samples to flooring choices. The proposal looked thorough and well researched. As he'd known it would.

"This is fine," he said, determined once again to get this meeting over with. "Let's flip to the budget."

Callie did as he asked. "The cost analysis is the final four pages. As I said, there may be options on the island I don't know about, but for the most part these figures should be close, if not completely accurate."

Turning to the last page first, Sam glanced at the bottom line. Not exactly cheap, but in the ballpark of what he'd been looking to spend. The shortened time frame would mean an increase in cost, but the number Callie had come up with was acceptable.

"You believe this number is realistic?" he asked, digging to make sure she hadn't provided a number for his approval with the intention of stretching the amount higher during the process.

Golden brows shot up. "Very realistic," she said. "For the amount of time we have and the condition the hotel is in, that's a solid number. I fully intend to get the best deal possible on everything I can, but there are some corners that simply can't be cut."

"I agree," he said. "Where is the color scheme?"

Surprise danced across Callie's face before she flipped through her own packet to answer his question. She must have expected him to drill harder on the numbers, but he didn't see any reason to waste time when he agreed with her estimations. They discussed the proposal for another twenty minutes and encountered only one speed bump, as they debated the shade of green to use for one of the room blocks. But all in all, the proposal was exactly what he'd been thinking, with touches he hadn't even considered. Which is why he'd brought Callie in to begin with—to capture the boutique aesthetic.

"We're ready to proceed," he said, once they'd agreed on the outside color, which would be a blue gray close to the current shade, and the addition of a gazebo near the water. Sam hadn't thought much beyond the initial building itself but appreciated Callie's broader view of the entire property.

"Then I'll get started," Callie said, slipping the proposal into a slender briefcase at her feet. "There is one more thing we need to discuss."

All his male instincts told Sam to brace for something bad. Callie's words were the equivalent of the dreaded "we need to talk."

"And what is that?" he asked, fighting the urge to say he had another meeting. Since she *was* his scheduled meeting, not meant to start for ten more minutes, the lie would be obvious.

"Us," she said. The word dropped like the pin being pulled from a grenade.

Sam did what any man would have done. He played dumb.

"I don't follow."

Callie sighed. "We can't keep pretending there isn't unfinished business between us, Sam. I appreciate this job and am looking forward to the renovation, but we're going to be dealing closely with each for the next three months. I can't keep up the farce."

"The farce?" Sam said, zeroing in on the word that struck him the hardest. "Is that what you think this is?"

"A poor choice of words on my part, but the last time we saw each other before Monday wasn't exactly normal. Or have you forgotten?"

"I haven't forgotten anything." Not for lack of trying. At least not in the past few days. "But I'm not interested in revisiting ancient history. The past needs to stay in the past."

"I've tried that," she said, leaning back in her chair, as if settling in for a long, leisurely discussion. "If three years of therapy taught me anything, it's that ignoring the past doesn't work."

"You've done therapy?" Sam had never been interested in examining his feelings and sure as hell had no intention of ever delving into the scars of his childhood. Both were the first requirements that came to mind when he heard the word *therapy*.

Callie kept her head up. "You know how my marriage ended, and you've met my mother. If anything, I'd expect you to be more surprised if I'd *never* had therapy."

While Sam had stuffed his demons into some dark recess of his mind, Callie had called hers out in a duel. Considering the confi-dent, seemingly well-adjusted woman before him, he thought she'd clearly won the battle. Which left Sam feeling outgunned and ill pre-pared for what she expected them to hash out in a morning meeting.

"What do you want to hear?" Sam asked, happy to say whatever it was she needed to get this over with.

Callie's ice-blue eyes dropped to the edge of his desk as she con-sidered her answer. After several seconds she said, "Maybe we could find some kind of reset button. Something that will clear out this cloud of awkwardness around us."

Sam felt relieved. Dealing with the present, he could do.

"What did you have in mind?"

That soft smile crossed her lips. "Ironically enough, we weren't all that close back then. Back when we were part of two couples who spent a lot of time together, each unaware there was a third couple in the mix." Her words carried a trace of sadness. "But we *were* friends. I know you're now my boss, but maybe we could also be friends again?"

Friends. Could he be friends with a woman he'd once had sex with? A woman he wanted to have sex with again and who hap-pened to work for him?

"That doesn't sound too difficult," Sam lied.

The lie earned him a full-on smile. "Good." Callie exhaled, blowing a lock of hair off her forehead. "I feel better already."

So long as one of them did. "Then we're finished here," he said. "Now, I believe you have a hotel to renovate."

～

The last guests of the season would be checking out on Sunday, which meant the renovation could begin in earnest on Monday.

The first order of business was the exterior of the building, and for that Callie needed workers familiar with stripping paint and getting it back on, in a hurry, but properly. No shortcuts or sloppy work.

Where was she going to find that? Surely there were other weathered buildings on the island that required maintenance. In a fishing village, there must be someone with the skills she needed. But who? Callie considered asking Sam, but if she couldn't take the first step without him, what tone would that set for the rest of the project?

Then she spotted Will's business card on the pegboard she'd installed the day before. Offering to show Callie around the island might not have been the same as offering insight for the project, but then, the renovation of the Sunset was as important to Will as it was to Callie. Maybe more so. Callie dialed the number before she could chicken out.

Will picked up on the second ring. "Destination Anchor. Willow Parsons speaking."

"Good morning, Will. This is Callie Henderson over at the Sunset Harbor Inn. I hope I'm not disturbing you."

"Not at all. What can I do for you? And please don't tell me this is bad news."

"No bad news here," Callie was happy to relay. "But we're starting the renovation on Monday, and that means I need a workforce on short notice. I need someone who knows how to handle the exterior first. Do you know who could do that?"

If they'd kept to the original schedule and stuck with a completion date in the late spring, Callie could have taken as much as a month to bring in the right team. She no longer had that luxury.

"I know the exact person you need," Will said.

"Really?" Callie had expected her to have to think about it. Maybe toss out a couple of names for consideration. Then again, on an island this size there might not be multiple candidates for this sort of thing.

"Yep."

When Will failed to elaborate, Callie asked, "Where can I find him?"

"Probably on the front porch," Will said.

"The front porch of what?"

"Your hotel. His name is Bernie Matheson. He and Olaf play checkers over there."

Callie sat back in her chair. That curmudgeon outside her door could not be her only option. "I'm not sure he's the person I need. The exterior of this building is going to need a complete revamping—"

"He's your guy," Will said with finality in her voice. "Bernie is a native and knows everything and anything that has to do with construction, carpentry, and repairing what the elements do to buildings around here. If you want the best, you want Bernie."

Scrubbing a hand over her face, Callie wallowed in frustration and dread for five seconds. Then she wrote Bernie's full name on a Post-it. "Sounds like you're right. I guess I need to head out and have a talk with him, then." Remembering his toothless checkers adversary, she asked, "What about Olaf?"

"He's a bit slow," Will said, "but I've seen what he can do with a piece of furniture. Whether he's building it himself or fixing up an older piece, his work is amazing. Floyd sells it up at the Trading Post if you want to check it out for yourself."

No wonder they'd offered to help out with the renovation. But Callie never would have thought her grumpy welcoming committee would turn out to be her go-to guys for this job.

"Then at least I don't have to go far," she said. Now she had to hope the men were willing to do more than offer casual help. "Thanks for the tip."

"Call anytime. And that invitation is still open," Will said. "My friends and I are meeting at Opal's bakery tomorrow around noon. Stop in, and I'll introduce you."

Since Henri and her mother were heading off the island before nine in the morning, Callie would be free the rest of the day. Though she'd need to start placing orders for the reno, a quick break for lunch wouldn't hurt anything.

"That would be nice. So long as I'm not intruding."

"Of course not. Opal's is on Silver Lake Drive, near the harbor. A few blocks before the Anchor Inn on the right, coming from your direction."

Callie pulled out the tourist map she'd been using to find her way around. "Got it," she said, circling Opal's on the map. "Noon tomorrow, then?"

"One thing," Will said. "If you have any finer sensibilities, you might want to leave them at home."

"Excuse me?" Callie asked.

"You'll understand when you meet Sid. See you tomorrow," she said; then the line went dead.

Callie had expected Will's friends to be women, but that had been a silly assumption on her part. She couldn't help but wonder who this Sid guy was, and what was so offensive about him.

As Sam passed through the lobby on his way to lunch, Rosemary Withers marched through the front doors of the Anchor Inn. Jaw set and her bushy brows nearly touching, the woman appeared ready for a fight in a floral-print dress that looked as if orchids were attacking her.

Sam sighed. This was not his day.

"Good morning, Rosemary," he said, employing his most charming smile. "Nice to see you, as always."

"I've told you before, those big-city charms won't work on me," his archnemesis barked in her bulldog way. "I hear you're starting renovations on the Sunset Harbor Inn. Why haven't I been consulted?"

As president of the Anchor Preservation Society, Rosemary Withers took it as her duty to protect and preserve anything and everything deemed "historic" with her life. Or at least with her formidable personality, which was as daunting as a merciless firing squad.

Sometimes Sam thought he might prefer the firing squad.

"We've finalized the plan only today, Rosemary," Sam said, crossing his arms over his chest. "We're not tearing the building down or adding on to it. This is a surface makeover to change the look and atmosphere, but I can assure you we fully intend to preserve the historic aspects of the facility."

"William Thomas erected the first walls of that building in 1911," she charged on, as if Sam hadn't spoken and didn't know the history of his own property. "That makes the center structure more than one hundred years old and impales upon us the need to preserve that history."

Sam wouldn't have minded being impaled with something right then.

"And preserve it we shall," he said. "Now, if you'll excuse me." Sam bowed. "I'm on my way out."

Rosemary persisted. "I'll need to see the plans."

Breathing deeply, Sam silently counted to ten. Since the Anchor Inn had been built in the 1960s, Rosemary had been a thorn in his side about the color scheme only, as the building needed to blend well with the historic sites around it.

He could see the Sunset Harbor Inn was going to be more of a fight. A fight Rosemary would enjoy a great deal more than he would.

"As I said, the improvements to the Sunset Harbor Inn are cosmetic. The structure is not being altered in any way, so you have nothing to worry about." Placating he would do, but Sam wasn't about to give this interfering old woman the power to approve or disapprove of his plans.

With narrowed eyes that accentuated the deep lines across her forehead, Rosemary stared him down. "What color?"

With a triumphant glare, Sam said, "Same as it was before. Blue gray."

Her response was a huff as she pulled her quilted purse tight against her shoulder. "I'll have my eye on the project and expect to be consulted if any structural changes get added later on."

"Of course," Sam said, more affirming the fact that they both knew she'd be watching and not that she'd ever be consulted.

Rosemary continued to stare until her face suddenly softened and she almost smiled at him.

Almost.

And then she exited the building, leaving Sam staring after her. What was she up to now? But then he knew. As Rosemary traveled everywhere via bicycle, Sam hoped he could reach the inn before the pushy old biddy did.

CHAPTER 8

Staring at the inside of her office door, Callie took several deep breaths in an effort to channel every ounce of inner confidence she could muster. Olaf had already said he and Bernie would help with the renovation. Heaven forbid they not get to play their daily game of checkers.

But now she needed them to take a larger role. To become team players and see her as their leader.

In other words, she needed to charm them into believing they would be in charge.

As expected, she found her quarry on the porch, huddled around their ancient checkerboard. Olaf was playing the red checkers and seemed to be winning. He'd ordered Bernie to king him with a joyous chuckle as Callie approached.

"Good morning, gentlemen," she said, shooting for a cordial tone. "Enjoying your game?"

"What do you want?" Bernie said, eyes glued to the board as he rubbed his chin between the thumb and forefinger of his left hand.

So much for a smooth approach. "I wondered if I might talk to the two of you about the renovations for the hotel. Olaf mentioned before that you'd be willing to help with the work."

"Then we can play on our lunch hour," Olaf said, flashing his gap-toothed grin. The twinkle in his green eyes stirred Callie to imagine he might have been handsome in his day. "You said that would work."

"Yes, I did." Callie hedged, unsure of how to proceed. "But you see—"

"You can't change your mind now," Bernie said, granting Callie his rarely given attention. "So what are you hemming about?"

Straightening her shoulders, Callie blurted, "I've been told you're the best person to handle the restoration of the exterior. Is that true?" she asked Bernie.

The grizzled islander scratched one ear, drawing attention to the gray hairs growing out of it. Callie returned her focus to his watery blue eyes. "I know more than most when it comes to fixing what the weather breaks down around here. If that's what you're asking."

"Do you believe we can save the shingles?" If Bernie didn't give the answer she needed, Callie wasn't sure what they would do. But instead of giving a yes or no, he rose from his seat, shuffled down to the end of the porch, and examined a few shingles that were exposed to the elements.

He rubbed a hand along the peeling surface, scratched, and even sniffed. Returning to the checkerboard, Bernie said, "We can save 'em. She'll need a lot of scraping, but we can get the old girl back to new again."

Callie exhaled as relief washed over her. "Thank goodness."

Jumping one of Olaf's checkers with his own, Bernie said, "We'll start in the spring."

"We can't wait that long," Callie argued. "The entire renovation has to be done by Christmas."

Olaf snorted. "Then you'd better bring back the blessed child, because that would take a miracle."

She aimed for the one thing she knew neither man could ignore. "Then we'll have to find a miracle, because this hotel will be renovated and open for business the weekend before Christmas. I thought you were the men for the job, but I'll have to find more skilled and knowledgeable islanders in the village."

"There ain't nobody got my skills and knowledge. You can search all the way up the Banks and you still won't find anyone who knows what I know."

Thank heaven men never outgrew their egos.

"Good," Callie said, as if she and Bernie were in perfect agreement. "We'll start first thing Monday morning. I'm assuming you can find the manpower we'll need?"

Bernie crossed his arms. "It's short notice, but I should be able to find a crew."

One down. One to go.

Callie turned her attention to the man on her right, flashing her brightest smile. "There's a great deal of furniture inside that could use a master's touch. Is it true that you have a way with such things?"

Olaf actually blushed, sending pink crawling over his forehead to disappear under his fishing cap. "Well," he said, "I don't like to brag."

Callie caught Bernie rolling his eyes but remained focused on her prey. "If I found the right fabrics, could you repair and refurbish the furniture?" She added an extra incentive. "We'll happily supply your name to any guests who express an interest in purchasing a one-of-a-kind piece of their own."

The twinkle gained several watts. "That sounds like a good deal to me."

"You'll still pay him," Bernie said. The words were a statement, not a question.

"Of course we will." Callie resisted the urge to pat herself on the back. "Then we have a team. Bernie's in charge of the exterior improvements, and Olaf, you're in charge of the furniture. We'll create a workshop right here on the premises."

Before Olaf could answer, the chime of a bell sounded from somewhere behind Callie, but it wasn't the front door this time. Bernie leaned to glance around her, then ran a hand through his salt-and-pepper hair, mumbling a profanity.

Curious as to what or who could cause such a reaction, Callie scanned the parking lot and found an elderly woman barreling toward the porch steps, looking like a flower-bedecked Wicked Witch of the West come to take her dog. The bicycle even had a wire basket on the front.

The new visitor pulled to a stop to the left of the stairs, threw a nylon-covered leg over the seat, and leaned the yellow bike against the railing. Tapping her hair into place, she pulled a quilted bag from the basket, pulled it onto her shoulder as if strapping on a weapon for combat, then stomped up the stairs.

"Are you the stranger Mr. Edwards brought to town to fix up this hotel?" she asked upon arriving on the top step.

Callie nodded, struck speechless by the enormous orchids engaged in a botanical skirmish all over the woman's dress. She almost expected petals and shredded leaves to fly into the air around her.

"Are you aware that the first walls of this structure were erected more than one hundred years ago?"

Having done her homework when she'd found the ad for the open position, Callie nodded again.

"And are you aware that we take historical preservation very seriously on this island?"

As she'd also researched the island as a whole, Callie knew there was an Anchor Preservation Society in charge of protecting the island's past. Perhaps she'd underestimated their dedication to the cause.

"My name is Callie Henderson," she said, extending a hand. "And you are?"

"The spawn of Satan," Bernie mumbled behind her, garnering a pinched-face look from their crusading visitor.

"My name is Rosemary Withers, and I am president of the Anchor Preservation Society. I've come to review your plans for the renovation of this hotel."

Callie had faced historical societies before and knew full well what one could and could not do with older properties. As they were not tearing down, altering, or adding on to the current structure, Ms. Withers had nothing to worry about where this particular renovation was concerned.

Callie also knew Sam should be the person dealing with this situation.

"Nice to meet you, Ms. Withers."

"Mrs."

"Excuse me?" Callie said.

"It's *Mrs.* Withers. I was married for fifty-two years, and the fact that Wilford Withers has proceeded on to meet his maker does not make me any less of a Mrs."

Nodding, Callie considered for the first time in her life that perhaps Evelyn Henderson *wasn't* the most difficult woman on Earth.

"My apologies. Mrs. Withers. I'm sure if you speak with Mr. Edwards—"

The woman cut her off. "I spoke with Sam before I came here. I'd like to see the plans."

There would be no plan sharing without direct orders from her boss.

"Would you like something to drink, Mrs. Withers?" Callie ushered the woman toward the entrance. "I did read up on Mr.

Thomas, who of course was the person behind the birth of this structure more than a hundred years ago, but I'm sure that your knowledge of the man and the building would put my meager research sources to shame."

Gray eyes turning softer, Mrs. Withers accepted the subtle compliment with the predictable amount of preening. "I would enjoy a cup of tea after my long ride over here." As Madame President stepped into the lobby, she said over her shoulder, "I'd grab a notepad, dear. You'll want to take notes."

Of course she would. Callie smiled and nodded, ordering Jack, who thankfully was manning his station, to bring them tea as she herded Mrs. Withers into her office.

～

Sam cursed under his breath at the sight of the bright yellow bicycle leaning against the railing in front of the hotel. How the hell had she gotten here so fast? Maybe she hadn't beaten him by much. If he hurried, there was still time to get inside before Rosemary ate Callie for lunch.

Racing through the front door, Sam looked over to the counter on his left, making eye contact with the wide-eyed teenager behind it. "Where are they?"

John or Jack or whatever his name was pointed toward Callie's office.

Sam nodded in thanks, crossed the lobby, and entered without knocking. The scene that greeted him was not what he'd expected. If he hadn't known any better, Sam would think Callie was throwing a tea party.

"Hello, Mr. Edwards," his employee said, rising from her chair with a smile. "Mrs. Withers and I are having a lovely chat." Smiling at the older woman still sitting at the edge of the desk, cup in hand, pinky in air, Callie said, "Did you know this building started as a warehouse for smuggled goods? Isn't that fascinating?"

As the floor seemed to shift beneath him, Sam struggled to get his bearings. "That's how the legend goes," he said. "I always assumed it was local lore created to entertain the tourists."

Rosemary tsked. "It's as true as the chair I'm sitting in. I told you he didn't understand, dear," she said to Callie. "He doesn't appreciate the history like you and I do."

These two were a team now? Exactly how long had Rosemary been here? Maybe that bicycle of hers could fly. A fact that wouldn't surprise him in the least.

"Now, Mrs. Withers, I happen to know that Mr. Edwards has great care for the history and character of his properties. When I was researching whether or not I'd like to work for him, I found an article about a factory he transformed into a hotel in downtown Charleston, South Carolina, in which he salvaged all the wrought iron and original wood floors of the structure. And all of it was repurposed and incorporated into the new plans." With a complete lack of guile, she fluttered her eyelashes in his direction and asked, "Is that story true, Mr. Edwards?"

Maybe he'd stepped into a play. Callie was certainly putting on an award-winning act. "Yes, it is." The hotel hadn't been his, but he'd been in charge of the renovation, and salvaging the building materials had made sense from a financial standpoint, as well as appeased the local historical society.

"You see?" Callie said. "We're all on the same page here. Preservation is key."

Getting the best product was key, but Sam had recovered his wits enough to know now was not the time to voice this fact. "Of course," he said instead. "Preservation." The word sounded less than sincere to his own ears, so Sam accompanied the statement with what he hoped would pass for a sincere smile.

Rosemary didn't look convinced. "Forgive me if I remain skeptical of Mr. Edwards," she said, pinning him with one of her evil-librarian glares. As she turned her attention to Callie, the weathered face softened. "But I trust that you'll keep him in line, my dear."

Sam nearly choked from the effort of keeping his mouth shut. If letting Rosemary believe that Callie could in any way "*keep him in line*" would keep the preservation society off his back, he'd gladly let the old woman have her illusions.

"There will be no need for that," Callie said, earning herself bonus points. "Mr. Edwards has already approved the proposal I submitted, which took all of the historical aspects of the hotel into account. In fact, he insisted on the Brookside shade of green for one block of rooms, specifically for its heritage as a historic American color."

Sam had insisted on the color to counter the more feminine shades Callie had proposed. Another point to Callie for creating the proper spin to appease Rosemary. She could have a future in politics if she ever left the hospitality field.

Rosemary's bushy gray brows nearly touched her hairline. "Really? Well . . . ," she said, looking as if she were sucking on a sliver of lemon. "Perhaps I judged Mr. Edwards too harshly."

He should be gracious, but Sam couldn't resist the temptation. "Apology accepted, Mrs. Withers. We all make mistakes now and then."

Callie shot him an unfriendly glare of her own, reminding him of their purpose here.

"We do appreciate your willingness to share your extensive historical knowledge with us," he said to Rosemary, bowing in her direction. "Your input is very important to us."

This insipid bit of acting seemed to put him firmly back in Callie's good graces, if the grin she gave him was any indication.

"Now, I do hate to put you off, but Mr. Edwards and I have a few details left to discuss before work begins next week." Callie helped Rosemary from her chair, then escorted her to the door. "I hope it's okay that I contact you with any questions as the project progresses?"

"Of course, my dear," Rosemary said, beaming and preening as if she'd been asked to consult on a Ken Burns documentary. "Call anytime. I'll leave my number with that sweet young man at the front desk."

"Perfect." Callie opened the door and nudged Rosemary into the lobby. "You have a wonderful day, Mrs. Withers." As she closed the office door again, Callie let out an audible sigh, her shoulders dropping as if a giant weight had been removed. "That woman is a piece of work."

"And you are one hell of an actor," Sam said. "Did she mention that she came to see me before coming over here?"

"She mentioned it," Callie said, returning to her seat. "How did you know she would head this way?"

Sam lowered into the chair Rosemary had vacated. "She smiled," he said. "Rosemary never smiles at me, so I knew she had to be up to something."

"She wasn't smiling when she got here." Callie laughed as she gathered the teacups, cream, and sugar onto a tray. "And Bernie's referring to her as the spawn of Satan didn't help."

"Bernie?" Sam asked.

"Bernie Matheson. You don't know him?"

The name didn't sound familiar. "Afraid not. Does he work here?"

Callie's brow furrowed. "Not for the hotel, exactly. He's going to be taking lead on renovations of the exterior work. How long have you been on Anchor Island?" she asked.

"Going on three years now. Why?"

"This is a really small island. I guess I expected most everyone who lived here year-round to know each other."

That might be true in some cases, but Sam wasn't big on socializing. "I know most of the business owners, but I don't encounter the other residents very often."

"Oh," she said. "Okay."

Something about her answer bothered him. "I'm not avoiding them," he said, not sure why he felt the need to defend himself. "I was focused on renovating the Anchor when I got here and then building it into the best hotel on the island. That didn't leave much time for bake sales and community picnics."

Callie's eyes softened as she propped her elbow on the desktop. "Do they really have community picnics? I had hoped but thought maybe that kind of stuff only happens in the movies."

There was nothing movie-like about snot-covered rug rats running around screaming their heads off and taking strangers out at the knee. Unless you liked that sort of thing, and Sam did not.

"There's always something going on in the park," he said. "I can hear the noise from my back deck."

Callie stood, lifting the tray with her. "That reminds me," she said. "I don't know where you live. Is it close to the Anchor?"

"Not far," he said, watching her carry the tray to the door. "But then, nothing is far on this island. I'm in a small cabin on Fig Tree Lane."

Balancing the tray against her hip, Callie spun in his direction. "Is that on the water?"

Sam shook his head. "No."

"Hold on a second." Callie opened the door, disappeared into the lobby, then returned empty-handed. "I'm confused. Why would you live in a small cabin in the village when you have that amazing property across the street?" She dropped back into her chair. "Or are you renting that on my behalf from someone else?"

"I own it." Uninterested in explaining his complicated relationship with Peabody Cottage, Sam said, "I'm fine closer to the Anchor. It's nice in the village."

One manicured brow went up. "You called picnics in the park 'noise.'"

She was making him sound antisocial. "A large gathering with live music tends to sound like noise from a distance."

Both elbows on the desk this time, she said, "There's music, too? This keeps getting better."

"If you like pirate shanties and steel drums."

"And you don't, I take it?" She was teasing him. Sam wasn't used to being teased.

"Not my favorites, no." He had yet to eat lunch and opted to use the fact as an escape. Not that he was running from anything. "I was on my way to lunch when Rosemary sidetracked me. I'll have to grab something on my way back to the office now."

"That brings us back to the subject at hand," Callie said. "Why *did* you race over here? You looked ready to do battle when you charged through that door."

He *had* been ready to save Callie from Rosemary's clutches. But that had really been about his property and his choices to renovate it. Not about Callie at all.

Keep believing that, big guy.

"Rosemary demanded I give her approval of the renovation plans. I have no intention of doing so, but you didn't know that."

Callie's lips curled up on one side. "You could have called me to let me know your wishes over the phone."

He couldn't have played the gallant knight saving her from a history-spewing dragon over the phone. "Yes, I could have. As I said, I was on my way out to lunch and not in my office when she caught me. I guess that didn't occur to me."

Neither of them believed what he was saying. Sam could see that on Callie's face. But that didn't mean he was going to change his story. Checking his watch, Sam said, "I'd better go."

"Of course," she said, rising when he did and following Sam to the door. "You wouldn't want to get in trouble with the boss."

She was teasing him again. He played along this time. "No, I wouldn't. *Our* boss can be a bit of a jerk at times."

"But he looks out for his employees," she said, walking beside him to the front entrance. "You have to give him credit for that."

When they reached the door, they turned toward each other. "Yes, he does. His people are important to him." A lock of golden hair fell loose along her temple. Sam fought the urge to tuck it behind her ear. Leaning in and lowering his voice, he whispered, "He isn't really a jerk. He just wants people to think he is."

Callie nodded. "That's what I think, too." Ice-blue eyes danced behind dark lashes, her cheeks slightly pinker than they'd been before. "But let's not tell him we know."

He laughed then. Sam couldn't help himself. "Deal." They shared a smile, and something sizzled between them. The teen behind the counter coughed, jerking Sam back to his senses. "I'll be going, then."

Before he could reach the handle on the door, the large slab of wood came flying at his nose. Sam stepped back in time to see Evelyn Henderson stepping through.

"Oh, good," she said. "We're all here."

CHAPTER 9

Callie cringed at the look in her mother's eyes. She knew that look. That look was bad.

"What are you doing here, Mother?"

"I've come to meet you for lunch, of course. I told you last night I want to try that little sandwich shop we passed the other day."

Why couldn't her mother be forgetful, like other people her age?

"You did, but I didn't realize you meant today," Callie said.

Evelyn propped a hand on her hip. "Well, I'm leaving tomorrow morning. When else did you think I meant?"

Of course. The old *why haven't you learned to read my mind yet?* thing. Another shortcoming on Callie's part.

"Then we'll go," she said, knowing it was easier to comply than to argue. And she did need to eat. "Is Henri coming with us?"

"Your cousin is out gallivanting around the island somewhere." Her mother's nose lifted an inch higher in the air. "She wanted to explore before we leave tomorrow." Lowering her voice, Evelyn added, "I told her not to rush back."

This meant lunch alone with her mother. Callie felt a severe headache coming on.

Sam had remained silent throughout this exchange, a choice for which Callie gave him extra points. He had to be aware that drawing any attention to himself could be dangerous. Evelyn already saw him as prey. Something she could toy with, like a cat with a cute, helpless little bunny.

Not that Callie would ever describe Sam as helpless, but her mother was a professional huntress and could make the bravest of adversaries run for their lives.

If only Callie had the option. To run as far away from her mother as possible. Unfortunately, there wasn't a corner on Earth where Evelyn wouldn't track her down. As evidenced by her very presence on this speck of an island.

"Fine," Callie said. "I have a couple things to wrap up here, and then I'll be over to get you." She shuffled her mother onto the porch. "I won't be long. I promise."

"But what about Sam?" her mother asked.

Callie froze. "What about him?"

"He has to come with us."

"Why does he have to come with us?"

"Because I'm leaving tomorrow." Evelyn rolled her eyes before adding, "Sometimes I wonder if you ever listen to me."

Callie heard every word her mother ever said. She just never understood them.

"Mother," she started, resisting the urge to inform her matriarch that she was nuts, "Sam is not required to entertain you while you're here. I'm sure he has more important things to do."

Ignoring her daughter's perfectly sane response, the blonde menace marched up to Sam. "You're going to lunch with us, aren't you, Sam?"

After a brief hesitation, during which his eyes flew to Callie, then back to his attacker, Sam said, "Yes, ma'am."

"As I said." Evelyn turned away to prance down the porch steps.

Callie looked at Sam and mouthed, "Why did you do that?" to which Sam mouthed back, "What could I do?" with a shrug of his wide shoulders.

"Don't dally," Evelyn chirped from the parking lot. "I'm assuming Sam drove over here. He can drive us to lunch. Which vehicle is yours, Sam?"

"The red Murano," he answered, though the only other vehicles in the parking lot were an old, rusty blue pickup and a dented silver Civic. It wasn't as if assigning ownership to the vehicles required possession of a genius IQ.

"You don't have to do this," Callie whispered after Sam pulled the door shut behind them and the pair walked together toward his car.

"It's one lunch," he said. "How bad could it be?"

He might as well have asked how hot could a raging volcano be? How cold could January in the Arctic be? How bad could an eternity in hell be?

Evelyn was climbing into the passenger seat as Callie whispered, "Imagine having your wisdom teeth pulled with no anesthesia." When Sam's brows rose, she added, "Times ten."

∼

As Callie had predicted, lunch with Evelyn Henderson had been an excruciating experience. Sam had been raised in the South by an unaffectionate mother and a demanding father. He'd endured cotillions, mind-numbing dinner parties, and silent family affairs where disappointment and repressed anger hung in the air like the seagulls hovered over sand, dive-bombing anything that moved.

Yet lunch with Callie's mother had felt exactly as she'd described it would. Like surgery without anesthesia. Except instead of losing his wisdom teeth, Sam felt more like he'd lost his liver. And surgery had been conducted with a butter knife.

"I'm really sorry," Callie said for the fourth time since they'd dropped Evelyn at the cottage. They were sitting alone in his Murano in front of the Sunset Harbor Inn, both too shell-shocked to get out. "I tried to warn you."

"She pinched my ass," he said, still stunned by the unexpected attack. "I feel like I need a shower."

Callie sighed. "I have to admit, I didn't think she'd go that far. I knew she had it in her, but jeez." Dropping her chin to her chest, she said again, "I'm so sorry."

Then the absurdity of the whole thing hit him. And Sam started to laugh. Really laugh. Something he hadn't done in longer than he could remember.

"Oh my God," Callie said. "She broke you. Sam, are you okay?"

He laughed harder, nodding his head. "I'm fine," he managed to say. "Just fine."

Soon Callie was laughing with him. "I guess it's better to laugh than to cry."

As their amusement faded, Sam looked over to see diamond-blue eyes staring at him. Blinking, she said, "I needed that."

Sam agreed. "So did I."

"There is one bit of good news in this," she said, choking back a giggle. "She'll be gone tomorrow."

Another round of laughter followed that statement. Clearly, they'd both lost their marbles, driven insane by a pushy Southern belle who believed the world danced to her tune. Sam could only guess what it must have been like to grow up as Evelyn Henderson's daughter.

The thought snatched the laughter from his lips. Not that his own mother had been a prize, but she'd never embarrassed him in front of others. Or belittled him in any way. She'd simply set high expectations.

And Sam had done his best to hit every one of them.

Something told him Callie could discover the cure for cancer and Evelyn would have little to say except "It took you long enough."

Unsure how to express what he was thinking, Sam blurted the words, "You're pretty well adjusted considering that woman raised you." Not exactly the best way to put it, but the words were true.

Callie took a deep breath. Her shoulders rose, then fell. She kept her eyes on her knees for several seconds, then faced him again, with a sad, self-deprecating grin this time. "Therapy does wonders."

He couldn't help but smile. "Maybe I should try it someday."

"Let me know," she said, reaching for the handle on her door. "I can recommend a good one in the Charleston area."

"If it makes you feel any better, you aren't the only one with a hard-to-please parent."

Callie's door remained closed as she turned back to him. "Oh yeah?"

Tapping on the base of the steering wheel, Sam nodded. "Yeah. Eugenia Edwards has some pretty high standards."

The snort was unexpected. "Then you must have been her dream child. Intelligent. Handsome. Total overachiever."

"True," he said, attempting to make a joke. Callie's laughter felt like a prize. "But I'm an overachiever out of necessity, not natural tendencies." Sam didn't know why he was telling her all this. He never talked about his childhood. To anyone.

But for some reason, he desperately wanted to make her feel better.

"I suppose I should thank her, though. Who knows what I'd be today if it weren't for Mother's high demands?"

"You call her Mother?" Callie asked, her blue eyes sparkling like icicles in the sunlight.

With a grin, Sam leaned toward her. "Not always."

Callie choked on a giggle as she reached for her door handle again. "Thank you," she said. "For enduring lunch with my mother, and for trying to make me feel better." One heel hit the gravel before she turned back his way. "And about thanking your mother? You'd still be the successful man you are today, Sam, no matter what she was like. I don't doubt that for a second."

Sam watched Callie climb out of his car with a mixture of feelings—protectiveness and a sense of peace—two things he hadn't felt in many years. As he watched her walk away, a feeling of unease came over him.

The return of Callie Henderson into his life was turning out to be more dangerous than Sam had first suspected. He'd worried she'd churn up old memories. Open old wounds. But if he wasn't careful, she might inflict some new ones.

~

"You need to land that fish, young lady," Evelyn yelled through Callie's bathroom door. "While you still have the looks to do it."

Standing at the sink in nothing but jeans and a bra, Callie fought the urge to smack her forehead against the porcelain. Maybe she could knock herself unconscious and not wake up until after her mother had left the island.

"I know you can hear me in there."

"Of course I can hear you, Mother. They can probably hear you in China."

"Don't you sass me, Calliope Mabel."

What kind of name was that? Calliope Mabel. She'd come to terms with the Calliope part years ago, but Mabel? The two names didn't even sound right together. If she ever had a daughter, Callie would name her something pretty. Like Olivia Jane or Isabelle Marie. No Mabels.

"And hurry up," Evelyn snapped. "We're going to be late for dinner."

Saturday morning could not come soon enough.

Out of spite, Callie took another fifteen minutes. She spent most of that time reading a magazine article about the newest trends in interior design. When she emerged from her private powder room, she found Henri sitting on her bed, reading a magazine of her own.

"You abandoned me today," Callie said, not yet ready to forgive her cousin for leaving her and Sam in Evelyn's clutches.

"If you think I can in any way control your mother, I'm going to suggest you cut back on the crack."

"At least with you around she has someone other than me to criticize." Expecting anyone to volunteer to spend more time with her mother was mean, but Callie was feeling too bitter and embarrassed to care.

"And I have to endure that criticism for nine hours tomorrow." Henri snapped the magazine shut. "Whatever she did must have been bad, to get you this pissed. Do I even want to know?"

Callie gave Henri a droll look. "She insisted Sam come to lunch with us."

Henri gasped. "No. And he went?"

"She didn't give him much choice."

"The poor guy." At Callie's glare, she added, "And you. Poor you."

Callie tossed her work clothes into the hamper. "When she wasn't hitting on him, she was suggesting that he and I would make beautiful babies together. She kept asking about his *vast holdings* of hotels and all but demanded to know his net worth."

Henri cringed. "That sounds like Evelyn."

"And then . . . " Callie hesitated, steeling herself against the image playing on a loop in her mind. "She grabbed his ass on the way to the car."

Her cousin had the gall to collapse into fits of laughter on the bed.

"I'm glad you find this amusing."

"Come on," Henri said, returning to a sitting position. "That's cheeky even for Aunt Evelyn. How did Sam take it?"

Dropping onto the bed, Callie smiled. "Oddly enough, he found it hysterical."

"He *is* the perfect man," Henri murmured.

"Not at first, of course," Callie said. "But after we dropped her off, we were sitting in his SUV and he started laughing. Out of nowhere. Uncontrolled mirth!"

Henri bumped Callie with her shoulder. "You have to admit. It's kind of funny."

Callie bumped back. "I was mortified. I still can't believe she did it." She fell back on the bed with a moan.

"Come on, Cal," Henri said. "She's done worse."

Eyes shut tight, Callie answered, "Never to one of my bosses."

"Sam isn't just another boss," Henri reminded her. "You've boffed him."

Callie jerked upright. "Shhhhh . . . My mother doesn't know that, and neither does anyone else around here."

"Except me."

"A confidence I'm starting to regret now," Callie said, rising to her feet. "Come on," she said, offering Henri a hand. "We might as well get this over with. One more meal, then she's gone in the morning."

"Then I'm stuck with her in a confined space," Henri added. "Which is why you're once again buying the drinks."

"Too bad the restaurant is too far away for us to walk," Callie lamented. "I wouldn't mind getting liquored up myself."

∾

Callie had never been so happy to be alone. Though Cecil was still with her, he wasn't going to tell Callie that her ass was getting too big or that she was going to die childless with a shriveled-up womb, denying him the rightful grandparrots he deserved.

At least she hoped a few days with her mother hadn't been long enough for him to pick up these particular lines. Though she loved her parrot dearly, a window might get accidentally left open if her feathered friend started talking that much like her mother.

After watching the taillights of Henri's truck fade into the distance, Callie poured herself a cup of tea, dragged a blanket out to the deck, and watched the waves pound the sand for a good hour. Watching the seagulls diving at the water or hovering on the wind, wings spread wide and strong, she breathed in the salt air and felt a vivid sense of home.

As if this was where Callie was meant to be. Which she was, for at least the next three months. Longer if Sam would keep her. Once she'd turned the inn around, and in record time, surely he'd ask her to stay.

Best to play it by ear. Something she'd learned in therapy was to take life one day at a time. And that was exactly what Callie was thinking about as she pulled into the parking lot in front of Sweet Opal's Bakery and Confections.

The building looked like an old, two-story house that had been converted into a storefront. A long, narrow porch ran across the front, with a door to the right and two Adirondack chairs on the left. An elderly couple occupied the chairs, the woman eating what looked like an éclair and the man some kind of pie.

Stepping onto the porch, she smiled at the woman, who offered up a salute with her treat. Callie assumed they were late-season tourists, since the man wore sunscreen on his nose and a camera rested on his large stomach, as if ready to catch a memory for the folks back home.

Entering the shop, Callie took in the large display case filled with an endless array of treats. Everything looked decadent and able to put ten pounds on her hips by Christmas.

"Callie," a voice yelled from her left. "Down here." Will Parsons waved from a table in the corner that she was sharing with a pretty redhead and a gorgeous brunette. It was official: Anchor Island was a refuge for incredibly beautiful people.

CHAPTER 10

"Hi there," she said, stepping up to the table.

"Glad you could make it," Will said with a smile. "This is Beth Dempsey," she offered, motioning toward the redhead. Then she nodded toward the brunette. "And the little tugboat in the corner is Sid Navarro. The one I warned you about."

Sid was a woman?

"What do you mean, you fucking warned her about me?"

With brows up, Will didn't give her friend so much as a glance. "And now you know what I meant. Guys, this is Calliope Henderson."

"Please," she said, "call me Callie."

"That's right," Will said. "Callie." Scooting over to the chair against the window, she tapped the one she'd vacated. "Have a seat."

Callie hesitated. "Are you sure I'm not intruding?"

"Of course not," the one named Beth said. "Will has been telling us that you're an old friend of Sam's. He's a bit of an enigma around here, so we find this fact highly intriguing."

If this meeting was to coax facts about Sam's past out of her, Callie would not be sticking around. "I wouldn't say old friends. We were more acquaintances."

Which was true. She'd been best friends with Meredith and therefore acquainted with Sam. But they didn't know each other that well. At least, they hadn't before that last night.

"We aren't going to grill you," Will said, offering her the chair once again. "We're discussing Beth's baby shower."

The redhead sat back with a smile, and Callie noticed her enlarged belly for the first time. "Oh, wow. Congratulations. Now I *know* I'm intruding."

"Nonsense," Beth said. "The more the merrier. Really."

"If you're sure." Callie settled into the red, retro-style seat and noticed each woman had a dessert in front of her. "Those look good."

"Opal is the best," Sid said. "She can bake anything. What's your favorite? Prego here will eat anything." She pointed a thumb in her friend's direction.

Beth looked slightly offended, then shrugged. "That's true right now. Bugger isn't choosy."

"Bugger?" Callie asked.

"That's what they call the munchkin," Sid answered. "The selfish asses won't find out if it's a boy or a girl so the rest of us can know what the hell to buy."

"For the umpteenth time, we want to be surprised!"

"That doesn't mean the rest of us should have to stay in the dark," Sid argued, sliding a fork into the chocolate cupcake in front of her.

"Yes," Beth said. "It actually does."

Sid huffed and Beth sighed and Callie wondered if these women were really friends.

"Besides," Beth said, cutting what looked to be a slice of carrot cake, "it's not as if you're going to buy anything other than tool toys, regardless of what gender it is."

This time Sid snorted. "That's true." The women laughed, and Callie realized this was more than friendship. Though she was an only child, she recognized what she and Henri had. These women were more like family.

Now she really felt like an outsider.

"We've already settled on yellow and green for the party colors," Will said, bringing Callie up to speed. "For obvious reasons. And we're having the shower at the Anchor Inn. We'd use Dempsey's, but Beth doesn't like the idea of having a baby shower in a bar."

"As a woman raised in the South," Callie said, "I thank you. That always bothered me, too."

"You see?" Beth said, glancing between her dark-haired friends. "She agrees with me."

"I'm sorry," Callie said. "I don't want to step on toes."

"Stomp away." Will slid her fork into a slice of rhubarb pie. "You won't hurt our feelings. She's the mom and what she says goes."

Sid rolled her eyes. "I don't give a shit where we have it."

Callie almost wished she could introduce this pint-size profanity machine to her mother for the shock value alone. The conniption would be epic.

Before Callie could ask what else they needed to work out, a short woman with gray hair, round cheeks, and a friendly smile stepped up to the table. "Hey there, darling. You must be the new gal fixing up the Sunset Harbor. Rosemary said you were pretty as a button, and she was right."

"Rosemary said that?" Callie asked, struggling to imagine the preservation patron saying quite those words.

The older woman waved a hand in the air. "Not exactly, but that's what she meant. I'm Opal," she said, wiping her hand on her apron. "Tell me your favorite dessert ever, and I bet I have it."

Callie smiled. "You probably don't."

Opal looked as if she'd been insulted, and the ladies at the table exchanged surprised glances.

"I don't mean anything by it. It's just that my favorite dessert is an English dish, and I rarely find anyone in America who makes it."

Well, this was going well. She'd managed to offend a sweet old lady and look like a pretentious ass to the women who were befriending her. Why couldn't she have asked for apple pie?

Opal put a hand on her hip. "What's it called?" she asked, the friendly smile no longer present.

"Eton Mess," Callie replied, longing to disappear under the table.

With pursed lips, Opal seemed to be searching her memory banks. Then she said, "I'll be right back," and disappeared behind the counter.

Silence reigned until Callie said, "I should have asked for pie. I didn't mean to offend her."

Sid laughed. "Are you kidding? You made her day."

"I what?"

"You gave her a challenge." Sid stabbed a piece of cupcake with her fork. "No one has stumped Opal yet. Kinzie—that's her granddaughter—says Opal prides herself on knowing every dessert out there. You'll have your mess thing in no time."

"Oh," Callie said, not sure how to respond. She would love to have the dessert, since she hadn't been to England in nearly ten years, but she didn't want to put anyone out. "It really isn't that complicated. I didn't mean to make any trouble."

"Don't be silly," Will said, sharing a look with her friends that Callie couldn't interpret. "Now that we've all settled into domestic bliss, so to speak, things have gotten boring. We could use a little trouble around here."

"Yeah," Sid agreed. "Stir shit up."

Callie felt the need to be honest. "I'm not really the shit-stirring type."

Beth tapped a fingernail on her glass of milk. "A gorgeous blonde harboring secrets about the island's most eligible bachelor?" A tapered brow danced over sparkling green eyes. "Don't underestimate yourself, Ms. Henderson. You could stir all sorts of shit."

And they were back to Sam again. "I'm not harboring anything," she said, knowing it for a lie as soon as the words were out. "Sam is my boss, and if he wants anyone to know about his past, he'll have to be the one to share." Knowing the more folks believed there was some deep, dark secret—which, in all honesty, there wasn't—the more they'd push for answers, Callie offered one caveat.

"I *can* say that whatever folks around here are imagining, it's probably nowhere near the truth. He's a nice guy who runs hotels." She shrugged. "There's nothing sinister to tell. No secret identity. No big bad lurking anywhere." With a laugh, she added, "That stuff only happens in the movies."

No one cracked a smile as Will murmured, "Not always."

"I'm sorry?" Callie asked, but Opal returned to the table before Will could explain.

Opal set a glass bowl in front of Callie. "There you go," she said. "I even tossed in a dash of port like the website said."

Everyone at the table grew silent, staring at the bowl as if it might explode.

"No fucking way," Sid said in hushed tones.

"Well?" Opal snapped. "Try it."

The concoction looked accurate, with the whipped cream and strawberries mixed together, and even a sliced strawberry on top. Callie removed the spoon stuck in the side and braced herself before sliding a bite between her lips.

And then her taste buds did explode. "Oh my God," she said around the sweetness in her mouth. "You did it."

The cheerful baker returned, clapping her hands in excitement. "I've been trying to think of something new I could add to the menu." Opal hugged Callie's shoulders. "Now I have it. Thank you, darling. You've got a free dessert here anytime you want it."

"Hey," Sid said, "you don't give me free desserts."

"Shush," Opal said, waving a hand at Sid. "What's your name, honey child?" she asked Callie.

"This is Calliope Henderson, Opal," Will answered for her. "But she goes by Callie."

"Calliope's Eton Mess," Opal said. "That's how it'll appear on the menu."

"What the hell?" Sid said. "What makes her so special? How come you don't name shit after us?"

Opal turned to Sid. "You eat a chocolate cupcake with chocolate buttercream, Sidney Ann. What exactly is unique about that?"

Sidney Ann sounded much too girlie for the dark-haired woman with the spicy tongue, who grew even prettier when she blushed. Though "pretty" wasn't the right word. "Sultry," maybe. And then Callie realized Sid wasn't wearing any makeup. Those long, dark lashes were natural. Since Callie's were practically transparent without mascara, she fought the stab of jealousy.

Then Sid stood up and charged around Beth to approach Opal. Despite the baggy T-shirt and loose-fitting cargo pants, Callie could see Sid's body looked amazing. What the hell did they put in the water on this island?

Wait. Hadn't Beth described Callie as a gorgeous blonde only moments ago? Maybe the water perfected their bodies while muddling their minds.

"If you loved me," Sid was saying to Opal, "you'd name something after me."

When had this become a competition? Opal could call the thing Sidney's Eton Mess if it meant that much to her.

Opal slammed both hands onto her ample hips. "How about Sidney Ann's Shit Cake?"

After several seconds of a tense stare-down, everyone burst out laughing. Everyone except Callie, who was beginning to question their sanity.

"Sorry," Beth said, noticing Callie's confusion. "We're kind of a family around here."

"We put the 'fun' in 'dysfunctional,'" Will added, still laughing. "Opal, you have to make Sidney Ann's Shit Cakes for Beth's shower. And throw in some of Calliope's Mess, too."

"Is it as good as it looks?" Beth asked, licking her lips.

Callie pushed the bowl across the table. "It is. Try some."

Beth slipped a bite into her mouth, then closed her eyes as her head dropped back, accompanied by a moan of ecstasy.

"That good, huh?" Will asked. "Let me try." After doing so, Will had a reaction similar to Beth's.

Feeling as if she'd shown them all a new invention, Callie gave herself a mental pat on the back. Though it was Opal who deserved the credit.

"You're a wonder, Miss Opal," she said, smiling up at the older woman, who was currently hugging Sid against her side.

"I've been called worse," she responded, giving Callie a wink.

As Will and Beth took turns with the Eton Mess, Sid said, "You're alright, Blondie."

Assuming this to be some kind of high praise from the rough-edged woman, Callie nodded. "Thank you, Sid. I'm glad you think so."

~

Regardless of the number of times Sam had told himself that he would not be the overbearing boss who checked in constantly, he arrived at the Sunset Harbor Inn early Monday morning to observe, and maybe supervise, the kickoff of the project. He told himself that Callie might need his input when dealing with the natives.

They could be an interesting group and preferred their own methods, which were often somewhat . . . unconventional.

Proven by the three men hanging from the roof as Sam pulled up.

Callie stood several feet in front of the inn, staring at the men dangling along the facade.

"What exactly are they doing?" he asked, startling her. "Sorry—I thought you heard me walk up."

"No," she said. "I'm too busy worrying about the possibility of a broken neck on our first day." Turning to face him, she asked, "Isn't there a safer way to do this?"

Nodding, Sam said, "I'm sure there is. Did you suggest they take another approach?"

Callie used her hand to block the glare of the sun off the hotel windows. "Of course I did. But Bernie says with the porch in the way, they can't run scaffolding along the center. He says this approach is perfectly safe." One of the danglers swung several feet to the left, and Callie let out a gasp. "I can't watch this anymore."

As they walked toward the entrance, two smaller crews were assembling scaffolding against each of the far ends. For the first time, Sam noticed the large number of people milling about.

"Where did you find all of these workers?"

"Bernie brought them," Callie answered. "I had to convince him that it wasn't necessary to start on Sunday. The last thing I wanted was the entire island resenting this project because they had to begin work on a weekend."

Smart move on her part. Sam wasn't sure he'd have thought of it. Knowing how quickly they needed the job completed and the intense amount of work there was to do, he likely would have taken the one-day head start.

"I suppose that makes sense," he said, unwilling to admit his own shortsightedness.

Callie pulled her jacket tight against the chill air coming off the water. "You suppose?"

Arguing would be pointless when he knew she was right. That didn't mean he had to concede, either.

"Where is this Bernie person?" he asked.

Callie nodded for him to follow and proceeded down the long porch. When they reached the end, she yelled over the side, "Bernie!" An older man with wiry black-and-gray hair crawled out of the base of the scaffolding.

"What do you want?" he yelled back. "I'm working here!"

Where had she found this disrespectful old coot? Sam fully expected Callie to put the man in his place and remind him that she was the boss here.

"And you're doing a wonderful job," Callie answered, taking Sam by surprise. "But I'd like you to meet the man who'll be signing your paychecks. It'll take only a minute."

The man mumbled the entire time he crossed the grounds in their direction but looked up with a grin once he arrived. "Nice to meet you," he said, then hitched around to return to work.

"Bernie," Callie snapped. "Are you or are you not the expert here?"

That seemed to get the codger's attention. "You know I am."

"Then let me introduce you to Mr. Edwards properly so we can make sure you get the recognition you deserve."

What game was Callie playing? Compliments and ego stroking, when she should have firmly reminded the codger exactly who was in charge here? Sam was about to show Callie exactly how to handle the situation, when the old man flashed a sincere smile and returned to the porch edge with what looked to be a blush on his cheeks.

"Thank you," Callie said, then turned to Sam. "This is Bernie Matheson, our foreman for the exterior work on the hotel. As an Anchor native, Mr. Matheson has extensive experience with structures battered by coastal weather. He has graciously offered to help us return the Sunset Harbor Inn to pristine condition."

Sam doubted this man had ever been gracious about anything.

"Mr. Matheson," he said, unwilling to play a part in this charade Callie was conducting.

"And, Bernie, this is Sam Edwards, owner of the hotel."

"I know who he is," Bernie barked. Callie shot him a look, and the man nodded. "Right. Nice to meet you." Pulling a wool hat from his back pocket, he returned his attention to Callie. "Now I'm going back to doing what you're paying me to do. Is that alright with you?"

"Of course," Callie said with a smile.

As the man stomped back to his scaffolding, Sam turned on Callie. "In the office. Now."

CHAPTER 11

Callie didn't like Sam's tone. She'd been dealing with fragile male egos all morning. Adding Sam's to the list was not on her agenda. "Sure," she said. "No problem."

She led the way, with Sam following close behind. Neither said a word until she'd closed the office door.

"What were you doing out there?" Sam demanded.

"What do you mean?"

Sam stepped closer, until less than a foot separated them. "That man was belligerent and disrespectful, and you acted as if he was in charge and you were some lowly secretary whose job it was to blow sunshine up his ass."

Of course that was how he would see it. Callie's jaw tightened as she struggled to control her temper.

"What I was doing was dealing with a specific employee in a manner that would get me what I wanted. Bernie Matheson is a cranky old man, set in his ways, who happens to have the skills and knowledge we need to pull off this renovation in the ridiculously short time to which *you* have committed us."

So much for controlling her temper. Tired of having to crank her neck to see Sam's face, Callie took a step backward. "I could let my pride get in the way and demand Mr. Matheson bow and scrape, which would have him quitting the project before we've even gotten started, or I can apply a little flattery and patience to get this renovation done. I choose the latter."

Sam's blue-gray eyes darkened to the shade of a menacing storm cloud. She considered he might fire her now, on the spot, but instead he took a step back.

In a deeper-than-usual voice, he said, "The man needs to know who's in charge."

"He knows who's in charge," Callie growled—the best she could do when she wanted to scream. "It seems to me you're the one who needs the reminder. Did you or did you not make me the lead on this project?"

Callie bristled as Sam backed her up against the desk. Though he didn't lay a hand on her, didn't touch her in any way, she could feel the heat radiating from him. Her own temperature spiked when she caught him staring at her bottom lip.

"You might be in charge of this project," he mumbled, his breath warm on her face, "but I'm the owner of this hotel and the one also signing *your* paychecks." Her body stiffened, with anger and something much more primal. "You'd do well to remember that."

Sam hovered above her, and all Callie could think was that she wanted him to kiss her. Hell, she'd clear the desk in one swipe if he wanted more.

Then his body heat was gone. Without another word, Sam threw open her office door and stormed out.

⁓

God, that was close. Sam hadn't needed to fight for control that hard in more years than he could remember. Maybe ever. What the hell kind of cliché was he? An attractive woman got firing mad, and he was suddenly as hard as a schoolboy with his first dirty magazine.

"Son of a bitch," he muttered, slamming his office door harder than necessary.

He should not have let her get to him. Maybe he should never have hired her in the first place. Callie brought back too many memories. Reminded him of too many weaknesses. Pushed him to want things he couldn't have and didn't deserve.

Sam muffled another curse when the buzzer went off on his phone. Pressing the INTERCOM button, he said, "Yes?"

"Mr. Dempsey is here to see you, sir."

He'd completely forgotten about his meeting with Lucas Dempsey. Sam was not in the mood to discuss legal matters, but he wasn't going to waste another man's time either. He'd made this appointment and he'd damn well keep it.

"Give me a minute, please," he said into the air, then released the button on the phone.

Sam prowled his office, removing his jacket and slinging it over the back of his chair. He loosened his tie, then the top button on his shirt. Mrs. Appleton had gone heavy on the starch this week, and Sam made a mental note to say something the next time he dropped off his laundry.

After pouring himself a glass of water, Sam dropped into his chair. He knew that firing Callie wasn't remotely an option, but he would need to keep a safer distance from now on.

Giving her the full autonomy she wanted was the only way to make this work. With that conclusion drawn, Sam took a deep breath, secure that the problem had been solved.

Pressing the INTERCOM button again, Sam said, "Send Mr. Dempsey in, please."

Within seconds, the lanky lawyer strolled through Sam's office door. Wearing khakis and a polo shirt, Lucas looked more like a man ready for the golf course than one meeting with a client. Reminding Sam once again that he was the only person around who hadn't caved to the laid-back island way of dressing.

Lucas Dempsey had been a man chasing a partnership at a large law firm in Richmond, Virginia, once upon a time. And he'd likely worn suits the price of a solid used car in doing so.

Sam rose from his chair as Lucas approached his desk. "Sorry for the delay," he said, shaking the hand Lucas offered.

"No problem," Lucas said, taking a seat. "I'm afraid you're not going to like my news."

Not what Sam wanted to hear. "Then you've had no luck?"

Lucas shook his head. "Sorry, but no. Your uncle's will is completely sound. The requirement that you keep the hotels, running them from here on the island for no less than five years, was locked in the minute you took possession."

Sam had taken possession only because he hadn't been given a choice. If he'd turned down the inheritance and the terms that came with it, both hotels would have been sold to the Anchor Preservation Society at a price well below value. A price that might as well have made them a donation.

"I never thought the terms would stand." Sam was too agitated to remain seated. Pacing, he said, "We can't even shorten it? The Sunset will be done by Christmas, and at that point I can bring in competent managers and get off this island."

Lucas sat back in his chair. "It isn't such a bad place," he said. Ironic coming from the man who'd grown up on Anchor and then hauled his ass off at the first opportunity.

"Not bad," Sam said. "Small."

"It is that," Lucas agreed with a chuckle. Sobering, he straightened. "Sam, I assure you I've tried everything I can think of. So long as he didn't make the terms contingent on marriage, divorce, or a change of religion on your part, the terms stand. The only other alternative is to prove him of unsound mind or under undue influence at the time the will was created."

Dropping into his leather chair, Sam let out a long-suffering sigh. "What's two more years, right?"

"Right," Lucas said, sounding chipper enough to make Sam want to punch him. "And there's a good chance that when the two years are up, the properties will have increased in value. Think of it as a two-year investment for a larger return in the end."

Sam tried to embrace Lucas's positive outlook, but the silver lining tarnished when he thought of all the larger hotels he could and should be running. He missed the bigger game.

"I do appreciate your time," he said. "And I'd also appreciate it if you kept digging a bit in case there's a loophole we've missed."

"I doubt I'll find anything," Lucas said. "Artie knew what he was doing when he drew up that will."

Arthur Berkowitz, known as Artie around the island, had been the only lawyer in town for more than three decades, before retiring a couple years ago. The loss of his practice had required the locals to seek legal counsel off-island, until Lucas had set up shop the year before.

Artie and Morty had been best friends for many years before his uncle's death, and Artie had made it clear to Sam whose interests he represented. In this scenario, that person had not been Sam.

"There is one colleague I could ask," Lucas continued, pulling Sam back to the discussion. "An associate who specializes in this sort of thing in my former firm, and who spent years practicing in Raleigh before moving to Richmond. If there's something we haven't thought of, he'd know about it."

With the glimmer of renewed hope, Sam joined Lucas on the other side of the desk. "I'll take any chance I can get."

"I don't want to get your hopes up," Lucas said. "The chances are slim."

The glimmer fading, Sam nodded. "Understood."

"I am familiar with the drive to get off this island." Scratching the back of his neck, Lucas offered an understanding smile. "But this place *can* grow on you. If you let it."

Like an itchy rash, Sam thought, but he kept the sentiment to himself. It also helped that Lucas had fallen for a woman deeply entrenched in the island.

"I'll be leaving in two years," he said. "If not before."

Lucas gave a knowing smile. "Don't be surprised if you change your mind."

~

By lunchtime, Callie still wasn't sure what exactly had happened with Sam. They clearly had two different management styles—of that there was no doubt. As a man used to being in charge, Sam hadn't taken well to Callie's brash and, now that she'd had some distance and time to cool off, totally inappropriate challenge to his authority.

But the encounter hadn't been all business, not by a long shot.

After spending her morning tracking down flooring matches for the hardwood already in the hallways, and having Jack and his friend Lot move the salvageable pieces of furniture into the dining room, Callie was ready to discuss the plan with Olaf.

Glancing at the clock, she knew exactly where to find him.

"Who's winning?" she asked, as she joined the men on the porch.

"Who do you think?" asked Olaf with glee, his fishing cap pushed back far enough on his head to reveal four red strands lying against his scalp. So he wasn't completely bald after all.

"Stick a sock in it, you old coot." Bernie carried his usual scowl. "You don't win all the time."

Olaf proceeded to take Bernie's last black checker and said, "Just most of the time."

Bernie growled as Olaf celebrated. Callie shook her head, wondering why two men who bickered like an old married couple would choose to spend so much time together.

"If you have a minute, Olaf," she said, "we've moved all of the furniture that needs your attention into the dining room. We need to see if there are any pieces you won't be able to save."

Olaf turned serious, and it was Bernie's turn to chuckle. "What makes you think there'll be anything I can't save?" Olaf asked, looking as if she'd somehow insulted his manhood.

Callie blinked. "Some of the pieces are really old. If they can't be made new again, I need to know so I can order replacements."

Olaf stood up, his fishing cap bobbing under Callie's nose. Looking down into narrowed green eyes, she felt yet another confrontation coming on.

"There ain't nothing I can't fix. You hear me?"

She did not have the strength for this.

"Mr. Hogenschmidt, I care about one thing and one thing only—completing this renovation to Mr. Edwards's specifications before the deadline. I appreciate your willingness to aid in that endeavor, and the last thing I would ever do is insult your capabilities."

Olaf blinked.

"Now, can we please proceed inside to assess these pieces?"

The man saved Callie the trouble of having to drag him by the ear.

"Yes, ma'am," he said. "Lead the way."

With relief, Callie escorted him inside the hotel. She'd made the mistake of not checking the room before she'd gone out to get Olaf. She should have known better. It was in shambles. Furniture stacked this way and that, some upside down or turned on its side.

As she was about to apologize to Olaf for the chaos, he moved farther into the mess. "This is going to keep me busy for weeks," he said. Callie thought she heard joy in his voice. "You'll need to pick the finish you want right away so I can order enough varnish."

"I have the samples in my office," she said, watching Olaf run a hand across the arm of a large parlor chair. "I apologize for how things are thrown in here. I'll get Jack and his friend to put them in order."

Olaf turned in her direction. "Nothing wrong in here. Looks like my workshop, except there's more pieces here."

If this was how Olaf liked to work, maybe he wasn't the person for this job. They did have a tight deadline and Sam had high expectations, as did she.

"This isn't too much for you, is it?"

"Course not," he said, testing the strength of a table leg. "Nothing's too much for me."

"Good," Callie said, feeling less confident than she sounded. "Then we need to find you a work space. We can recruit some men from the crew to help you bring over what you need."

"Eh," he said, spinning a loose spindle in the back of a chair. "Bernie and me loaded up the truck yesterday." Olaf pointed to a back corner of the room. "Plenty of room back there, and we can use those double doors to go in and out."

Callie hadn't thought of using the dining room as an actual work space, especially since it would need a lot of attention, removing wallpaper and applying new paint, as well as a good buff on the floor.

Speaking of the floors: "Won't the work be messy?" she asked, hoping Olaf wouldn't take this as another insult to his skills. "I mean, we can't have stains on the floor."

"Cardboard," the older man said.

The look on Callie's face must have revealed her confusion.

"We'll cover the floor with large pieces of cardboard, same as I do in the shop." Olaf raised his bushy brows. "If I get started right away, the room will be cleared in plenty of time for whatever you have planned in here. Nothing to worry about."

He sounded so certain, Callie couldn't help but believe him. "Thank you," she said. "I doubt I'd be able to get this project done without you. Or Bernie." The irony of this fact was not lost on Callie. If someone had told her two old and weathered islanders would be her saviors . . .

"We're doing it for Morty." Olaf said the words with a shrug, as if this was something Callie should have known.

"I'm sorry," Callie said. "Who is Morty?"

Green eyes met hers. "The owner of this place. You know, Morty."

Callie tapped her chin as she pondered this statement. Maybe Olaf was senile.

"Sam Edwards owns this hotel." She said the words slowly, emphasizing each word as if speaking to a person hard of hearing.

"Only 'cause Morty let him have it."

A throbbing pain pulsed in Callie's right temple. Mondays were known to be trying, but three cranky, overbearing, and now senile men before lunch was too much.

"Could you explain to me what that means?" she asked Olaf. There was clearly a piece to the puzzle Callie didn't have. "Who is Morty?"

Olaf dropped into a chair and wiggled, as if testing its sturdiness. "Morty was Sam Edwards's uncle. Left him the hotels in his will. Whole island thought the nephew would sell 'em and be done with it, but he came and he stuck."

Sam had inherited the hotels? Somehow Callie had missed that in her research. That explained how the man who'd always been looking for the next big challenge had ended up on this almost-unheard-of island. But why had he kept them, instead of selling them off, as, according to Olaf, the islanders had expected him to do?

Sentimentality was the first thing that came to mind, but Sam wasn't the sentimental type.

Olaf hopped out of the chair. "Better get started," he said. "I'll back my truck up to the door and load in."

"Good," Callie said, still focused on the mystery of Sam and these hotels. "Olaf?" She waited for the older man to give her his attention. "If you're doing this for Morty, I'm assuming he was well liked on the island?"

"Everybody loved Morty." A toothless grin split Olaf's face. "He was family around here. Can't say his nephew has the same way about him, but Morty loved this place. So we'll fix it up for him."

No, Sam didn't have the same way about him. From what Callie could tell, he didn't even know most of his neighbors. He didn't like the picnics in the park. Didn't know the tradesmen from the village. Maybe the hotels were too lucrative to give up. She had yet to see the island in the full swing of the season, so it was possible.

But even if the hotels did exceedingly well financially, this little tourist destination couldn't come close to what Sam could do at a hotel in a larger city.

So why Anchor? She didn't have the answer. Maybe Callie knew as little about the real Sam Edwards as the folks of Anchor Island did.

CHAPTER 12

Two weeks into the renovation of the Sunset Harbor Inn, and Callie was ready for a vacation. Or maybe a really long nap. Like, a month long. In her previous experience, Callie had been part of a team. A group of planners and runners with each person carrying part of the load.

Not this time. At least she had Yvonne. Or, as Callie had begun to think of her, the miracle worker.

Callie spent her days picking out linens and rugs, upholstery and curtains, artwork and accent pillows. Once she finished sufficiently debating with herself about whether she'd made the right decision, Callie emailed the final info to Yvonne, who then placed the orders, tracked the dollars spent, and reported the current budget status every few days.

When this ordeal was over, Callie would be campaigning hard to make sure Yvonne received a much-deserved raise in salary.

Until then, she'd learned Yvonne was a sucker for Opal's raspberry tarts, and took the necessary steps to make sure the woman had a solid supply in her fridge at all times.

Contact with Sam had been slim over those same two weeks. Callie hadn't even gotten the chance to apologize for losing her temper that day in her office. Yes, he'd pushed the wrong button, but that was no excuse. She'd crossed a line, and Sam deserved an apology.

As she was scheduled to appear in his office the following morning, Callie fully intended to deal with the issue so they could move on. Well, so *she* could move on. Every time she thought about the encounter, about Sam so close and his eyes so fierce and his body so hard and hot . . .

Yes. Well. A little closure on the whole thing would put her back on solid ground. It was a disagreement and nothing more. Or so she deluded herself.

Due to the shortened time frame in which they had to finish the project, the workers accepted a six-day workweek, with Sundays off. As today was Sunday, Callie took the opportunity to walk around the hotel to gauge their progress without the crew in the way. Not that she disliked the workers. Some of them were quite interesting.

And nearly all of them enjoyed sharing stories about Sam's Uncle Morty. From what Callie had heard, the man had been quite a character, always ready with a smile and a helping hand. He'd chaired entertainment committees, done magic tricks for the kids in the park, and was beloved by all who knew him.

In other words, the complete opposite of his nephew. And the islanders were not bashful about saying so. Callie doubted Sam would disagree with their assessment, but she still experienced a sliver of guilt over not defending him.

Then again, Sam could take care of himself, and with Morty as their motivation, Callie was getting a great deal of dedication from Bernie's crew. Which was exactly what she needed to pull this miracle off.

Now, if only she could line up a similarly dedicated group for the inside.

TERRI OSBURN

Staring at the back side of the inn, Callie marveled at how much Bernie and his men had accomplished in such a short time. They would be ready to apply the new paint soon, which was good, since November was coming fast and they needed the exterior painted before the temperatures dropped even lower.

Feeling good about where they stood, Callie turned to face the harbor behind her. Sun glistened off the water, forcing her to squint against the glare. She could see the marina on the other side but only faintly, the white sails bobbing up and down with the waves. Breathing deeply, Callie let the wind whip her hair around her face.

Anchor Island was truly the most peaceful place she'd ever been. Though she'd yet to visit much of the planet, Callie doubted many sites would top Anchor for tranquility and calm. Especially on a clear fall day like this one. She thought longingly of spring and how glorious it must be, with its warm gusts buffeting the coast.

Then she remembered she might not be here in the spring. Callie was reluctant to broach the subject with Sam, wanting to wait until she'd made enough progress to really show what she could do. And, in all honesty, she had never run a hotel in her life. She wasn't even sure she wanted to, since her real love was designing. Did she want to give that up?

Callie dismissed the questions. No sense in worrying over something that would likely never be offered.

"Beautiful day," said a deep voice behind her, sending Callie whirling through the air. She lost her balance, and her arms flailed like dueling propellers as she careened forward and back.

As gravity looked to be the victor in this comedy sketch, Sam caught Callie around the waist, righting her to a standing position and pulling her close against his chest. The wind whipped a lock of dark hair across his forehead as his blue-gray eyes stared into hers, looking surprised but not wholly unhappy to have her so close.

116

"Thank you," Callie said, the words barely a whisper. She shook her head to get the hair out of her eyes, but the wind blew it back again.

Releasing one hand from her hip, Sam tucked the errant lock behind her ear. Heat danced along her skin where his fingers brushed her temple.

"I didn't mean to scare you," Sam said, still holding her close. One brief glance down to her lips, and then he stepped back. "Sorry about that."

Callie shook her head but had to force the words to come. "No," she said. "I mean, no apology necessary. I didn't expect anyone else to be out here."

He smiled, drawing attention to his stubble-covered chin. "I could say the same. I wanted to take a look around while the place was empty."

So they'd had the same idea. But then Callie remembered she was scheduled to give him an update the next day. Was he there to assess the situation for himself, not trusting what she might tell him?

"I was doing the same," she said, her voice firmer now. "To make sure my report would be thorough and accurate."

Sam chuckled as if she'd said something funny.

"I'm sorry," Callie said. "Did I make a joke?"

Sliding his hands into the pockets of his brown suede coat, Sam met her eyes. "You can stand down, Callie. I have complete faith that your report will tell me everything I need to know." With a one-shoulder shrug, he cut his gaze to the building. "The inn landed in this condition because of my neglect. I don't want to make the same mistake twice."

If that was supposed to make her feel better, he'd missed the mark by a nautical mile.

"I see that didn't appease you either." Sam took Callie by the elbow, turning her toward the end of the building. "Show me around. We can do the visual now, and then deal with the financials tomorrow."

Callie opted to remain silent as they trudged across the uneven grass to the front of the building. Withdrawing the key from her pocket, she pulled her arm out of Sam's grip and preceded him up the stairs. It would do no good to throw another temper tantrum when she had yet to apologize for the last one.

But Sam Edwards was quickly turning into the most infuriating boss she'd ever had. And Callie had worked for some real doozies.

Determined to say what needed to be said, she closed the door once Sam followed her into the lobby, then spun to face him. "I'm sorry that I lost my temper a couple of weeks ago. Your comments on my management style hit a nerve, and I lashed out. It was unprofessional and uncalled for, and I apologize."

"Already forgotten," he said. That was it. Nothing else. No apology for having insulted her or for his boorish, pig-headed behavior.

Pressing her teeth together so hard she feared one might chip, Callie counted to five. She loosened her jaw enough to say, "I appreciate that."

"I told you," Sam said, "I don't like to dwell in the past."

Six years into the past was much different than two weeks, but Callie managed not to say so. Barely.

"Fine," she gritted. "Then let's get started."

≈

Sam knew he was being an ass, but sticking with the demanding-boss act was the only way to keep his bearings where Callie was concerned. Not that he wasn't a demanding boss, but he'd been as much at fault for their encounter that day in her office as she'd been. Him more so, if he were being honest.

But being honest with himself and admitting the truth to Callie were two different things. Theirs wasn't only a complicated history; they were dealing with a complicated present filled with the demands of an employer-employee relationship that happened to be laced with an attraction Sam was barely able to control.

Signified by the way he'd once again nearly crossed the line outside. He would never have let her fall, especially when he had been the one to startle her, but Sam shouldn't have held her so close. Or for so long. What had likely been only seconds had felt like hours, and the pull she had on him had revealed a weakness Sam didn't like to think about.

Following her through the inn, watching her blonde hair dance over the back of her neck, and listening to her rattle off the small bits of progress they'd made, explaining in clipped tones what steps would come next, highlighted his weakness all the more.

If she had any idea what he was thinking, what he'd like to do to her on that antique chaise awaiting its turn for new upholstery, she'd . . . What would she do?

"So that's what we've accomplished so far," Callie said as they stepped out of the dining room, now a makeshift woodworking shop, and into the lobby, where they'd started. "I'll have full financial reports tomorrow showing what we've spent and where we've managed to generate savings."

"Sounds enlightening," he said, struggling to pull his mind away from the images of what they could do on that chaise.

Callie's nostrils flared. "I'll try to make my report as enlightening as possible."

Sam sighed. He'd wanted her to dislike him, and he was doing a damn good job of making sure she did.

As Callie locked the door, Sam waited for her on the top step, fighting the urge to apologize in some way. When she joined him, he said, "I'm impressed with what you've done here and have complete faith in your ability to see this project through."

He sounded like an idiot.

Callie's jaw stopped ticking for the first time since he'd asked her for the tour. "Thank you." Her next words proved she was still perturbed. "I'm happy we could impress you."

"You," he said.

"Excuse me?"

"*You* impressed me." Sam nodded toward the inn. "I know this isn't an easy project. You're running this almost single-handedly and deserve credit for doing so."

She softened. Finally. "Yvonne has been a huge help. I might have switched from tea to tequila by now if I didn't have her support."

"Good to hear we haven't driven you to drink."

"Yet," she said. Callie gave him a half smile, her eyes on his for only a second before they shifted to the cottage in the distance. "Speaking of tea, do you want to come over for a drink? I can make coffee, if that's what you prefer."

He followed her gaze, considering taking her up on the offer. Which was a very bad idea. "I don't know."

"Sam," Callie said, "the work stuff is over. It's Sunday. We can be friends today."

Friends. Why had he agreed to that, again?

"Besides, I want you to meet Cecil under better circumstances." Callie hopped down the steps, turning at the bottom and walking backward. "I promise I won't let him attack you." The smile on her face was a challenge, as if he might be afraid of a little bird.

There was no way his ego could let her believe that, even in jest. Stupid ego.

"I could use some coffee," he said, stomping down the steps, then using his long stride to catch up to her. He slowed as he drew even. "Do you have plans for the linens and other items we won't be needing anymore?"

"I was going to ask you about that." Callie pulled her coat tighter as the wind off the ocean hit them full-on. "I'd like to donate them somewhere, but I wasn't sure if you'd approve."

She made him sound like an ogre.

"There's a homeless shelter over in James City that could use the bedding and towels. The curtains could be recycled, and everything else I'd like to send back to Charleston. My mother does charity drives, and they can always use items for the auctions."

Callie hesitated, falling a step behind him. Sam stopped to wait, turning to see what held her up. To her wide-eyed stare he said, "What?"

With a shake of her head, Callie stepped forward, keeping pace once again. "Nothing."

He wasn't letting her off that easy. "Don't 'nothing' me," he said. "What did you think I was going to say?"

Brows drawn, Callie shrugged. "I don't know, but not that."

Reminding himself that playing the role of a jerk was his idea, Sam glanced to the left as they crossed the street. The inn and Peabody Cottage were the only structures at the end of this dead-end lane, but you never knew who might venture this way to take in the view.

"I'll get an address from Mother and pass it on to Yvonne. She already has the information for the homeless shelter." They'd donated the discarded items from the Anchor renovation to the same facility, something he didn't bother to tell Callie. "I'm sure she can set up the shipping whenever the items are ready to go."

They traveled the remaining distance to the cottage in silence, Callie taking the lead up the driveway and through the front door.

"There's a man in our midst. There's a man in our midst," echoed the bird. Sam wondered how many phrases the creature had in his repertoire.

"Say hello to Mr. Sam, Cecil," Callie said, removing her coat and offering to take his. "You met him a few weeks ago, remember?"

Did she always talk to the bird as if it understood every word she said?

"Right. Right. Hunky man Mr. Sam. Cecil needs a cracker."

Callie hung their coats over the back of the couch. "You had a cracker before I left."

"I'm telling Mother." The parrot puffed up, as if putting all his plumage behind the threat.

"Good luck with that," Callie said, turning her attention to Sam. "You want to hang out in the kitchen while I make the coffee, or stay in here with Cecil?"

As tempting as it was to test the limits of the pet's vocabulary, Sam opted for the kitchen. "I'll follow you."

She once again led the way, and Sam took in the small changes she'd made as they passed through the cottage. The large blue chair had been moved closer to the window. A few family photos were scattered along the end tables and bookshelves, and an old quilt was draped over the end of the couch opposite their coats.

"I see you're making yourself at home," he said, genuinely happy to see life back in the cottage. As it should be.

Glancing over her shoulder, Callie asked, "Was I not supposed to?"

"No," Sam replied. "It's your house for now. You should make it your own."

Reaching the cupboard, Callie pulled down a canister and plopped a filter packet into the top of the coffee machine. "About that," she said.

"About what?" Sam was distracted by watching her move around the kitchen as if she belonged there. As if she'd lived there forever.

"The 'for now' part," she said, replacing the canister and pulling two mugs from the next cupboard over. Turning to face him, she leaned a hip on the edge of the counter. "I wasn't going to bring this up, but I realize I need to know. Will I have a job here once this project is over?"

CHAPTER 13

Sam looked as if she'd punched him, and Callie wondered if maybe being direct wasn't the best approach. As much as she didn't want to ruin this job, she couldn't find herself unemployed again at Christmas and end up right back where she'd been before this chance came along. If she needed to line up job leads for the new year, it was better to know now than to be an idiot and wait until the last minute.

Floundering like a fish desperate for air, Sam opened and closed his mouth several times before finally getting out a "huh" and tapping his chin.

"I guess that's my answer," Callie said, turning her attention to the tea. She'd wanted to know, and now she did. As usual, she'd learned the "careful what you wish for" lesson the hard way.

"Do you want to stay on?" Sam asked. Callie couldn't tell from his tone whether he was asking because the job was open to her or out of mere curiosity.

Callie went with honesty. "I'm not sure. Do you want me to stay?"

They sounded like a pair of prepubescents trying to ask each other to a dance.

"I didn't think you'd be willing to stick around," Sam said, which didn't really answer her question. "You transition hotels. If you stay on when this one is finished, then you'd be giving that up."

It was something she'd thought about. Callie would miss the design aspect, but the inn would require regular freshening. A change of linens. New area rugs when the current ones wore out. And there would be event planning. Being involved in making someone's big day go off without a hitch might be a trade-off worth giving up the constant grind and pressure of the massive renovation projects.

Not that weddings didn't come with their own stress. The details of a design were what Callie loved the best. Those details would still be there when she was designing an event instead of a hotel lobby.

Before Callie could say what she was thinking, Sam said, "I'd think this island would be too small for you."

Callie poured the coffee into Sam's mug. "I could say the same about you."

There. She'd asked. Sort of. He'd really brought it up.

Sam didn't respond right away. In an effort to make it appear she wasn't all that interested in his answer, she asked, "Cream and sugar?"

"Lots of cream," Sam said. "A little sugar." He glanced over her shoulder as she poured in the creamer. "That's good. Thanks."

She slid the mug and sugar bowl his way so he could put in as much as he wanted. With her back to the counter, Callie blew softly across the top of her tea, waiting for Sam to finish. Once he'd slid the bowl to the back of the counter, she repeated her question.

"So?" she said. "What made you leave the big city for this tiny island?"

Blue-gray eyes met hers briefly. "I got an offer I couldn't refuse."

Since she knew he'd inherited the hotels, his answer didn't make much sense. But his evasion was an obvious sign he didn't want to get specific. So she changed the subject.

"What was your Uncle Morty like?"

Dark brows drew together. "How do you know about Uncle Morty?"

"Olaf mentioned him," Callie said. "A lot of the crew knew him, and they've been sharing stories with me."

Sam set his mug on the counter with a thud. "Then you know what he was like."

She'd apparently hit a nerve. "I know he was well loved on the island. That he was very active in the community. And that he owned the Anchor and Sunset Harbor Inns before you took over."

A muscle ticked in Sam's jaw. "That sums it up. But the next time you want to know something, ask me, not the locals."

Callie bristled. "I didn't ask anyone anything. I told you, Olaf brought him up."

"Olaf needs to work more and talk less." Sam crossed his arms.

If the man was looking for a fight, she would not indulge him. Not again.

"Sam," Callie said, "they all loved your uncle. I'm not sure why talking about him bothers you, but I promise they don't have a bad word to say about him. He sounds like a lovely man."

The ticking slowed. A little. "He was," Sam said. "When he wasn't trying to get his own way."

She was going to need a translator to understand that one. Since none was readily available, she let the subject drop. Sam seemed relieved as he lifted his coffee mug to take a drink.

"I'm guessing you're not as active in the community?" Callie had found it curious that Sam knew none of the locals with whom she'd managed to become acquainted in a matter of weeks. On an island this small, a person would have to make a concerted effort *not* to know his neighbors after living among them for three years.

"I'm an active member of the Merchants Society," he said. "I don't have much time for socializing."

The picture was starting to come together. "So, you don't like the picnics in the park, you complain that the festive events sound like noise, and you don't have time for socializing." Callie nodded like a wise man on a rock. "I see."

"You see what?"

"You're antisocial."

"I am not."

"Do you work evenings?"

"No."

"But you have no time to socialize."

She knew she'd won when his mouth did the dying-fish impression again. Callie let him flounder while she sipped her tea, then said, "It's nothing to be ashamed of. There are lots of people who feel insecure in social situations."

Callie knew this statement didn't describe Sam at all. Back in the day, he could work a room better than any politician in the great state of South Carolina. That meant there had to be a good reason he wasn't engaging his fellow man on Anchor Island.

"I'm starting to think you're the one lacking in social skills." Sam looked incredulous. "Did you just call me insecure?"

"You're avoiding people for a reason," she said with a nonchalant shrug.

"I'm not avoiding anything."

"Then you'll come with me tonight?"

"Then . . . ," Sam stammered, "I'll what?"

"I've been invited to a small gathering." She'd dreaded attending what Will had assured her would be a casual dinner and drinks, but if she had Sam with her, at least Callie wouldn't arrive alone. And he really did need to socialize. As far as she could tell, most islanders did not have a positive opinion about the buttoned-up hotelier. "You can come with me. Dinner is at six."

"I'm not going to dinner with a bunch of strangers."

"I believe you know these ones," she said, brushing aside his protest. "The dinner is at Will Parsons's place. I know you know her. You probably know her fiancé as well, since I think he owns a couple of businesses."

"Randy Navarro," he said.

"That's his name."

"I'm still not intruding on—"

"I'll be there to help you get through it." Callie set her mug in the sink. "Think of it as a trial run. Your first step to getting out more."

"You'll help me through . . . I don't need . . ."

Callie strolled out of the kitchen, leaving Sam to stay or follow. "Will says it's casual." She stopped near the front door to see that he'd indeed followed her. She assessed his dress pants and shiny brown shoes. "Do you own a pair of jeans?"

"First you're going to tell me where I'm going, then you think you can tell me what to wear?"

"Jeez," Callie said, holding her hands up in surrender. "Wear what you want, but be here by five forty-five." She pulled the door open with a smile. "I'll be ready."

Looking unhappy and a bit battle-worn, Sam huffed. "Fine. Five forty-five." Then he marched through the door.

～

If Sam had been a religious man, he'd have sworn Morty had sent Callie to torture him. His uncle may have been more affectionate than the parents Sam had grown up with, but he was still Sam's mother's brother, and the absolute determination to have his way ran deep in the bloodline.

Which was probably why Sam was so determined *not* to do anything that even hinted at pleasing someone else. So why in the hell had he agreed to accompany Callie to this dinner party? Sam hadn't done the fake-smile, bad-wine, mix-and-mingle thing since he'd come to Anchor. He had to admit, that was one positive of this miniature hamlet. Less of the pretense he'd never enjoyed about his previous jobs.

Sam was a sucker for a challenge. He got a rush out of taking something everyone else dismissed and transforming it into what no one believed it could be. That was one of the reasons he'd pursued the boutique route for the Sunset. Anchor Island was known as more of a roughing-it island destination, not the kind of place where one would expect to find a boutique anything.

No one except Sam.

And once the project was finished, he'd have done his duty. Both of Uncle Morty's properties would be completely renovated, operating as he'd always dreamed they would and offering what Anchor needed to keep tourists coming to her shores.

Which meant Sam *should* be able to return to his life. To walk away instead of being tied to this speck of sand for two more years.

Damn it.

"I see your mood hasn't improved," Callie said in greeting as she opened the cottage door. "I'm sure you'll feel better once we get there."

"I feel fine," he said, and he meant it. Once his temper had flared out, Sam recognized what Callie had done. Which was another reason he imagined Morty had put her in his path. A little push of that button, a little pull of that string, and the puppet would do what you wanted.

The only reason Sam hadn't stood her up was that he didn't believe Callie was being malicious in her manipulations. She didn't know how much he wanted to leave the island. Didn't know he'd kept himself apart for a reason.

Doubtless, she thought he was lonely and that getting him out would do him good. It wasn't Callie's fault her impression was completely off. He certainly hadn't done anything to show her differently, and Sam didn't intend to, either.

When Callie stepped out of the cottage, pulling the door closed behind her, Sam moved to the side to let her walk in front of him. But instead of heading toward the car, she once again looked him up and down. "You *do* own a pair of jeans."

With a smirk, Sam said, "And I wore them, as ordered. Happy?"

He had debated wearing the jeans, but to have refused would have been juvenile, and Sam would not give Callie the satisfaction of saying so.

"I don't know," she said, tapping the side of her chin. "Turn around."

"I'm not prancing around this porch for your amusement."

A mischievous grin danced across her face. "Can't blame a girl for trying."

Heat trailed up Sam's neck, reaching the tips of his ears in seconds. He was thankful for the darkness surrounding them as they walked away from the porch light. Sam was not a man prone to blushing.

"I have the address written down," Callie said as he opened the car door for her. "I planned to use my GPS until I remembered the no-service thing."

Sam caught the scent of Callie's perfume on the breeze and resisted the urge to lean into it. She smelled like a sugar cookie. His favorite.

"I know where it is," he said before closing the door.

As Sam circled the vehicle, he sent up a prayer that the night would go by quickly. He worried that being in close proximity to the woman in his passenger seat for very long would be more temptation than even he could resist.

Especially when she smelled good enough to eat.

That thought alone threatened to short-circuit his system.

As he climbed behind the wheel, Callie put a hand on his arm. The overhead light revealed an apologetic smile. "I really do appreciate your doing this. I'm not sure I'd have mustered up the courage to walk into this thing alone."

Sam nodded, because all he could think about was how glossy her lips looked, and whether she'd believe him if he said he'd kissed her only to see what they tasted like.

"No problem," he said, talking more to himself than to Callie. He could do this. All he had to do was keep his hands off her. And not look at her lips. And not breathe in.

Piece of cake.

~

The moment they walked through the door, Callie was relieved to have Sam by her side. Not that they were officially on any kind of date, but the party consisted of three couples—Will and Randy; Beth and her husband, Joe Dempsey; and Sid and her fiancé, Lucas Dempsey—which meant Callie would have very much been the odd woman out.

Exactly as she'd feared. After Sam had left that afternoon, she'd felt a little bad about how she'd coerced him into coming with her. Or maybe "bulldozed" was a better word for it. But the man really did need to get out more. He was a prominent business owner on this island. He should be part of the community. As he'd been six years ago, before both their lives had imploded with one blown tire and the death of two unfaithful people.

Was that why Sam didn't inject himself into this community? Was he refusing to let people in so no one could hurt him like that again?

Callie dismissed the thought as quickly as it came. That was the coward's way, and Sam was no coward.

"You won me five dollars," Will said, handing Callie a glass of white wine.

Will and Randy's home looked rustic and quaint from the outside but was startlingly different on the inside. An open floor plan linked the kitchen, dining, and living areas, with clean, contemporary furnishings accented by a Far East piece here and there.

The home emanated elegance and simplicity but somehow offered warmth as well. Callie was eying a particularly beautiful white sculpture on the fireplace mantel as she accepted the drink. As if hanging in suspended animation, a tall, slender female figure stood regal with her head tilted to one side and her long, flowing dress dancing around her.

The piece was absolutely captivating. Callie longed to add something similar to the Sunset's décor.

"How did I do that?" she asked, only half paying attention.

"You got him to come."

That statement earned her full focus. "Excuse me?"

"Sam," she said. "When I told Randy you were bringing him, he bet me five dollars that our hermit hotelier would be a no-show."

They had a name for him? "Hermit hotelier?"

"Not as insulting as what some others call him." Will nodded toward the corner of the dining room where Sam was in deep conversation with Lucas Dempsey. "Other than Merchants Society meetings, Sam doesn't socialize much."

"He told me he doesn't have time for socializing." Callie knew that to be an excuse, but a sense of loyalty drove her to defend him. "I doubt he deserves to be called a hermit."

"The only time in three years that he's attended anything other than an official meeting was last spring." Will took a sip of wine before continuing. "That was Beth and Joe's wedding, and he didn't stay long."

Still in defense mode, Callie said, "Maybe he doesn't mingle well." It was a bold lie, but she delivered it with as much confidence as possible.

"He doesn't seem like the type to be intimidated by a roomful of people."

At that moment, Randy and Joe joined the two men in the corner. Sam looked completely at ease. "You're right," Callie said, having to concede the point. "I've never known Sam to be intimidated by anything."

Beth and Sid joined them near the fireplace. Beth was carrying a tray of hors d'oeuvres.

"The Weeble here needs to eat," Sid said, pointing at Beth, who instantly rolled her eyes.

"Must you call me that?" Beth said. "I don't wobble that much."

Sid's brows went up as she snatched a spanakopita off the tray. "Give it a few weeks."

"Remember," Will said, "everything you dish out now, we're going to dish right back when it's your turn."

Sid stuck out her tongue, revealing a green blob.

"It's time to eat," Will said to the room at large. "Houseboy, you're on."

Callie wasn't sure whom Will was talking to until Randy excused himself from the men and strolled toward them. The extremely large man dropped a kiss on his fiancée's cheek.

"I expect something extra in my pay for that remark."

Will's blue eyes turned dark as she wiggled her perfectly plucked brows. "After everyone leaves, I'll wear the apron," she whispered loud enough for the ladies to hear. "And nothing else."

That earned her a kiss on the lips that lasted long enough for Sid to yell, "Get a room!"

The food had yet to be served, and this was already unlike any dinner party Callie had ever attended.

CHAPTER 14

Callie doubted she had met a more animated group of friends before tonight. The Dempsey brothers were surprisingly amicable, considering what she'd learned during the first course. It seemed Joe's wife, Beth, had been engaged to his brother, Lucas, before the loving couple had met. In fact, that engagement was the reason the future parents had been thrown together.

Watching how affectionate and deliriously in love Lucas was with Sid probably explained the lack of tension. Clearly, everyone had ended up with the person he or she was meant to be with. And though Sid took credit for matchmaking her brother and Will Parsons, the pair argued that they'd gotten together in spite of Sid's efforts, not because of them.

Callie wasn't sure what that meant, exactly, but she enjoyed being among these people. Their bond was real and went beyond familial connections. And it didn't hurt that the food was amazing. This may have been the best fettuccine Alfredo she'd ever tasted. Signified by the fact that she all but licked her plate clean.

"If I had any cooking skills at all," Callie said, "I'd ask for the recipe for this."

"It's easier than you think," Randy said, with one of his wide smiles. Callie was still getting used to the gentle giant. He seemed friendly and kind and moved with the grace of a man half his size. And seriously knew his way around a fettuccine noodle.

"Really easy for me," Will added. "Gotta love a man who can cook."

"Amen," chimed Sid.

"Stop gloating," Beth said, rubbing a hand across the top of her pregnant belly. "We didn't all get so lucky."

Joe Dempsey draped an arm across the back of his wife's chair. "I make up for my lack of cooking skills in other areas," he said, nibbling on the pretty redhead's earlobe, making her face match her hair.

With a nudge of her shoulder, Beth said, "And that's the reason I can't get any closer to this table." She extended an arm to reach her water glass but couldn't quite make it. Joe moved the drink closer.

The whole scene was incredibly charming, and Callie could have sworn she felt a twinge in her uterus. As if the constant reminders from her mother weren't bad enough, now her own body was dropping hints.

"So, Sam," Will said, "how do you and Callie know each other?"

As Sam was sitting beside her, Callie hadn't been able to watch him during the meal. Now she glanced over to see stormy gray eyes cut her way. The look was brief, almost nonexistent, before he turned his attention to Will.

"Excuse me?"

"Callie mentioned that you two knew each other a long time ago." Will plopped her chin into her hand like a child about to hear a story. "Did you work together at another hotel?"

"I wasn't in the hotel business back then," Callie said. Then she turned to Sam. "It seems you're considered a mystery man on the island." She included a smile with the words, though something more like panic was racing through her system. "I tried to tell them you're a regular person. Flawed, even."

Please smile. Please make a joke.

"I wouldn't go that far," Sam said with a grin. Callie felt the deep timbre of his voice down to the tips of her toes as relief replaced her brief bout of panic. Returning his attention once again to Will, he added, "Callie and I shared a mutual acquaintance. But she's right. It was a long time ago. We actually lost touch until she applied for the position here on the island."

That was more than she'd expected him to share, but then, he'd also not told them anything specific. Thank goodness.

"Oh." Will looked disappointed. "What a coincidence."

Desperate to change the subject, Callie said, "I was admiring that beautiful sculpture on your mantel. Where is that from?"

Will turned to Randy. "That came from Lola's, didn't it?"

"That's right," Randy said. "It reminded me of you, so I bought it."

Will dropped her hand to the table. "But you had that before we got together."

With a self-satisfied grin, Randy said, "Yep."

The dinner guests exchanged glances as the meaning of Randy's words sunk in.

The lanky brunette smacked her fiancé's arm as her eyes turned misty. "How come you never told me that?"

His brown eyes turned soft. "Because you never asked, gypsy."

A collective "aw" echoed around the table, before Beth said, "What's for dessert?"

Will laughed. "We have an assortment from Opal's, of course. I'll set them out on the counter."

"I'll help you," Beth said, struggling to push her chair back.

"You stay there," Will ordered. "Sid will help."

"I'll what?" The tiny woman across the table from Callie had remained all but silent throughout dinner.

"If you can rebuild an intake manifold, you can help set out desserts."

"I might have to take pictures," Lucas said. "We'll need to document this rare occurrence."

"Shove it, smart-ass," Sid muttered, setting her napkin on the table. "Keep it up, and your night won't end nearly as well as Randy's is going to."

Lucas hopped out of his seat. "You're going to need a third set of hands, Will. I graciously volunteer."

"That's what I thought," Sid said. She was tucked against Lucas's side before they reached the kitchen.

Beth didn't argue about staying in her seat. Instead, she leaned over and laid her head on Joe's shoulder. The older Dempsey brother had darker hair and was stockier than his younger brother, but both men were affectionate with the women they clearly adored.

Callie's uterus gave another twinge. Stupid uterus.

～

Sam escorted Callie to the car shortly after nine. They were both filled to the brim with pasta and sweets, as well as a glass or two of wine, though Sam had switched to soda more than an hour before they left.

For most of the trip back to Callie's, the pair traveled in silence. Sam had done enough mingling for one night that he was content, even relieved, to be off the conversational hook. But there was something else he needed to say before they reached their destination.

"Thank you," Sam said, keeping his eyes on the road.

"Hmm?" Callie murmured. "Thank you for what?"

Sam gave her a quick glance. "For making me go tonight. I had a good time."

"So did I," she replied, sounding sleepy. "I like these people. Sid is a bit of an acquired taste."

He couldn't argue with that. Sam's only interactions with the ballsy boat mechanic before tonight had been at Merchants Society meetings, where she definitely felt no compunction about sharing her opinions. And in rather colorful language.

"Yes, she is."

"But I like her the best, I think. She's the most genuine person I've ever met. No frills. No pretense. What you see is what you get."

"And what you get is a lot," Sam added.

They laughed softly together as Sam pulled into the cottage drive. He slid the car into park as he said, "And thank you for not telling them about the past."

Callie snorted. "I wouldn't know how to tell them. Saying, 'I was his wife's best friend but then she started schtupping my husband and on a secret lovers' getaway they were both killed in a car accident so we had a one-night stand to spite them' doesn't seem like dinner-party repartee."

"Callie."

"Well, I wouldn't really say that last part," she murmured, as if he hadn't said her name.

"Callie," he repeated. Once she turned his way, Sam said, "We didn't have sex to spite them."

"We didn't?"

"No." He might not have known exactly what he'd been thinking back then, but Sam knew exactly why he'd made love to the woman beside him. And spite had played no part in it.

"I always wondered," she said, her voice small. "But I was never sure. And you weren't around for me to ask."

Sam took a deep breath as he contemplated how to respond. Finally, he said the only thing that came to mind. "I'm sorry that you were left to wonder."

Silence loomed again, neither making a move to exit the vehicle.

"Do you want to come in?" Callie asked, as Sam had feared she might.

"Not a good idea."

"Why not?" she asked, her voice no more than a breath in the dark.

Leaning his arms over the steering wheel, Sam turned to look at the woman beside him. "Because if I go in there now," he said, pointing toward the cottage, "I'm not going to leave again before morning. And we both know that wouldn't turn out well."

"It wouldn't?" Her quiet questions were making this harder than he'd anticipated.

"I'd say we're already complicated enough, wouldn't you?"

"Right," she said, straightening in her seat. "I'm a complication you don't want."

"That's not what I said." Not wanting her would have made this whole situation a hell of a lot easier.

"No. I know. You're right." Callie pushed her door open and climbed out of the car, then hesitated before closing it. He could see by the look in her eyes, illuminated by the overhead light and the glare of the moon, that she hoped he might change his mind.

That he would step out of the car and follow her in.

But he didn't.

He couldn't.

Damn, he wanted to.

Instead, he rolled down his window and let the cool, salt-scented air fill his lungs. He'd always liked the way that scent lingered over the island. The punch of the ocean ever present in his senses. Which was likely what had him turning right instead of left at the end of Lighthouse Road.

Sam drove the Murano up Highway 12 toward the ferry station and pulled over at one of the more narrow parts of the island. He ambled through the sand to reach the top of a dune, where he sat and watched moonlight glimmer off the waves. For one dark moment, he wallowed in his loneliness, let the anger and frustration sink into his bones until he could feel himself vibrating with it.

Six years ago, he'd lost his wife to another man. She'd wanted more from Sam, but he'd been unwilling to change. Unwilling to even try to be what she wanted. More attentive. Less work-obsessed. A doting husband who was more interested in having a good time than in studying financial reports.

But Sam couldn't be that man, so Meredith had turned to someone else. And the fact was, there was nothing more he could have given. His drive and ambition would always win out, meaning work would always come first. Sam knew that now. Whatever dim light might have been flickering inside him had died a sudden and violent death, along with his adulterous wife and her philandering lover.

And, as he'd feared, Callie's reentry into his life was bringing it all back. The pain of Meredith's deceit. The shame of *his* failure. If Callie knew who Sam really was, she wouldn't have invited him in tonight.

And if she hadn't invited him in, Sam wouldn't be sitting on a dune, getting sand in his shoes while trying to figure out how he could have her and not hurt her.

If the moon had any answers, he was keeping them to himself. The thought made Sam chuckle at his melodramatic pity-fest. He'd reminded Callie more than once that he didn't like dragging out ancient history. And this was why.

Because when he did, the uselessness of it always hit him full force. He couldn't go back in time. He couldn't change who he was, not then and not now. Callie's question earlier in the day about whether she would be staying on after the project ended was answered in that moment.

She wouldn't see it right away, but sending her packing was the best thing. Sam might not be able to go back and change the mistakes of the past, but he could damn well make sure they didn't get repeated.

∾

Callie stood with her back against the door for a long time after the sounds of Sam driving off had faded in the distance. What had she been thinking? That was easy. She hadn't been thinking at all. She'd been feeling. Which had always been her problem.

Callie was notorious for letting her heart rule her head—something even therapy couldn't fix. She was tougher now, not as eager to do others' bidding or to contort herself into what they wanted her to be. She'd twisted herself into a pretzel to please Josh, and he'd still jumped into bed with Meredith.

Dr. Langdon's voice echoed in her mind. *You have no one to please but yourself, and you should demand others accept you for who you are. Don't let anyone tell you you're not enough.*

The reminder helped. So she'd invited her boss in for the night and he'd turned her down. So what?

But then, she hadn't really invited him in for anything more than a coffee. Maybe some conversation. Sam had been the one to take it to morning.

She would have liked to say his arrogance was misplaced, but Callie never had been very skilled at outright lying. A bit of fluffing the truth? Sure. Direct deception? Not even a little.

Shaking off the self-pity threatening to undo the progress she'd made, Callie stepped away from the door, removing her coat as she went and laying it across the couch.

As she turned on the lamp on the end table, Cecil greeted her with his usual request. "Did you get crackers?"

"Not tonight, Cecil." Crossing the room to reach her sole companion for the last six years, the only creature who'd been faithful through thick and thin for six years before that, Callie let her troubles go for the night. "I'll give you an extra one tomorrow, okay?"

"Cecil needs a cracker now."

"As I was reminded once again tonight," Callie sighed, "we can't have everything we want." Lowering his blanket over the cage, Callie added, "Don't ever try to make sense of the opposite sex, Cecil. It's a losing endeavor."

With that, she turned off the light and headed to the kitchen for a little ego soothing.

"Nothing a cup of hot chocolate and a good book can't cure."

As she swiped at the light switch, Callie added, "Better get the peanut butter cups, too."

CHAPTER 15

Four weeks later, Callie found her first gray hair, struggled to button her jeans (the damn things had obviously shrunk), and had started her third bottle of antacids.

Things were not going according to plan.

In fact, things hadn't gone her way since she'd received an email from Sam the morning after their little dinner-party excursion to inform Callie that her services would no longer be needed once the Sunset Harbor Inn was back in business. And he'd been so formal in the message that Callie imagined it must have been hard to sit at his desk with that giant stick up his ass.

Ms. Henderson,

In your capacity as project lead, your responsibilities include over-seeing the renovation and redesign of the Sunset Harbor Inn, up to and including the relaunch event. To answer your inquiry as to whether the position will continue after said relaunch, I'm afraid your services will no longer be required once these duties have been completed.

Respectfully,

Sam Edwards

Just. Freaking. Dandy.

No matter. She'd intended for this project to be her launching pad to running larger and more involved hotel transitions. To be the star attraction on her résumé. That beacon would shine even brighter if she managed to pull off the task in such a short period of time.

Which meant she had to hit that deadline *and* the hotel had to be the next best thing since peanut butter met chocolate and they lived happily ever after.

On a side note, Callie really needed to cut back on the candy.

Two quick knocks sounded on her door before Jack popped his head in. "I hate to bother you," he said, his voice dropping to a reverent whisper, "but the boss is on the phone."

Callie jerked back in her chair. Not only had she not seen Sam in the month since the dinner party, but he'd communicated with her exclusively through email. She'd been pissed about it for the first two weeks, but once the project had hit several bumps and delays, Callie had become relieved Sam wasn't all up in her business.

Shoving her in-dire-need-of-a-cut hair out of her eyes, as if Sam would be able to see her over the phone, Callie took a deep breath, squared her shoulders, and said, "Put him through."

"Right," Jack said with a nod.

To Callie's surprise, Jack the goofy counter clerk had been indispensable over the last few weeks. He'd made sure the crew had food so they didn't have to leave the site to have lunch—an expenditure Sam had approved via email, of course—and he'd even picked up a paintbrush and done a better job than she did.

Today he'd been helping Callie strip the wallpaper in the dining room, which was part of the reason she could barely lift the telephone receiver to her ear. The first order of business when this job was over would be a visit to an expensive and thorough spa.

"Callie speaking," she said, managing not to wince when the receiver reached her ear.

"I'd like to visit the inn," Sam said, forgoing a greeting of any kind.

Panic latched onto her heart as her brain shuffled through possible excuses. "Um, this inn?" she asked, stalling for time.

"As I'm currently sitting in the only other inn I own, yes," he said. "That inn."

"Right." What was she going to do? They weren't far enough along. Callie glanced down at herself. She looked like hell. Then she closed her eyes and gave herself a mental slap for thinking it mattered one iota how she looked to Sam.

I'm a complication, nothing more.

"The place is a bit of a mess right now," she hedged. Possibly the understatement of the year.

"I would hope so," he said. "The hotel *is* under renovation. I'll be there in ten minutes."

"But . . . ," she started. Then the line clicked dead and Callie's forehead hit the desktop. Rolling her head from side to side, she moaned, "This is so not good."

Jack stuck his head through the door again. "What'd he say?"

"He's coming over," she answered, not bothering to lift her head. "We're dead."

Technically, *she* was dead. Jack was an innocent bystander who would be left alive to find another job. Maybe Sam would make him the new manager. She ignored the taste of bitterness that thought put in her mouth.

Sitting up, Callie said, "We can do this."

With a grimace, Jack motioned toward his forehead.

"What?" Callie asked. "I have no time for charades, Jack."

"You've got a little something there on your forehead."

Callie dug through the mess on her desk to find the small compact she hadn't used in weeks. Popping it open, she glanced in the mirror. There, in bold red letters, like a neon sign across her forehead, were the words PENDING APPROVAL—though it took her a second to figure that out, since the words were backward in the reflection.

Looking down, she spotted the smudged image of those same words where she'd just stamped them on an invoice. Callie fought the urge to crumple under the desk.

If those words didn't describe the story of her life, Callie didn't know what did. In fact, when she finally got around to writing that scathing memoir that would make her mother look like the non-nurturing hoyden that she was—long after her death, of course—that would be the title.

Pending Approval.

Snagging several tissues, Callie wet them on her tongue and rubbed feverishly at her forehead. Then she took a drink of water to get the paper off her tongue. After dropping the tissues in the trash, checking her reflection to make sure the ink was gone, and straightening the piles on her desk to give the impression of organization, Callie stood, tugging on her gray T-shirt.

Holy crap. She was wearing jeans and a T-shirt. But she couldn't exactly wear her good business suits to strip wallpaper. In her short career of hotel flipping, Callie had never been forced to do manual labor. But this wasn't a normal flip, and she certainly wasn't above getting dirty to get a job done.

Maybe she had time to run home and change. Callie glanced at her watch. How long ago had he called? There probably wasn't enough time. Screw it. Maybe Sam would be impressed that she was willing to pitch in a little elbow grease to hit his ridiculous deadline.

And if not, what did it matter? She was finished in six weeks anyway. One way or another.

"Where do we stand outside today?" Callie asked Jack.

"They're painting the end walls," he said. "Which at least means they aren't blocking the entrance."

"Or hanging from the chimneys like circus performers." Callie would take whatever good news she could get. "That's something. The floors?"

Jack pinched up his face. "Only three rooms done. And the ripped-out carpeting is still stacked in room fourteen."

"I told them to get that into the Dumpster last week!"

"I'll see if I can find Lot, and we'll throw it out the window, then haul it around."

Callie laid her hands against Jack's smooth cheeks. "Your mother did a fabulous job with you, Mr. Barrington. Make sure you tell her I said so."

Her teen phenom blushed, flashed one of his crooked half smiles, then dashed out of the office, a blur of green shoes and flailing, skinny legs.

Employing several deep breaths to calm her racing heart, Callie stepped out of her office in time to see Sam climbing out of his Nissan. If there was a god in heaven, may she be paying attention to a tiny island in the mid-Atlantic and send a miracle hurtling down toward Callie's little inn.

◇

Sam was relieved as he pulled into the parking lot. The front looked fresh and polished. The once-peeling shingles shining like new in the morning sun. The porch still needed attention, but that would come. There were still six weeks to go.

Before he could reach for the handle on the front door, Callie swung it open. She wore an old gray T-shirt, jeans with a small hole above the right knee, and stained tennis shoes.

His mouth went dry. Staying away from her had clearly been the right decision. The physical reaction he was having to this casual look stood as confirmation that distance was best.

But he couldn't ignore the project completely. The hotel *was* his responsibility.

"Good morning," he said, stepping inside. "I see things are going well so far."

A chuckle that sounded more maniacal than humorous echoed around the lobby. "So far," she said, closing the door, then retreating to the edge of the counter. "Can I get you some coffee? Or a soda?" She jerked a hand toward the area behind the counter. "We're well stocked on sodas. Can't let the guys go thirsty."

For a second Sam wondered if the job was maybe too much stress for her. Her eyes were darting too much. Her movements were jerky and stilted.

"I'm good, thanks." Sam stood his ground, afraid any sudden moves might spook her. "Are you okay?"

"Yeah," Callie said, louder than necessary. "I'm good. I'm great. Peachy."

"Good," he said, more convinced that she was anything but.

"Good," she said, crossing, then uncrossing, her arms. "Well."

"Well?"

"Right." The woman had gone completely over the deep end. Regardless of the progress he'd seen out front, Sam worried he'd put too much on Callie's shoulders. He'd neglected the project for too long.

But he needed to see where they stood to determine how far he should step back in.

"A look around, then," he said, adding a smile to appear as non-threatening as possible.

"Oh," Callie said, holding her place at the counter. "Are you sure you don't want to sit in my office and talk? I could tell you about what's going on." Her voice trailed off a bit. "How well we're doing."

Sam was pretty sure he knew how well they were doing. Not well at all.

"I'd rather see it," he said, willing to coddle her only so much.

"Of course you would." Callie ran her hands across the counter as she turned, offering a half bow. "Have at it."

The panic seemed to subside into forlorn surrender. Sam accepted the invitation, heading for the stairs.

"No need to go up there," Callie said.

"The work hasn't reached the second floor?"

She shook her head. "But, as you can probably smell, we have lots going on down here." Callie motioned toward the hall behind her that led to the downstairs rooms. "Want to see how the green you picked looks on the walls?"

Maybe things weren't so bad after all. Painted walls were a good sign.

"I would, yes."

"Room nine," she said, allowing him to lead the way.

He'd barely taken a few steps down the hall, when Sam heard "Heave!" coming from a room nearby. Spinning to face Callie behind him, he asked, "What is that?"

"What is what?" she asked, the crazy Callie back again.

"You don't hear that?"

"Timber!" came the voice again.

Sam lifted his brows. She couldn't possibly pretend she didn't hear that.

Callie smiled. "One moment, please."

She squeezed past him, brushing her breasts across his chest. He might have found it arousing if she didn't have that crazy look on her face. Like she was about to cut him into small pieces and use him for fishing bait.

When she reached room fourteen, Callie opened the door, stuck her head in, and mumbled something he couldn't understand. Then she pulled the door shut and said, "Shall we proceed?"

A trip to the clinic might be in order. This woman needed a tranquilizer. Or a lobotomy.

As Sam followed Callie down the hall, scenes from *The Shining* filled his head. He definitely had her in height and weight, but if she had him in crazy, those two advantages might not matter.

"Here we go." Callie swung open the door to room nine, then motioned for him to enter ahead of her.

"Why don't you go first?" he said, unwilling to turn his back on her.

"Eh," Callie said, walking into the room.

He took his eyes off her long enough to examine the walls. The color was definitely the right choice. It looked great in the natural light from the window and was the right balance of masculine and feminine, as he'd hoped.

Then he looked at the floor.

"There's no flooring in here," he said, moving around as if that would make something different appear beneath his feet.

"Not yet," she said, that trilly little laugh back again. "They're working at the end of the hall." As if on cue, hammering sounds came from somewhere in the distance. "It's taking a little longer than anticipated," she added, holding his gaze.

Her left eye was twitching. Time for an intervention.

"Let's go," he said, motioning for her to exit the room in front of him. "We need to talk."

Callie sighed, her shoulders dropping so far, she looked like Quasimodo. She kept her head down as she trudged all the way to her office. He'd definitely let this go too long. A mistake he kept repeating.

When they reached the office, Callie opened her mouth to speak, but Sam held up a hand to stop her. "I'll go first," he said. "I owe you an apology."

If the look on Callie's face was any indication, that was the last thing she'd expected to hear.

CHAPTER 16

That was the *last* thing Callie expected to hear. Maybe losing your hearing was part and parcel of losing your mind.

"Did you say what I think you said?"

Sam sighed. "Sit down, Callie."

It was a good thing her desk chair was right behind her, because Callie dropped at the order. The chair rolled backward away from the desk, with her in it.

"I knew this was going to be a major undertaking, even before the Christmas wedding opportunity came about," he started. Callie watched his lips move to make sure she didn't miss anything. "Against my better judgment, I took a backseat and let you handle the brunt of the project. A mistake on my part."

Callie let those words sink in. Tilting her head to the side, she asked, "Are you implying that putting me in charge of this project was your *mistake*?"

"Not at all," he said, face stern. "I stand by my decision."

Then she'd fried every last brain cell, because Sam wasn't making any sense. "Tell me again what exactly it is you're apologizing for."

Sam lowered himself into the chair in front of her desk. Finally. Callie was getting a crimp in her neck from looking up at the man.

"I shouldn't have taken the hands-off approach."

Again, not a vote of confidence.

"So you should have been more hands-on?"

"Yes."

"Because I clearly was not the right person to be in charge."

"Not at all."

Maybe she was asleep and this was some psychotic dream. Callie pinched her leg. It hurt. Sam was still there. So . . . not a dream.

Scooting forward, Callie propped her elbows on the desk and massaged her temples. "I can get this," she said. "One more try." She looked at Sam through narrowed eyes. "You're confident that I'm the right person to run this project?"

"Yes."

"But you made a mistake by not being more involved?"

"Exactly."

She waited for something more, but Sam remained silent. Callie considered how much it would hurt her career to walk out now and never look back. Surely her mental health was more important than any job. And right now, she was seriously worried for her mental health, because someone in this office was nuts, and Sam looked perfectly normal.

"Why are you wearing that outfit?" Sam asked, confusing her even more with the abrupt change of subject.

Callie glanced down to remind herself what she was wearing. Oh yeah, the work clothes. "I'm wearing these clothes because I've been scraping wallpaper off the walls in the dining room. And last week I wore something similar because I helped rip out the carpet." She wasn't going to apologize for getting her hands dirty. "If I had the skills, I'd probably be at the end of the hall, helping lay the new floors. If somehow that means I'm unfit to run this job, then I'm sorry, but I don't agree."

"The only thing that means," Sam said, "is that I've been an idiot."

Was this exasperating man incapable of giving a clear answer?

"Part of me wants to agree with you," she said, too tired to keep this up much longer. "But an idiot on what grounds?"

Sam leaned back, propping an ankle over his knee. "On the grounds that I should be doing my part as well." He stood up, prompting Callie to leap out of her seat. "I'll report back after lunch, ready to work," he said.

Wait, what?

"Ready to work?" she asked, absolutely certain this time she'd heard him wrong.

"That's what I said." Sam exited the office while Callie was still standing stunned behind the desk.

She ran after him. "What work do you plan to do?"

"Is there more wallpaper to be scraped?" Sam tossed over his shoulder as he pulled the front door open.

"Well . . . yeah," Callie said.

"Then we'll start there." As he practically hopped down the steps, he added, "Make sure there are enough scrapers to go around."

Callie slumped against the door frame, too confused to process his last comment. Sam was going to work beside her? Like, manual-labor work?

There was no way.

Jack chose that moment to sneak up behind her. "What happened?" he asked, ignoring Callie's startled gasp. "Did he can you?"

"No," she said. "He's coming back to help."

"Help with what?"

"Scraping wallpaper."

"There's no way," Jack said with a snort.

"My thoughts exactly," Callie chimed.

Guilt was Sam's constant companion for the next hour as he stopped at the Anchor to let Yvonne know where he would be the rest of the day, then drove by his cottage to change clothes. He hadn't been joking with Callie. If she had to pitch in with manual labor, so would he. Especially since he'd left her to completely fend for herself for the last month.

All because he'd wanted to have sex with her.

When he'd turned into a ball-less wonder, Sam didn't know. But he didn't like the feeling.

To his relief, and to Callie's credit, the project wasn't nearly as behind schedule as it had looked on his first visit of the day. As luck would have it, the kitchen had been updated shortly before Uncle Morty had passed away. Since it didn't need any work, Callie had used the kitchen as a staging area. As furnishings, linens, and décor pieces arrived, the boxes were labeled and organized into zones for more efficient distribution later.

The idea was brilliant and further proof Callie knew what she was doing. Right now, though, she didn't look brilliant. She looked like a woman about to snap.

"You're back," she said, twitching more than she'd been earlier.

"I am." Sam plopped a large bag of tacos onto the counter. The two teens lingering behind the check-in desk perked up as the scent hit their noses. "And I brought food."

Callie ran a hand through her hair. "I'm not really hungry—"

"No working on an empty stomach," Sam interrupted, tossing another bag to the boys. "This one has paper plates, utensils, and napkins. Is there someplace we can all sit to eat?"

"All?" the taller kid asked. Dark hair run with a shock of white hung over one eye as he hugged the bag he'd caught to his chest. Brown eyes darted from Sam to Callie and back again.

Chewing on her bottom lip, Callie shrugged at the teen, then slid her hands into her back pockets. "We could sit on the old chairs in the dining room that Olaf hasn't gotten to yet."

"Works for me," Sam said. He dragged the bag back off the counter. "Lead on."

Thirty minutes later, the boys he now knew as Jack and Lot had eaten four tacos apiece and departed the dining room to return to their work. Jack had called it hurling duty, but Callie explained they were discarding the old carpeting through a window to be carried around to the Dumpster at the end of the building.

That sounded a lot better than the image that had first come to mind.

Once they were alone, Sam asked, "Why aren't we stepping over a work crew at this point? I'm assuming you didn't plan to do everything yourself."

"The winter festival," Callie answered, as if he should know what the hell that meant.

"I'm sorry?"

"They're all over in the village, setting up for the winter festival coming up this weekend." She collected the empty taco wrappers the boys had left near their seats and tossed them into one of the bags. "It's only for a few days, and then they'll be back." Keeping her face averted, she added, "I hope."

Sam ignored the last bit. For now.

"The outside looks good."

"Doesn't it?" Some light returned to her eyes, revealing the capable, reasonable woman who was still in there somewhere. "Bernie says they should finish with the shingles in the next day or so, then they can start on the porch."

Having the exterior finished before the brunt of winter arrived was a good sign. "Where do we stand on the interior?"

Callie's errant twitch returned. "Well . . . ," she hedged. "About that."

Adding his own trash to the bag, Sam said, "Show me the plans marked up to where we stand right now. I know you've got it on paper, so show me."

"Of course I have it on paper," she said. "But it's on my office wall. You'll have to come see it."

As he followed her, Sam noticed how good her bottom looked in the tight-fitting jeans. The denim showed off the curve of her hips in a way fancy skirts did not. And no heels were needed to put a swing in Callie's step. By the time they reached their destination, Sam had to remind himself why he was there.

And then he saw it.

On the back wall of Callie's office was a giant blueprint of sorts of the entire Sunset Harbor Inn. Both floors were broken out, one on top of the other. All rooms were numbered and included the color scheme, as well as the décor pieces and even what area rug would go in each. She'd cut out pictures of the curtains and linens and pinned them to their intended destination.

All the guest rooms on the bottom floor were marked as PAINTING COMPLETE.

"So, once the workers return, they'll begin painting the second-floor rooms?" Sam asked, marveling at the precision and detail of the diagram.

"That's right." Callie stepped up beside him. Pointing at the rooms at the far end of the bottom floor, she said, "The flooring is complete in the two end rooms, but it's slow going. Since we can't start putting things together until the floors are in, I'm afraid this is going to be our biggest speed bump."

"Why so slow?"

Callie sighed. "I could only find two people on the island with any experience installing this kind of hardwood flooring. They're actually quite quick, but we couldn't start until the painting was done. By then, Elder was in the middle of another job, so we had to wait."

"Elder Wonnamack?"

"That's right," Callie said. "He and Frank Ledbetter are doing the floors. You know them?"

"I had Elder do some repair work at the Anchor. I didn't realize he installed floors."

With brows drawn, Callie asked, "How much work did you put into the Anchor to renovate it? And where did you find the workers?"

"Thankfully, the Anchor didn't need as much work as this one does," Sam said. "I brought a crew in during the off-season and put them up over here."

Ice-blue eyes went wide. "You didn't use locals?"

"I wanted a trusted crew I knew would do the job right." Sam hadn't thought much about it at the time. "The only reason I didn't suggest we do the same over here is that we're still doing steady business at the Anchor and I didn't want to tie up the rooms."

Callie rubbed her hands over her face, emitting what sounded like a groan between her fingers. Then she shoved them into her hair and said, "Let me get this straight. You brought in outsiders, bypassing any skilled local workers who might have been available."

"I . . . ," Sam started, but Callie held up a hand to silence him.

"It's no wonder these people don't like you."

"Excuse me?"

"Several of the villagers have refused to join the crew." Callie paced the small space behind her desk. "I couldn't figure it out before, but now it makes perfect sense. I wouldn't want to work for you either."

"What are you talking about?" Sam asked.

"It's you!" Callie exclaimed, poking him in the chest. "All this time, I thought they didn't want to work on a job run by a woman. I was so pissed I could barely sleep. And I couldn't tell *you* because I was already a complication you didn't want to deal with, so why give you more reason to replace me?"

The pacing resumed, quicker this time. "All that stress for nothing. It's you they have a problem with, not me."

Sam didn't care who liked or didn't like him, so long as his peers respected him and his businesses did well. Life had never been a popularity contest, and he wasn't about to play that game on this inconsequential little island to keep the natives happy.

"Are you done now?" he asked, once Callie had finished her rant. Sam took her huff as a yes. "I did what I had to do to bring the Anchor Inn up to my standards and get back to business as soon as possible. I don't need approval from you or anyone else on how I choose to do things. The existence of a high-quality hotel with spotless views and incomparable amenities for an island this size directly contributes to bringing more tourists to town, which in turn benefits every person in that village."

Pausing to rein in his temper, Sam attempted to button his suit jacket before realizing he wasn't wearing one. Crossing his arms instead, he said, "I will not have my tactics questioned. Not by anyone."

Callie stared at him for several seconds. Her eyes searched his, for what Sam didn't know.

"You really believe that." The words were a statement, instead of a question, so Sam held silent. "You don't know how to be part of a community."

"I don't give a shit about community," Sam growled, tired of feeling judged. He'd endured enough of that in his early years.

"What I care about is business, and getting this one back up and running in time for that wedding in six weeks."

"And if we're going to make that deadline, we need bodies," Callie said matter-of-factly. "Solid, hardworking bodies, of which there are plenty on this island."

"So hire them and get on with it," he said.

"There's only one way I can do that," Callie said, a devious smile spreading across her face. "You're going to make them like you."

"The hell I am," Sam barked. "I told you, I don't care what these people think of me."

"Well, I have a job to do," Callie argued, pointing to the giant diagram on the wall. "And unless you make an effort, it's going to be the two of us attempting to whip this place into shape in the next six weeks."

Sam had no intention of doing the heavy lifting on this project, and he would never expect Callie to do so either.

"How do you suggest I make them like me?"

Callie tapped the side of her nose. "I have two words for you: Sam and Cecil."

CHAPTER 17

Contrary to what Sam proclaimed, Callie had not, in fact, lost her mind. If anything, she'd found it. She needed villagers willing to help put this hotel back together, and if Sam was the reason they refused, then it was his responsibility to change their minds.

The man would become a social butterfly, friend to the common man, and supporter of the community if it killed her. And based on the look on his face, it just might.

"I am not doing this," Sam repeated for the fifth time. "I am not making a fool of myself because some small-minded islanders don't like me."

"I highly recommend you not call them that while entertaining their children."

Sam rolled his eyes while throwing his hands in the air in exasperation. They'd taken the conversation from the inn over to Callie's cottage, where the other half of the act resided. Callie stood beside Cecil's cage, while Sam remained obstinate on the other side of the room.

"How would you like to meet some new friends, Cecil?"

"Rather have a cracker," her pet squawked.

Callie expected this response. "What if these new friends gave you crackers?"

"New best friends," he chirped enthusiastically. "New best friends."

"That bird is going to be a solo act," Sam said, looking ready to bolt.

Callie shot Sam a narrowed look, but it was really an excuse to look at him. The man who always looked pressed and ready for the boardroom cut a striking image in worn denim and a tee that hugged his shoulders like a second skin. Though he'd worn jeans to the dinner party, as Callie had suggested, those must have been his dress jeans.

Today Sam wore his get-dirty jeans, and they were giving Callie plenty of dirty thoughts. Just because they wouldn't be exploring a more physical relationship didn't mean she couldn't enjoy a little mental fantasy about the man. It wasn't as if he would know.

"Stop looking at me like that," Sam barked. She feared he could read her mind until he added, "This circus-act idea is never going to happen."

"Fine," Callie said. "Then call Will Parsons and tell her the Sunset Harbor Inn will not be open for business until spring."

Sam's jaw flexed, but he didn't argue. Instead, he stalked across the room like a lion ready to attack. Callie couldn't help but admire how he moved. Maybe she should make outlandish demands more often.

Stopping on the other side of the cage, he said, "There has to be another way. I'll donate to the preservation society. Or buy a new scoreboard for the high school football field."

Throwing money into the community might help his case, but Callie doubted a donation would do enough to garner the immediate reversal they needed. "They don't want your money, Sam. They need to get to know you as a person, not this hermit-hotelier image they have of you."

Sam frowned. "Hermit hotelier?"

"That's what they call you," Callie said, hoping a poke to his ego would gain his cooperation. "Doesn't that bother you?"

He looked to be considering the idea. "I've been called worse."

The man had to have a weak spot. Callie grasped onto the stories she'd heard about his uncle. "Did you know Morty well?"

The change of subject seemed to take him off guard. "Of course I did. He was my uncle. I spent every summer here with him when I was a kid. At least, until high school, when my mother felt I needed to do internships with the larger family properties."

"Wait. You came here as a kid?"

"Yes. Why?"

"Do the natives know that?"

Sam shook his head. "I have no idea. If they were around and remember me, maybe. I don't walk around talking about it."

"But that's a connection," Callie said. "You weren't new to this island when you took over the hotels. Do you remember the stories your uncle used to tell the kids in the village?"

"I don't know." Sam dropped into Callie's favorite blue chair and ran his hands over his face. Leaning back, he kicked a leg up on the ottoman. She'd never seen anything sexier. "But it doesn't matter. I'm not the storyteller he was. And I don't have the patience to deal with children."

Callie doubted that was true. He may not have much experience with them, but her woman's intuition told her Sam would be great with kids. Once he stopped treating them like miniature adults.

Unable to help herself, Callie sat down next to Sam's leg on the ottoman, resting her hand on his knee. "Would it be so bad for people to like you, Sam? To see you not as a buttoned-up hotel owner but as the nice guy you really are?"

Leaning forward until their faces were mere inches apart, Sam stared into Callie's eyes. "I have my reasons for not reaching out to the people on this island. For not ingratiating myself with this community."

"Why?" she asked, feeling a bit drunk from the heat of his body so close to hers.

Sliding his knuckles along her jawline, he said, "Because I have other plans."

The statement made no sense to Callie, but that might have been because she'd lost the ability to think clearly. Or breathe normally. Or concentrate on anything other than Sam's full lower lip and his eyes, the color of a storm cloud over the sea.

"That's good," she mumbled, referring to something that had nothing to do with the current conversation.

Sam leaned closer, saying, "To hell with it."

And then he kissed her. An onslaught of feelings and emotions, pent-up passion and forbidden longing, crashed into Callie's system. His lips were hot and demanding, and she gave the same in turn. Her head was swimming, her senses coming alive.

Sam leaned back in the chair, pulling Callie with him until she was draped across his body—his big, powerful body that was hard in all the right places, while his lips were soft and his hands kneaded her bottom, pulling her tighter against his arousal.

Oh, yes. He was definitely hard.

Callie couldn't get close enough. She slid her knee up and over his hip, grinding against him. Sam drove a hand into her hair and moaned in response. Finding the bottom of his T-shirt, Callie dragged her nails over his abs, feeling the muscles bunch and twitch beneath her touch. She wanted to taste those abs. To run her tongue along his skin until he was begging for more.

"Don't forget the condom," Cecil chimed, jerking them both back to reality.

Holding her by the shoulders, Sam panted, and his now-dark-gray eyes stared up at her as if surprised to find her there.

Without a word, he shifted Callie gently to the side, set his feet on the floor, and dropped his head into his hands. After what looked to be a silent argument with himself, Sam bolted off the chair. "This is what I was trying to avoid."

The adrenaline pumping through Callie's veins turned to anger. She wanted him and she knew very well he wanted her. She could still feel his hands on her skin. Taste him on her lips. Feel him throbbing between her legs.

"We're two single, consenting adults, Sam. Stop trying to avoid what you know we both want."

"You work for me, Callie," he argued, turning to face her. "I will not take advantage of that."

"Then I'll take advantage of you," she replied, rolling off the chair and closing the distance between them. Sam looked as if he wanted to step back, but she knew his ego wouldn't let him. "I'm not screwing you to get a job, and you're not screwing me as part of my job description. There's no reason we can't fall into bed together."

The storm continued to rage in his eyes as Sam fought the messages his body was sending. She knew he was weakening when his hands flexed open then closed. As if he were struggling to keep them off her.

"I have no intention of marrying again," he growled, as if that would put her off.

"Good," Callie said. "I don't want to have your babies, I want to have sex."

And she meant it. The uterus twitches were annoying and real, but Callie had no intention of letting some instinct as old as time override rational thought. This wasn't the 1800s, for God's sake. Sam stared in stunned disbelief, as if she'd suggested they steal a car and drive off a cliff.

"You can't deny you want me," she said, exploiting her advantage. "Loosen up, Sam. Have a little fun."

He didn't move when Callie slid her hands beneath his shirt. He didn't so much as flinch when she slid her nails along his rib cage. But when she reached for the button on his jeans, he grabbed her hands.

In a ragged voice, he said, "I'm not sure I remember how to have fun."

Callie gave him her most seductive smile. "Then let me remind you."

∾

Sam wanted to argue. To set her away from him and do the right thing. Only in that moment, doing Callie felt like the right thing.

"Are you sure about this?" he asked, clinging to the last remnants of sanity he had. "I can't promise you anything, Callie."

"You forget," she said, lifting his shirt and dropping a moist kiss on his abs, "we've done this before. I know exactly what you can do for me." She kissed him again. "And to me."

Callie wasn't playing fair. How was he supposed to think with her hands on him? With her mouth tempting him like that? She'd said sex only, and that was all he could give. Callie deserved more. She deserved everything.

Sam didn't have everything to give.

"You deserve more," he said, but speaking was growing more difficult as the blood quickly rushed from his head.

"Then we'll have to do it more than once." Callie pushed his shirt up his torso. Without thought, Sam lifted his arms and helped her take it off. Her purr of appreciation shot straight to his groin.

Cupping her face in his hands, Sam caught her gaze and held it. "You're killing me, Callie. I'm trying to protect you."

"From what?" she asked, her eyes dropping to his mouth.

"From me," he said, before giving in and tasting her again.

She was spice and sex, and the combination threatened to fry his brain. His body was already beyond saving. Her fingers were like matches to a flame as she slid her fingertips over his nipples, then replaced them with her tongue.

If she kept this up, he was going to finish long before she got his pants off.

The only way to save himself from embarrassment was to turn the tables. Forcing himself to interrupt Callie's ministrations, Sam yanked on the bottom of her shirt, then slipped his hands under the cotton and up along her sides. Though he'd meant to remove the shirt with one swift movement, his hands found the undersides of her breasts and his intentions took a detour.

Warm lace danced under his palms as her nipples pebbled behind the delicate material. He filled his hands with her, massaging, until Callie let out a moan, then laid her forehead against his chest.

"Bed," she mumbled, her breathing unsteady. "We need a bed."

Taking his hand, she led him out of the living room and down the hall. Another wall of windows brought the ocean into the bedroom space. It was an element Sam had added when he'd had Morty's cottage redone.

Sam had picked every item in this house. Personally oversaw each minute detail of the renovation. He'd even picked the blue-and-white linens that covered the California king in the center of the room.

Common sense began to creep back in. This was crazy. It was the middle of the day. Sam didn't even take holidays off. What the hell was he doing taking a Monday afternoon to have sex?

Then Callie turned, smiled, and pulled the gray T-shirt over her head. Right. That's what he was doing.

As she returned to his arms, all supple and hot and ready, the winged beast in the living room called out his condom reminder once again. Sam didn't have anything with him.

"Do you have something?" he asked between long, wet, mind-blowing kisses.

"My cousin left a box," Callie answered, trailing her teeth across Sam's ribs. She slid lower, and he forgot what they were talking about. "She thought I might need them."

Who thought she might need what? The top button on his jeans was undone now. Callie lowered the zipper, then pressed the denim over his ass as her tongue lit a fiery trail from his navel down.

One slender finger dipped behind the band of his boxer briefs, scorching his skin and threatening to send Sam to his knees.

"Bed," he said. "Now."

Callie followed the order, shuffling backward, never breaking the contact between them. As she lowered onto her back, Sam followed, running on instinct and mindless desire. He pressed a thigh between her legs, and she hiked a knee over his hip. They rolled across the large mattress, playing some kind of sexual-king-of-the-hill contest.

Every time Sam had Callie right where he wanted her, she'd push against his shoulder and take the top position again. When she took the lead for the third time and started working down his body, Sam decided to let her have her way. There would be plenty of time for both of them to have a turn, and giving in seemed smart when she started tugging his jeans off.

The Levi's hit the floor and Callie straddled his hips, sitting up with a triumphant look on her face. With a smile that promised all sorts of wickedness, she reached behind her and undid the lacy black number that was the only thing between his hands and heaven.

As the lingerie landed somewhere beside the bed, Sam's mouth went dry as his hands took what she offered. She was perfection. He massaged and tweaked, enjoying every sensation as it danced across her face. The waves of pleasure drove her to move against him, grinding in circles, then leaning forward far enough for him to take one nipple into his mouth.

And then the phone rang.

Sam froze, reality cutting through desire as if it had come crashing through the wall of windows. Callie ground harder.

"Ignore it," she said, her eyes closed and her hands on his to hold them in place.

"We can't," he said, using every ounce of strength to remain still. "You need to answer it."

The only reason that phone would ring was because one or both of them was needed. Either Yvonne was looking for him, and that she would do only for a good reason, or Callie was needed back across the street.

His ingrained sense of responsibility reared its ugly head. Sam could not ignore the call. No matter how much he wanted to. Removing his hands, he waited another second for Callie to move. After a brief hesitation, she climbed to the side of the bed, pressed a pillow against her naked breasts, and answered the phone.

CHAPTER 18

Callie wanted to scream into the phone, *What do you want?* but instead said, "Hello?" She could barely comprehend the words coming from the other end through the flood of humiliation washing over her.

It seemed there'd been a delivery that Jack didn't know what to do with. Callie let him know she'd be right over, then ended the call without saying good-bye. Sam shuffled around behind her. She wanted to stay there, hugging the pillow with her head down until he left, but the shuffling stopped. No footsteps left the room.

Reminding herself she'd endured worse, Callie turned to find Sam staring out the wall of windows at the waves crashing in the distance. She knew exactly how the sand felt. If only she could be washed away from this scene.

"I was wrong," Sam said, and Callie pulled the pillow tighter, as if it could protect her from what would come next. "I thought the Anchor had the best views on the island." He turned to face her. "But this is better."

She'd expected anger. Assumed the cold and distant Sam would reappear and tell her all the reasons that what they'd been about to do was wrong. To reject her again.

Instead, she found a Greek god standing in her bedroom in nothing but a pair of jeans, looking like the answer to a prayer. A very dirty, explicit prayer.

"The view is pretty good from here, too," she said, relieved that the warm and willing Sam was still with her. Callie wanted to pick back up where they'd left off, but Jack was expecting her. She had a job to do and should never have let her libido get the better of her.

That didn't mean they couldn't finish this another time. Or was the moment gone?

Unsure of what to do next, Callie scooted down the bed until she could reach her bra where she'd tossed it on the floor. "Duty calls," she said, her voice still ragged and breathy.

Grabbing her shirt from the other side of the bed, Callie continued to hug the pillow, which was asinine, since he'd been kissing her breasts only moments ago. But awkwardness brought with it a strong sense of modesty. If only Sam would move or say something else.

And then he did.

"Come here, Callie."

As if drawn by an invisible thread, she obeyed, crossing the small space to reach him. Sam took the pillow, tossed it on the bed, and pulled her against him. The live wire that had been sizzling beneath her skin went into overload.

Callie slid her arms around his middle and laid her cheek against his warm chest. His heart rate was racing like hers was. This wasn't over.

Sam held her there, his chin on the top of her head and his strong hands lingering at the small of her back. "We need to work on our timing," he said. Pulling back far enough for her to look up at him, he asked, "How about dinner tonight?"

"You want to take me out?" Callie asked.

Dropping a chaste kiss on her forehead, he said, "I was thinking we could stay in."

That sounded promising. And then a thought occurred. "Are you suggesting I cook?"

Sam chuckled, and she felt the vibration throughout her entire body. She seriously hated Jack right now.

"How about if I bring something with me? If I remember correctly, you have a weird penchant for British food. Dempsey's fish and chips are excellent."

A budding warmth that had nothing to do with their current state of undress developed somewhere behind Callie's breastbone. He had paid attention all those years ago. She put an immediate wet blanket on that thought.

Callie didn't want or need romantic gestures. What she wanted was sex. With Sam.

"I'll have the wine ready to pour," she said, sliding her breasts against his chest to remind herself this was entirely physical.

To her delight, Sam groaned, kissed her until her bones felt like pudding, then leaned his forehead against hers. "Dinner at six," he said.

And sex by six fifteen, Callie thought.

~

The rest of the day was torture. Callie and Sam worked side by side, removing wallpaper from the dining room walls. Olaf had yet to finish with the furniture, but enough space had been cleared to give them room to work. And since Olaf was off helping with the festival, the pair worked alone, accompanied only by a small radio set to the local station.

As Van Morrison sang about going into the mystic, Sam reached for a high spot on the wall, revealing a wide expanse of abs as his shirt came up and his jeans rode low on his hips.

Callie nearly jumped him right there.

They'd discussed a plan of attack going forward on the project, which was contingent upon signing on more workers. Bernie had maintained enough of a crew to handle the exterior but wasn't willing to transfer to the indoor tasks, and neither, it seemed, were his men.

Apparently, dedication to Morty went only so far.

That left them back at the campaign to improve Sam's reputation.

"How is this circus act you suggest going to change anything?" he asked, and not for the first time.

"We've been over this," Callie said. "Win over the kids, and we win over the adults. Win over the adults, and we get our workers."

"Not everyone has kids," he argued, saying the word *kids* with extra derision.

Callie took a break from scraping to stare at her gorgeous helper. "What is your problem with children?"

"I don't have a problem with children," he said, peeling a large section of paper off the wall in one piece. "I just have no desire to entertain a bunch of them."

She wasn't signing up for babysitting duty herself, but Callie liked kids well enough. Though she couldn't remember the last time she'd played with one.

"Cecil will do most of the work," she said. "All you have to do is ask him questions. You're the straight man, and he delivers the punch lines."

"Speaking of," Sam said, dropping his scraper to his side, "where the hell did you find that bird? He's like a freak of nature."

Now he'd crossed a line. "Cecil is *not* a freak of nature. And don't you ever say that around him. He's sensitive."

"He's a bird."

"He has feelings," Callie said. "And I got him from the circus."

"You what?" Sam stared as if Callie had claimed she'd given birth to her colorful pet.

"His owner was old and had trained Cecil from birth to be part of his circus act," Callie explained. "I happened to know the man's son, who couldn't keep the bird after his father died. He said the bird had an attitude problem and his wife refused to live with it."

Sam leaned against the wall. "So you took him?"

"Honestly?" she said. "I was seventeen, and I thought he would annoy my mother."

"Did it work?"

Callie shook her head in the negative. "They were made for each other. But I fell in love with him, too. Which is why I took him with me when I moved out. I knew she'd make him meaner. He can be very sweet when he wants to be," she added. Which was true. Cecil had seen Callie through many dark days.

Sam didn't argue or say anything at all. He simply returned to the task of scraping wallpaper. But nearly a minute later, he said, "I've never had a pet."

It was Callie's turn to stare in amazement. "Never?"

He gave a noncommittal shrug. "Mother believed all pets were dirty and useless." With a quick glance, he added, "My father was never around, so I have no idea how he felt about them. My guess would be that he agreed with her."

The image of a poor little Sam sitting all alone on some fancy staircase, sad and forlorn and longing for a puppy, popped into Callie's mind. Every little boy should have a puppy.

"I'm sorry," she said, "but that's the saddest thing I've ever heard."

Sam snorted. "I wouldn't go that far. And if I ever got one, it wouldn't be a parrot who thought the world revolved around him."

"That parrot is going to save our asses," Callie said. "I suggest you be nice to him."

∾

By five o'clock, when he and Callie had called it a day, Sam's arms were sore and the rest of his body was still riding an adrenaline high from earlier in the day. The untimely phone call could have been the slap of reality that put an end to anything happening between him and Callie. And for the first few minutes after, that was exactly what it had been.

But then he'd slid on his pants and walked to the window while Callie dealt with whatever crisis needed her attention at the inn. As he'd stared out at the surging waves, Sam hadn't been able to think of one reason why they shouldn't enjoy each other. Callie was right about the lack of conflict due to their positions as employer and employee.

They had a history. A complicated one, yes, but maybe the complications were all in the past. Callie wouldn't be staying on Anchor. And as of right now, Sam wouldn't be leaving. At least not for two more years, unless Lucas pulled a legal miracle out of thin air and broke the terms of the will.

If there was one thing Sam had mastered in the last six years, it was ignoring the past. That meant focusing on the now, and the now Callie was offering was a whole lot better than any now he'd experienced in too damn long.

He'd been honest with her. Let her know marriage was not an option where he was concerned. And that was exactly how she wanted it, too. They were two consenting adults, both aware of the rules and limitations involved in falling into bed together. Sam had been out of this game for far too long, as proven by the fact that he'd nearly lost himself before they'd even gotten started.

Tonight would be different. This encounter wasn't about consolation or giving in to some adolescent-like urge and ripping each other's clothes off. He might not have a heart to give, but Sam could give Callie pleasure, and that was exactly what he intended to do.

But first he needed to do a bit of research.

"Thanks for meeting me here," Sam said as he joined Randy at the bar in Dempsey's. "I know this was short notice."

"Not a problem. Will is over at Tom and Patty's, helping stuff goodie bags for Beth's shower, so I'm on my own for dinner." Randy nodded toward the dining room. "Should we get a table?"

"Afraid I wasn't clear," Sam said. "I'm not staying to eat. I need some answers."

A dark brow floated an inch above the other. "Answers about what?"

Sam tapped the bar, feeling like an idiot for even asking the question, but he needed to know if Callie's guess was correct.

"I hear the natives don't like me. Callie says they won't help out at the inn because of me." He looked Randy in the eye. "Is that true?"

The big guy screwed up his mouth, staring at the bottle of green tea before him. "I can't say for sure about them refusing to work at the inn, but it's true that you're not the most popular business owner around here."

"Because I brought in my own crew to handle the Anchor?"

"What?" Randy said, meeting Sam's eye again. "Nobody cares about that."

"Then what the hell is the problem?" Sam struggled to keep his voice down. "What did I ever do to these people?"

"You haven't done anything, and *that's* the problem." Randy leaned back on his stool. "In case you haven't noticed, this village is on the small side. Makes for a tight-knit community. But you refuse to be knitted in, for lack of a better term. The islanders believe you think you're better than they are."

Sam heard the words *I am better than they are* spoken in his mother's haughty, Southern-belle voice in his head. That was exactly what Eugenia Cumberland Edwards would say, and Sam hated that she'd ingrained the sentiment in his brain. He wasn't an idiot or a snob. Sam had avoided becoming part of the community because he knew that was Morty's intention, not because of some egotistical illusion that he was better than anyone.

The ridiculous requirements of his uncle's will were there only because Mortimer Cumberland had been certain that, given time, Sam would become part of the island and never want to leave. The idea that he could be manipulated and have his life's ambition altered so easily was what had driven Sam to keep his distance. To *not* get involved.

Now he had to go above and beyond to change these people's impressions of him, or else push the renovation deadline back to spring and likely damage Will's budding business in the process.

His selfish, stubborn determination had come back to bite him in the ass, and Sam grew even angrier knowing all of this could have been avoided.

Short of taking out an ad in the island newsletter to explain his motivations to the natives, which he wasn't willing to do, Sam was short on ideas.

"How do I change their perception of me?" he asked Randy, glancing at his watch to make sure he was still on time to arrive at Callie's by six. "I don't have to tell you how important it is that we have the inn finished and ready for business by Christmas. If we don't get more workers, that's not going to happen."

Randy looked to be taking the problem more seriously once Sam pointed out what the lack of island help would mean for his fiancée. "Most of my guys went south to pick up work during the off-season. I can lend my own services."

"You may be the size of three men," Sam said, "but I don't think you alone are going to cut it." At that moment, Tom Dempsey, the owner of the bar, approached with a large paper bag.

"Two orders of fish and chips, ready to go."

"How much do I owe you?" Sam asked.

"Twenty-one twenty-five."

Sam pulled twenty-five dollars from his wallet and slid it across the bar. "Thanks, Tom." The action gave him an idea. Turning to Randy as Tom walked away, he asked, "What if I donate money to an island charity?" He already gave a sizable annual contribution to the preservation society—another stipulation set forth in Morty's will—though Sam would have given the money regardless. "Or maybe the school."

Randy looked dubious. "Throwing your money at them isn't going to make them like you. If anything, it'll make them *dis*like you even more." The big guy rubbed his chin. "You need to get involved somehow. Give your time. Get in the mix with them."

That was what Sam was afraid of. "Callie wants me to do some kind of storytelling session with the kids during the festival this weekend."

"Like Morty used to do." Randy nodded, and his wide smile returned. "That's not a bad idea. Though you don't strike me as the entertaining-children type."

"I'm not." So much for finding another way. "But I guess I will be this weekend."

~

Callie checked her reflection for the third time in the last fifteen minutes, then kicked off the strappy heels for the second. It wasn't as if she was leaving the house. And the slinky dress did enough to show off her curves without having to highlight them with the shoes. She tucked her hair behind her ear, then changed her mind, running her hands through it to achieve what she hoped was a tossed, sexy look.

Happy with the results, Callie sent up a prayer of thanks that the little black dress still fit. She hadn't worn this particular number in more than six years. The midsection felt tighter than she remembered, but it zipped, and that was all that mattered. However, cutting back on the peanut butter cups was definitely in order.

Spinning to check out the back—again—Callie asked herself the age-old question of whether her ass looked fat in the dress. But then the doorbell rang and she conceded her ass was as big as it was and there was no doing anything about it now.

A quick glance at the clock as Callie struggled not to sprint through the living room indicated the time was 5:50. Ten minutes early. She could only hope that meant Sam was as anxious as she was to resume their afternoon activities.

Reaching for the doorknob, she struck a pose, hoping the effect was more sex kitten than desperate goober.

"Well, hello," she said, pulling the door open with a smile. And then the smile disappeared. "Henri? What the hell are you doing here?"

"You sent me a melodramatic email that said, and I quote, 'Things aren't going well. If you don't hear from me in a week, assume I took a long walk off a short pier. Promise you'll take care of Cecil for me.'" Charging into the house, Henri set her duffel bag on the floor, then propped both hands on her hips. "That was eight days ago. You haven't answered any of my messages from the last two days, so here I am." With an exaggerated head nod, she added, "You're lucky I didn't tell your mother. If I'd have gotten here to find you *had* actually turned yourself into fish food, she would have kicked my ass for keeping the secret."

This was not good. Sam would arrive any second. Henri was *not* going to ruin this night for her. Did she have any idea how long it had been since Callie had sex?

Too long!

"I'm sorry," Callie appeased. "I'm fine." Grabbing the duffel from the floor, she pushed Henri toward the exit, which was still open and sending cold wind up Callie's dress. "Now you can go."

"I'm not leaving," Henri said, pulling out of Callie's grasp. "I just got here. That's a nine-fucking-hour drive. Are you crazy?"

Callie had to get rid of her. She stuck her head out the door, relieved not to see headlights coming down the lane. "Get a room at the Anchor Inn," she said, tossing the duffel onto the porch. "I'll pay for it. Order room service. Get a steak. You love steak. I'll pay for that, too."

"Did you really just throw my bag out the door?" Henri glared in disbelief. Then her eyes went wide. "Oh my God. You're wearing the fuck-me dress. Why are you wearing the fuck-me dress?" She shot a look out the door. "Is he coming over right now? Please tell me it's Sam. If you're fucking some gap-toothed, balding dude who smells like fish, I will never forgive you."

Callie waved her hands in front of her face. "Of course it's Sam, you crazy woman. Do you really think I'm *that* hard up?"

Henri shrugged. "It's been a long time. You never know."

"I know," Callie said. "Now you have to go. He'll be here any second."

"Well, shit. Where is the Anchor Inn?" Henri asked, grabbing her bag off the porch. "I don't remember."

"Follow this road back to the main strip and make a left. The Anchor is past the marina on your left. You can't miss it." Callie all but pushed her cousin down the steps, then remembered her bare feet. "Holy moly, I don't have shoes on." Rubbing her arms for warmth, she hopped back inside the house. "I'll call you tomorrow."

"You'd better!" Henri yelled back, tossing her bag into the back of her truck as she ran around to the driver's side. Climbing up into the cab, she waved. "Have fun boinking your boss!" And then she disappeared.

Callie rolled her eyes and continued to shiver. As Henri backed out of the drive, another pair of headlights rounded the corner. Ducking back inside, Callie slammed the door shut and scooted over to the window to make sure it was Sam. She didn't need any more surprises this evening.

Sam's burgundy Murano pulled into the drive, and Callie exhaled in relief. The sex was saved.

CHAPTER 19

S am would have sworn he'd passed Callie's cousin's truck. But that was impossible. Maybe the floor guys had worked late. Had there been a truck like that parked at the inn today?

He couldn't remember. Callie would likely know who it was, but as soon as she opened the door, all thought of asking about old, run-down trucks drifted out of Sam's mind.

Standing in her bare feet, toes of one foot curled under and a tight black dress riding high on her milky-white thighs, Callie was the hottest thing he'd ever seen.

"Hi," she said, nervous anticipation clear in the shy smile. "You're right on time."

"Hi," Sam said, unable to say anything more.

With a shiver, she asked, "Are you going to come in?"

He instantly felt bad for making her stand in the cold. "Of course," he said, stepping into the cottage. Callie closed the door, brushing her breast across his arm in the process. He felt it like a kick to the head.

All he could do was stand there and stare down at her. The choppy blonde hair, usually tucked behind her ears, looked messy, as if she'd just crawled out of bed. The gray makeup smudged around her lashes made her eyes look brighter than usual, and the deep red she'd applied to her full lips carried a glossy sheen. When she bit down on her bottom lip, Sam's brain went fuzzy.

"Is that our dinner?" she asked, her voice sultry as she stared up at him through thick lashes.

"Yeah," he murmured, unable to look away. His clothes felt tighter. Restrictive.

"Well," she said, tilting her head and drawing Sam's eye to the expanse of bare shoulder exposed above the low line of the dress, "are you hungry?"

The brown bag hit the floor. "Very." Giving in to temptation, Sam laid his hands on Callie's bare shoulders, testing the black bands around the top of her arms that served as sleeves. They slid with little effort, and he knew he could have the dress around her ankles in no more than a breath.

Slipping her hands beneath his sport jacket, Callie slithered against him. "Maybe we should start with an appetizer."

"Yes," Sam said, pushing his hands into her hair, then tilting her head back. "We should."

She tasted of heat and white wine, and Sam was lost instantly. He was hard within seconds and unable to pull Callie close enough to appease the carnal need racing through his system. He needed to be on her. In her.

"We need to find a better location," she muttered, between nips to his bottom lip. "And you're wearing too many clothes."

"So are you." Unwilling to break contact, Sam picked her up and Callie wrapped her legs around his waist. "Tell me the condoms are near the bed."

"On the nightstand," she said, before returning her attention to sucking on his earlobe.

When they reached the bed, Sam settled Callie on her back, following her down and catching himself on his elbows so as not to crush her. The black dress rode up to her hips, and as he slid his fingers along the soft skin of her thigh and higher, what was missing had Sam smiling against her lips.

"You're trying to kill me," he said, tracing a hand over her bare hip.

"I didn't see the need to put them on when they were going to come right back off."

Sam didn't know practicality could be hot, but her words had him ready to melt in her hand. Which reminded him, they were both still wearing too many clothes.

Rising off the bed, Sam kicked off his shoes while pulling the jacket off his shoulders and flinging it through the air. As he unbuttoned his shirt, Callie leaned up on her elbows. "Dinner *and* a show. Excellent idea."

Her eyes, illuminated by the moonlight pouring through the wall of windows, shone like ice as she watched him, appreciation and raw lust in her gaze. Sam took his time with the buttons, something that required considerable restraint on his part, as Callie's dress had slipped higher, revealing a hint of blonde hair between her thighs.

She dropped one knee to the side, and Sam feared permanent damage if he didn't get his pants off in the next few seconds. Letting his dress shirt fall to the floor, he removed his belt and made quick work of his khakis.

"My God, you're gorgeous," Callie whispered with awe in her voice. Sam's temperature spiked as he stood there, allowing her to look her fill. Then he crooked a finger for her to join him. Though he considered letting Callie return the favor and provide her own show, he preferred to remove the dress himself.

Without argument, she went onto her knees and crawled to the end of the bed, never taking her eyes off his. "You beckoned," she said, returning to her feet before him.

Sam didn't speak. Instead, he reached for the zipper at the back of the dress. The front gaped loose, and he withdrew far enough to watch the swath of black fall to the floor in a wisp. His breath caught.

"So beautiful," he said, reverence in his touch as he trailed one finger down the side of a breast, then over her belly. Callie flinched as if he'd touched a flame to her skin, but stood her ground.

As he knew she always would. Her strength made him want her even more.

A smile that was both sexy and shy crossed her lips as Callie pulled him silently to the bed. When they reached the edge, she sat down and ran her hands along the outside of his thighs, stopping him in place. Her hands explored further as she blew a gentle breath across his tip.

His body jerked in response.

When she replaced her breath with her tongue, Sam had to lock his knees to keep from dropping. Without further hesitation, Callie took him deep at the same moment she cupped his balls, and every nerve ending in his body came alive.

She really was trying to kill him.

Enduring the torture for as long as he could, Sam growled when he felt his breaking point creeping closer. Stabbing his hands into her hair, he pushed the words through his lungs.

"Callie. I can't . . ." Then he shot over the edge, the ripples of the climax echoing through his limbs. If this was how he went, Sam thought, at least he would die a happy man.

~

Callie waited for Sam to stop shaking before she slid her hands around the backs of his thighs and nudged him onto the bed. "How was that for an appetizer?" she asked, relishing the look of hunger and ecstasy in eyes that had turned charcoal gray.

"Amazing," he said, his voice low and heavy and sending quivers to her core. "But now it's your turn." Sam followed words with action, sliding two fingers inside her at the same moment he took her mouth with his.

She nearly came off the mattress, spreading her legs wider as she clung to his shoulders to keep herself grounded. Not that Sam wasn't anchor enough. He stroked his fingers in and out while making circles against her clit with his thumb. The storm built to a crescendo in her body faster than anything Callie had ever experienced.

"Come for me, Callie," he said against her ear.

His finger curled against something inside her, and she screamed his name as her nails dug into his forearms. Panting and out of breath, she rode the waves that came one after another with every flick of that magical finger. She thought she might drown in the pleasure, until he eased out of her, leaving her bereft and wanting more.

But then he was there, his tip pressing against her core.

"Get a condom," he said, his teeth clenched, as he pressed close again but didn't enter.

By some miracle, Callie was close enough to the nightstand to reach the box without having to shift her position. She removed a packet and opened it with her teeth before sliding it over his rock-hard erection. Letting the box fall to the floor, she guided him home, lifting off the bed to show him what she wanted.

With a moan that seemed to emanate from deep in his chest, Sam drove into her, sinking to the hilt and stretching her to accommodate him. Callie moaned in turn, hitching on a breath when he started to move. The fire built again, spinning through her and setting her alight from the inside out.

They found a rhythm, each thrust going deeper than the one before. Callie slid her nails along Sam's rib cage, then around to the powerful muscles bunching and flexing beneath his hot, slick skin. Dipping lower, she clenched his firm ass, pulling him tighter as if there were some way they could get closer.

With his forehead against hers, Sam gave one final thrust before his body went rigid and a growl escaped his lips. Callie lifted, holding on tight as they shattered together.

～

Nothing could have prepared Callie for this experience. She would be sore for a week, but if spending the rest of the night enjoying Sam's body would put her in traction, she'd accept the prognosis with a smile on her face.

Though at the moment she was moaning for a completely different reason.

"This is the best fish and chips I've had since the last time I was in England." Callie caught an errant flake of breading trying to escape from her fork. "I think they put the food equivalent of crack in the batter, whatever that might be." She tried to steal a bite from Sam's plate, but he was too fast.

"I don't think so," he said, pulling the plate out of her reach. "You already ate half of my fries."

"You made me work up an appetite," she said, enjoying the flash of heat the words ignited in his eyes. "Don't you want me to keep my energy up? It would be a shame if I fell asleep when we have the whole night ahead of us."

Leaning close, with a sexy grin curling one side of his mouth higher than the other, Sam said, "I'm perfectly capable of keeping you awake all night long without having to sacrifice my dinner."

The cocktail of charm, confidence, and practicality gave Callie more of a buzz than the wine Sam had poured. They'd opted to eat at the table, with Callie on the end and Sam to her left. Since she'd commandeered his shirt as dinner attire, Sam was left with nothing but his khakis. The sight of his bare, broad chest was giving her all sorts of ideas for dessert.

"I had a talk with Randy Navarro while I was at Dempsey's, picking up the food," Sam said, keeping his eyes on his plate. Maybe she wasn't as fetching in the button-up as she'd hoped.

"About what?" she asked, popping a fry into her mouth.

"How the islanders feel about me."

Callie tried not to bristle at the idea Sam had sought confirmation elsewhere about something she'd already told him. "And what did he say?"

Sam dropped his fork and sat back with his glass of wine. "That you're right. They don't like me. Except your reason is off."

Of course. She had to be wrong about something. "Then why don't they like you?"

After taking a sip, Sam set the glass back on the table. "Because I don't *mix* with them, Randy says. They believe I think I'm better than they are."

How, exactly, that made her wrong, Callie wasn't sure. "Which is why I suggested you *mix* with them during the festival this weekend. At what point does this prove me wrong?"

"You said it was because I brought in outside workers."

Callie took a deep breath, waiting to see if he was joking. Sam's face remained serious. Her appetite waned. For several things.

"And you don't think that has anything to do with their dislike?"

The smugness receded, but only marginally. "I guess there's no way to know for sure." She raised her brows, shooting a challenging look across the short distance between them. "I admit," he said, "the choice could be a contributing factor." She stared harder until he added, "Fine. It didn't help."

"So now you're willing to team up with Cecil, as I suggested?"

"Yes."

"But only because Randy said it was a good idea." She made sure her words came out as a statement, not a question. Did he have any idea how insulting it was that he required someone else's input over hers?

"I did tell him that you thought my taking part in the festival was a good idea."

"It isn't a good idea. It's the perfect idea."

"Regardless," he said, "it's our only idea at the moment, and we don't have time to wait for alternative inspiration."

"You're right," she said, wadding up the napkin in her lap and dropping it onto her plate. "I'm feeling less inspired by the second."

Ever an astute man, Sam leaned his elbows on the table. "I've pissed you off."

Callie tapped the side of her nose but remained silent. If he was going to see the light, he'd need to find it on his own.

"Because I'm reluctant to make a fool of myself to gain acceptance that I couldn't care less about?"

"Try again," she said.

He leaned back, rubbing a hand across his abs. Callie was distracted by the narrow trail of soft hair that disappeared behind the button of his trousers. Lust momentarily squelched her anger, but she raised her eyes a second later, reminding herself how little he'd respected her opinion.

Fortunately, Sam was contemplating his plate and not her face.

"Because I discussed the situation with Randy."

He was quicker than she'd expected. "You're getting warmer."

"Am I?" he asked. "Because for a second there, I felt it get quite cold in here."

"Did you happen to run into Randy?" she asked, unwilling to let him off the hook just yet. "Or did you seek him out?"

"I set up the brief meeting. Why?"

"By doing so, you dismissed my opinion as insufficient, that's why. But when Randy—a man, I might add—told you the same thing I did, then it had to be true." Callie carried her plate and wineglass to the sink, fearful her face would reveal more hurt than anger.

If Sam knew he'd hurt her, he'd have the upper hand. She would be the sensitive woman who couldn't take being questioned, and they would never stand on equal ground again.

"How long have you been on this island, Callie?" Sam asked, his voice revealing nothing. No anger. No annoyance. Not even arrogance.

"Six weeks," she answered, rinsing her plate in the sink.

"Randy Navarro has lived on this island for more than fifteen years." She didn't have to turn around to know Sam was advancing on her. "I didn't dismiss your opinion," he said into her ear. "If anything, seeking secondary confirmation proves I took you seriously. I simply wanted insight into the people on this island that neither you nor I could have."

He trailed one fingertip along the side of her neck as he pressed his warm body against her back. Callie let the dish drop to the bottom of the sink as she braced her hands against the counter.

"You have a brilliant mind, Calliope Henderson, and I respect that you understood a problem before I knew it even existed." His hands slid under the tail of the shirt, caressing her hips as he ground against her backside. The proof of his arousal had her pushing back in response.

Callie tried to speak, but Sam slid one arm across her abdomen as the other went lower, pressing between her legs. Her head fell back on his shoulder as her knees threatened to fail her.

"Now I believe it's time for dessert," Sam breathed into her ear. His hands were definitely serving up something delicious. "It's my turn to taste you, Callie." He put words to action as he licked the top of her shoulder, exposed by the open collar of the shirt.

She rode the hand that nearly had her ready to come right there at the counter. With a guttural moan, Callie nodded the yes she couldn't say, and Sam lowered her to the floor. For the rest of her stay in Peabody Cottage, Callie would never again look at that blue kitchen area rug without thinking of Sam pressed between her thighs.

CHAPTER 20

The next morning, Sam struggled to concentrate on anything other than memories of the night before. He'd left Callie's place around four that morning. They may have nodded off for a couple of brief naps, but for the most part Callie had kept him up all night, in every way possible.

She was sexy, demanding, enthusiastic, and flexible. And Sam feared he might never get enough. The thought set off warning bells in his brain.

Their current arrangement, outside of their professional connection, involved mutual physical satisfaction and nothing more. But every time Callie demanded respect, challenged him on an intellectual level, or displayed her impressive ability to analyze a situation and solve a puzzle before he'd found all the pieces, his admiration for her grew. And then there were the moments she let down her guard—when she was sweet, kindhearted Callie, with the bright smile and brighter eyes.

That was the Callie who posed the greatest threat to his well-being.

And likely to her own. If she understood how little Sam had to offer on a personal level, she'd make sure their relationship went back to business only. Throughout their night together, Callie had never given the slightest hint she wanted more than sex from him. That lack of expectation both nullified his guilt and pricked his ego.

"Good morning, Mr. Callie's Boss," said a voice from the far side of the lobby. Sam had come out to the main desk to pick up the reservation report for the month ahead. With his nose in the report, he hadn't noticed anyone else in the area.

He also didn't expect to be addressed as Mr. Callie's Boss.

Turning, Sam found a familiar blonde smiling from the end of the counter.

"So that *was* your truck last night," he said, tucking the folder beneath his arm.

"I was hoping you didn't recognize it," Henri answered, looking unconcerned. "My timing has always been a little off."

"How long had you been there?"

Henri smiled, revealing one deep dimple in her right cheek. "Long enough to realize Cal had plans for the night that didn't include me."

Sam fought the urge to glance around for open ears. He wasn't worried about what others thought of anything that went on between him and Callie, but he didn't see the need to broadcast their private lives either.

"Does your presence in my lobby mean you stayed here last night?" he asked.

"I did." Henri held up her key card. "The place is so nice, I think I'll stay another night or two."

He should have told her there was no need, since he and Callie could always use *his* cabin. And then Sam realized what he was thinking. Did he plan to spend every night with Callie? They hadn't talked about it before he'd left that morning, but her stay on Anchor was only temporary. No sense in wasting what little time they had.

His thoughts drifted into what they could do with that time. Graphic images played through his mind. Erotic images.

"You alright there, big guy?" Henri asked.

Sam shook his head. "Yes. Yes, I'm fine. I'm glad you're enjoying your stay."

At that moment, Yvonne appeared from the back office, a wide smile spreading across her face at the sight of Henri. "Good morning," she said, with more warmth than Sam would expect for one of their guests. "Did you sleep well?"

"Great," Henri replied, her eyes lingering on Yvonne almost affectionately. "I thought maybe we could grab some lunch."

"I'd like that." Yvonne stared at Henri for several seconds, until Sam cleared his throat. "Oh," she said, jumping back a step. "I'm sorry, Mr. Edwards. I didn't see you there."

"Yes," he said, "I know." He'd never thought much about why Yvonne, one of the most beautiful young women he'd ever seen, didn't have a boyfriend on the island. Now he knew.

Yvonne gave the clock behind her a quick check, then said to Henri, "I can't leave for another half hour. Do you mind waiting?"

With a slow shake of her head, Henri said, "Not at all." She wore a goofy grin on her face and Sam felt like an interloper.

"I've got work to do," he said, waving the file he'd been holding against his side. "You two carry on." Yvonne nodded as if to acknowledge his departure, but she was too busy smiling at Henri to spare him a glance.

"How about that," a familiar voice said from the lobby behind them. "The exact three people I came to see. It's as if you knew I was coming." Callie delivered the greeting with an equal smile for each of them, though her eyes lingered on his for an extra second.

If he'd had a mirror in that moment, Sam would have seen the same goofy face Henri had made moments before.

"Hey, Cuz," Henri said. "How was your night?"

With one arched brow, Callie replied, "Fine, thanks. How was yours?"

"Good," the dimpled blonde said. "So good, I'm going to stay here a little longer." Henri cast a smile in Yvonne's direction, gaining a blush that brought out the freckles scattered across the woman's mocha cheeks.

Sam enjoyed watching the realization come to Callie. Her eyes darted between the two women several times before she said, "Ooooooh. Well. Good for you."

"What did you need from me?" Yvonne asked Callie.

"Oh yeah." Callie pulled a folded piece of paper from her bag. "Bernie made a supply list for the gazebo construction." Handing the paper over, she asked, "Could you place the order for delivery on Friday?"

"Sure can," Yvonne said, glancing over the order. "I'll do this real quick before lunch."

"Which she's having with me," Henri said.

"Then I guess I don't need to see you," Callie said. "I was going to take you to lunch after I met with Sam, but if you're busy . . ."

"We don't have to—" Yvonne started, but Henri interrupted.

"Yep. I'm busy."

With a chuckle, Callie said, "Tossed over for a pretty girl. I see how you are."

As she had yet to address him, Sam said, "Did we have a meeting scheduled this morning?"

"No," Callie said, finally giving him her attention. "But I took a chance you might have a few minutes free. If not, I can come back later."

"I have time," Sam said, a little too eagerly.

Yvonne looked confused. Henri looked smug. And Callie looked good enough to eat. Which Sam knew from firsthand experience that she was.

Instead of the work clothes she'd worn the day before, Callie had slipped back into her business attire today. Though he couldn't see much of the outfit hidden beneath her coat, the glimpse of skin between the hem of the blue skirt and the black boots that reached her knees was enough to make his mouth water.

"Should we go into your office?" she asked, wearing an innocent look on her face.

"Yes," Sam croaked, then cleared his throat. "After you." He let her lead the way, catching her scent as she walked by. Memories of the night before hit like a physical blow. Not touching her before they were alone in his office took all of his self-control.

Which was the reason Callie found her back pressed to the door the moment it clicked shut. Sam drove his hands into her hair as he took her mouth with his, driven to taste her like a starving man stumbling upon a feast. One night hadn't been nearly enough. He wanted more.

Needed more. The thought was the only reason Sam broke the kiss. Callie could easily become an addiction, but she wasn't his to keep. He had to remember that.

With their foreheads pressed together, Sam closed his eyes and struggled to catch his breath. "Sorry about that," he said between pants.

"I'm not," Callie said, nipping at his bottom lip. "I think all of our meetings should start this way."

"Then we'd never get down to business," he said, pushing against the door to put space between their bodies. With her lips swollen from his kisses, and her eyes hazed over with lust, Sam considered having a couch installed in his office. Then again, there was his desk.

Shaking himself back to reality, he stepped back, buttoning his suit jacket.

"Don't do that," Callie said, halting his hands with her own. "Don't revert to buttoned-up Sam. Not with me."

"Buttoned-up Sam?"

"Yes. Serious. All business. Cold and impersonal." She smoothed her hands over his lapels. "It's like an armor you wear." Looking into his eyes, she flattened her hands against his chest. "You don't need the armor with me."

But he did. Today especially.

To appease her, Sam left the coat unbuttoned. "You make it sound as if I'm two different people."

"You are," Callie said. "There's Mr. Edwards, the competent and confident man in charge. And then there's Sam."

"And Sam isn't competent and confident?"

"Oh," Callie said, her voice growing husky, "I would never say that." The wicked smile that flashed across her lips nearly had him reaching for her again. "But Sam feels a little less intimidating."

"Funny," he said. "I've never gotten the impression you felt intimidated around me. If anything, I'd say the exact opposite."

She shrugged. "If I were to let you see when I feel intimidated, then we'd never be on equal footing. Therefore, I don't let you see."

"But you're telling me now."

"Because I'm talking to Sam, not Mr. Edwards."

Unable to help himself, Sam let his body have what it wanted and pressed against her once more. "How can you tell the difference between the two?" he asked, truly curious.

"There's a way you look at me." Callie trailed a finger along his brow, then down his jawline. "A softness. An openness. A longing."

Sam withdrew from her touch, buttoned his jacket, and left Callie standing at the door while he returned to his desk. Taking a seat in the leather chair, he clenched his hands on his desktop. "What did you need to see me about?"

∼

Callie knew the moment he went cold that she should have kept the words to herself. Kept the exchange flirtatious or even seductive. Then Sam would have stayed with her. But she'd taken it a step too far. Been too honest and revealed more than he could handle.

With a sigh, she took a seat across the desk from him, dropping her bag to the floor and crossing her legs. She knew the skirt rode high enough to reveal an ample amount of thigh. Nothing said she couldn't use temptation to ease Sam out of his cold front.

"I made some calls this morning in regard to the winter festival. They had an open slot on Saturday at eleven thirty."

"An open slot?"

"Yes," she said. "In the kids' tent, for you and Cecil. Luckily, they aren't sending the program to the printer until this afternoon, so you'll be on the schedule and we should have a good crowd."

Sam looked as if she'd put a plate of rotten meat under his nose. "I doubt anyone in town will miss the chance to see me make a fool of myself."

Callie managed not to roll her eyes, but only barely. "You are not going to make a fool of yourself. You're going to make children laugh and show the people on this island that you do not think you're better than they are. That *is* what you agreed to last night, correct?"

Now he looked as if she'd sentenced him to death. "I'm not sure I know how to make children laugh."

This, Callie didn't doubt. "That's why you'll have Cecil. You two can rehearse in the evenings for the rest of the week, and then you'll be a smashing success come Saturday."

"Ah, yes," he said, leaning back in his chair. "The circus act."

"Are you really afraid of sitting in front of a group of little kids?" Taking a shot at his ego could backfire on her, but Callie took the chance.

"It isn't in my nature to play the fool," he said, but his tone carried less arrogance.

Callie leaned forward and set a hand on the edge of his desk. "I would never make a fool of you, Sam." The words seemed to placate him, as he nodded but remained silent. "Think about it," she said. "The kids are going to think you're brilliant. I mean, you'll have a talking bird."

"And what if the talking bird is the one who comes across as brilliant?"

The insecurity was unexpected and brought relaxed Sam back to the conversation. To keep him, Callie rose from her chair and strolled around the desk. "I promise you," she said, settling onto Sam's lap, "there is nothing to worry about. After this weekend, the locals will see you as the kind, generous man that you are. And you'll be the hero who is going to save this project, doing Will a huge favor and giving one lucky couple the wedding of their dreams."

As she'd hoped, Sam pulled her close, rubbing a thumb against the inside of her knee.

"Hero, huh?"

"Uh-huh," Callie whispered into his ear, before taking the lobe between her teeth. "My hero."

The hand on her knee slid higher. "You're playing me, aren't you?" Sam asked, his voice deep and free of censure.

"I needed to touch you," she said, which was scarily true. "Is that a bad thing?"

His answer was a kiss that threatened to short-circuit Callie's brain. She squirmed closer and wondered if the fancy leather chair had a recline feature. When Sam brushed his fingers over the cotton of her underwear, Callie twisted hard enough to nearly eject them onto the floor.

"Now you're trying to kill us both," Sam said, pulling Callie's skirt back into place. "Since that door isn't locked, this will have to wait until later."

The hum rushing through her body didn't want to wait, but practicality won out. The last thing she needed was for Yvonne to walk through the door and catch them having sex on Sam's desk. Though the thought had Callie calculating how quickly she could lock the door and return to Sam's lap.

"You do need to spend the next several evenings at my place," she said, allowing Sam to put her back on her feet. "Since I own the other half of your act."

He followed Callie out of the chair, looming over her with their bodies pressed intimately together. "If you think I'm coming over to spend all my time with your parrot, you're sadly mistaken."

Callie knew the silly grin splitting her face likely made her look like a lovesick schoolgirl, but she didn't care. Rising on her tiptoes, she said, "That's the sweetest thing you've ever said to me, Mr. Edwards." Then she kissed him with everything she had. As he kissed her back in kind, Callie's heart came dangerously close to getting involved.

CHAPTER 21

By Saturday morning, Callie couldn't imagine sleeping without Sam beside her. It had taken until Thursday to convince him not to leave in the middle of the night, but she'd done it. When he'd arrived with personal items on Friday, with the intention of leaving them for future use, she tried not to let the panic show on her face.

She was already in danger of giving more of herself than she'd planned. Was she setting herself up for heartbreak? Was she confusing sex for something more? But then she'd remember that it was during those late-night moments when Sam completely let his guard down, when he was gentle and caring and held her as if he never wanted to let her go, that she imagined a future together.

In other words, this was all Sam's fault.

The man had even painted her toenails. After a rambunctious bout of incredible sex, Callie had lamented her lack of time for a pedicure, so Sam had volunteered. She'd never had a man paint her toenails before. The simple act had been incredibly arousing, and she'd made sure Sam was adequately rewarded.

"You look rather pleased about something," Henri said, joining Callie at the edge of the kids' tent. "Where's your hunky bedmate?"

"He's around the back, practicing with Cecil," Callie said. "I hope this goes well."

"Cecil's a pro," Henri said. "He'll be fine. It's anyone's guess about Sam."

"He's been so good with him, Henri. So patient. Sam will be a better dad than he thinks."

Henri spun so that her back was to the crowd inside the tent. "Please tell me you're not pregnant."

"What? No! Where would you get that idea?" Callie's heart beat double time at the mere thought of having kids right now. She wasn't ready for that. They weren't ready for that. "Are you crazy?"

Taking her by the hand, Henri dragged Callie to a tree not far from the tent entrance. "Did you hear yourself?"

"I said I'm not pregnant." Callie pulled her hand away and rubbed her shoulder, which Henri had nearly pulled out of the socket. "What is wrong with you?"

"You said Sam would make a great dad." Henri jabbed her in the arm. "You've been sleeping with him less than a week, and you're already in love with him."

Callie met Henri's glare. "I am not!"

Henri stared into her eyes as if trying to read her mind. "You're going to get hurt, Cal."

"I'm *not* in love with him," she said. "But even if I were, I'm a big girl. I can take care of myself."

"Like the last time?" Henri asked.

"That's not fair, and you know it." Callie had been a different person when Josh died. Weak and insecure. She wasn't that person anymore. "I'm not going to fall apart if Sam doesn't want me," Callie argued. "But this conversation is pointless. It's sex."

"Every single night?"

"What does that have to do with anything?"

"What if he still expects you to leave after Christmas?"

Callie held Henri's gaze. "Nothing has changed. When this job is over, I move on. We both know that."

Her cousin stood there shaking her head, her eyes solemn. "You're setting yourself up for a fall."

"You're entitled to your opinion," Callie said. "Now I need to get back inside."

"I hope I'm wrong," Henri said, sincerity and concern clear in her eyes.

After a brief hesitation, Callie returned to the tent without responding.

Sam couldn't remember the last time he had been this nervous. Which pissed him off even more about having to do this. He could practically hear Morty cackling from wherever he was in the afterlife, saying, *I knew you'd come around eventually.*

"Screw you, Morty," Sam said, only to have Cecil echo the words back to him. "That is not part of this act, Feather Brain."

A squawk was the bird's reply, followed by "Don't ruin the act. Don't ruin the act."

Sam rubbed damp palms down his denim-clad thighs. Callie had insisted he wear casual clothes. Heaven forbid he not look like any other islander. He didn't see how dress slacks would have made a difference, but his wardrobe wasn't something worth fighting about.

Not that he and Callie fought. They passionately debated now and then, but even when she was arguing some business approach or political stance contrary to his own, she was still intoxicating. The combination of a quick intellect, professional confidence, and mouth-watering curves made Callie the sexiest woman Sam had ever known.

And he wanted to keep knowing her, both biblically and personally. Which was all the more reason to let her go after Christmas. Besides, if Callie knew he was having more permanent thoughts, she'd likely break it off before then. She'd wanted sex and nothing more. That was what Sam had agreed to, and that was the deal he would keep.

Though the thought of her in another man's bed was like a knife in his gut, Sam wanted her to be happy. And someday she would meet the guy who could give her everything she deserved and more. That man simply wasn't him.

"You're on in one minute, Mr. Edwards," said Helga Stepano-vich. As proprietor of the day-care center on the island, Helga was the logical choice to run the kids' tent at the festival. "Step up this way, and when you hear me introduce you, come on in."

Sam moved close to the tent flap where Helga had indicated, carrying Cecil's cage with him. They'd considered letting him sit on Sam's shoulder, but since he'd been away from the circus for so long, there was no way to know how Cecil would react to a tent full of kids. Better to keep him in the cage, where everyone was safe.

Helga's voice came through the thin material. "I hope you're all ready for a very special treat. Put your hands together for Sam and Cecil."

Right on cue, Sam stepped into the tent and carried Cecil to the front of the crowd, taking a seat on the stool next to him. Kids bustled about, a couple of parents having to restrain their little ones from running closer to get a better look at the colorful bird in the cage.

"Hi there," Sam said, flashing the biggest and fakest smile of his life. They were a bunch of little people. How hard could this be? "I'm Sam, and this is my good friend Cecil." Pointing to the cage,

Sam waited for Cecil to greet the crowd, as they'd rehearsed. The bird held his beak.

"Say hello to the kids, Cecil."

Silence.

"He's a little shy," Sam said, ignoring the drop of sweat that slid down his spine. "We're here to tell you a few stories today. Would you like to hear some stories?"

The kids cheered, and Sam's confidence grew. This was not that difficult. He was sitting next to a talking bird, for Christ's sake. The *bird* had to do the heavy lifting.

Once the excited cheers faded, Sam turned toward the dangling cage. "Are you ready to tell the stories, Cecil?"

Several seconds of silence passed before Cecil, staring straight ahead as if he'd been stuffed and mounted, made a gurgling noise.

Sam glanced around until he found Callie standing off to his left. He raised his brows and she shrugged, then mouthed the word *crackers*.

"You need to earn your crackers, Cecil," he said, smiling and nodding at the children as if to reassure them this was all part of the act. Sam wished someone would reassure him that this bird's beak would start flapping soon.

"Is he real?" a little girl in the front asked.

"He's very real," Sam answered, flicking the side of the cage. The damn bird didn't so much as flinch. "He's nervous. Aren't you, Cecil?"

"I don't think he's gonna talk," said a little boy.

Sam swiveled on the stool. "Sure he is." Leaning close to the cage, he whispered, "Don't do this to me, Cecil, or I'll turn you into shish kebab."

To Sam's amazement, the bird whispered back, "Feather Brain."

Really? The bird was pissed because Sam called him a name? This had to be a joke.

"The kids are excited to hear your stories," he said, loudly enough for the crowd, then dropped his voice again. "I'll buy you all the crackers you can eat. Even those oval party ones Callie won't let you have."

"Hey there, boys and girls," Cecil bellowed, stirring the room into a frenzy of excitement once again. "My name is Cecil, and I'm the pretty one in this act."

Relief flooded Sam's body. He didn't care how much the poultry insulted him, so long as he kept talking. The kids were practically buzzing, clapping and hopping around, with joy evident on their tiny little faces.

So this was what Morty had experienced when he told his stories. Sam could see the attraction. The munchkins were kind of cute, in an I-don't-have-to-take-them-home kind of way. For some reason, he looked over to Callie in that moment and recognized a similar joy on her face. And maybe a hint of pride, though whether for him or her bird, Sam wasn't sure.

"Which story do you want to tell first?" Sam asked once the crowd had hushed a bit.

"The Three Bears," Cecil replied, as he'd been trained to do. Sam told the story of Goldilocks and the Three Bears, allowing Cecil to recite all of the dialogue, which he did to perfection.

The kids were enthralled. Even the adults in the tent looked to be absorbed in the show. By the time Sam and Cecil finished telling the stories of the bears, The Three Little Pigs, and Hansel and Gretel, the adult population inside the tent outnumbered the kids, and for their first performance ever, the pair received a standing ovation.

Through it all, Callie had smiled and laughed, beaming her support from the sidelines. And she'd been right. Less than twenty minutes after the show ended, Sam and Callie had been approached by nearly a dozen people offering to lend a hand with the renovation. He'd deferred to Callie, letting her carry the conversations to learn the skills of the volunteers and give them instructions for when their services would be needed.

She'd taken the lead without hesitation, then handed out business cards to anyone interested, even those who weren't sure if they would be able to help or not.

"I don't remember authorizing business cards," Sam said as they walked to his car. He was carrying the other half of Sam and Cecil, while Callie carried the cage stand.

"Yvonne found some business-card stock that was already perforated. All I had to do was design the card using the template, and voilà," she said. "I'm all fancy official-like."

Sam took her free hand and gave it a squeeze. "You could have ordered business cards," he said, "though I'm not sure why you'd need them for such a short-term position."

Callie tensed. He could feel it all the way down to her slender knuckles. "I knew I'd be dealing with both employees and vendors. I needed to make it clear I carried the authority to make decisions." All casual laughter was gone from her words. "Having business cards helps make people take me seriously."

"Then I'm glad you made them." Sam buckled Cecil onto the backseat, then took the stand from Callie and slid it across the floorboard. "I have to give you credit," he said, climbing into his driver's seat. "You were right about today."

"I nearly died when Cecil clammed up," she said, clicking her seat belt. Her voice had lightened again, but she had yet to look at him since he'd mentioned the temporary condition of her job. "What did you say to get him talking?"

"Puttin' on the Ritz," chimed the passenger in the backseat. Sam sighed. He hadn't intended to deliver on the promise.

"You didn't?" Callie said, looking his way with a twinkle in her eye.

"I was desperate."

She turned to glance at her pet, then back to Sam. "You know you have to buy them now, right?"

Unable to help himself, Sam dropped a quick kiss on Callie's mouth. "This is why it's never good to overpromise."

As if the words had another meaning, Callie's eyes went dim again. She pulled away from him. "Wouldn't want to do that."

Sam didn't like the way this conversation was going. If he didn't know better, he'd think Callie was upset with him about something, but what, he didn't know. "Have you started looking for positions opening up around the first of the year?" he asked, choosing to change the subject.

"Not yet," she said, keeping her eyes on the passing scenery.

"I could put out some feelers for you," he offered, cutting his eyes her way to gauge her reaction. "I have a friend who owns a few properties in Florida. That would be the perfect place to look in the dead of winter."

Gnawing on the edge of a nail, she said, "I can take care of myself, thanks."

"I'm happy to help."

"I said I'll be fine." The words were clipped and louder than necessary. "I'm sorry," she said. "I'm tired today." Finally looking his way, she said, "I think I'll take a nap before dinner. You probably have something else to do besides watch me sleep."

Sam wasn't dismissed often, and he didn't like it. He preferred to spend the day with her, whether she was sleeping or awake, but that was all the more reason to give her the room she seemed to want.

"That's fine," he said, keeping his tone casual. "I need to check in on a few things at the hotel anyway."

Her only response was an empty smile before returning her gaze to the passing trees. The rest of the short drive passed in silence, broken intermittently by Cecil singing about his Ritz from the backseat. Sam carried the cage and stand into the cabin once they'd arrived at the Peabody, accepted her chaste kiss good-bye, then left.

He didn't know what had upset her but didn't believe it was a change of heart. Callie was honest to a fault. If she wanted something more from him, something that carried beyond the end of the renovation, she would tell him. Maybe she'd decided she wanted less. Perhaps she'd had enough of him and wasn't sure how to say so.

If that was the case, he'd deal with it. An early ending was probably the best way to ensure no one would get hurt. Then again, considering the ache in his chest as Sam drove away, it might have been too late to prevent that.

CHAPTER 22

By the time Callie met Sam that evening at the Marina restaurant, she felt like a complete ass. She'd promised Henri that she was not in love with him, that their relationship was strictly sex with a definitive end date, and then gotten pissed off when Sam mentioned her impending departure.

What was wrong with her? Less than a week ago she'd been ripping Sam's clothes off with the claim that all she wanted was sex. Something she wholeheartedly believed at the time. Then, out of the blue, all these long-buried emotions had started clogging up the works. This was no time for her heart to overrule her brain.

She'd offered up the apology Sam deserved as soon as they'd ordered their drinks. As expected, he'd tried to dismiss her words with the whole *that was in the past* thing. It had been the same damn day, for heaven's sake. But getting snippy while trying to apologize for being snippy seemed counterproductive, so she'd said what she'd needed to say and let him do with it what he would.

She'd also taken him up on his offer to help her find another job. There was no reason not to use his connections if Sam was going to offer them. He'd agreed to make some calls and get back to her, which, she had to remind herself, was exactly what she'd wanted.

"Was it really necessary to make the punch green?" asked Sid as she stepped up next to Callie near the dessert table. The punch looked like a kale smoothie. Thankfully, it didn't taste like one.

"Maybe red was too close to pink?" she asked, trying to give Will the benefit of the doubt. Speaking of Will, Callie watched her slide up next to Sid with a plate full of finger foods.

"Red would wire the mom, which would wire the baby, and she's getting kicked enough," Will said, before shoving a celery stick into her mouth. "If I've learned anything in the last eight months, it's to do everything the pretty pregnant lady tells me to do."

"That hormonal, huh?" Callie asked, never having had the pleasure of spending a great deal of time with a pregnant woman.

"You should have seen her while we were planning the wedding." Sid plopped a chocolate cupcake on top of the empty wrapper on her plate. "When you thought you were talking to the sweet and pleasant Curly, she'd threaten to cut you and spit in your eye."

Callie nearly snorted green punch out her nose. "You're kidding. Beth is so sweet and . . . mild-mannered. I can't imagine her threatening to cut anyone."

"Wait until she waddles this way," Will said. "Last I checked, she was still pissed about the flowers."

"Flowers?" Callie asked, looking from Sid to Will in confusion. Who could possibly get mad over flowers?

"The centerpieces are yellow daisies," Will said, as if this explained everything.

"Which were a bitch to get this time of year," Sid added.

So Beth was upset that they had gone to so much trouble? "What's so bad about that?"

"They're girlie," Will and Sid said together.

It took several seconds for Callie to catch on. "And the party was supposed to be gender neutral."

"You're quick for a blonde," Sid said, then received an elbow jab from Will. "What?"

"That's rude."

"It was a compliment."

"In your world, maybe." Will leaned toward Callie. "Rough around the edges, but she means well."

"Nothing I haven't heard before," Callie said, telling the truth. She'd been a natural blonde since birth, making her the butt of many jokes over the years. Smiling at Sid, she said, "I appreciate the observation."

Will rolled her eyes. "Do not encourage her."

"What are you rolling your eyes about?" Beth asked, doing as Will had said and waddling their way. "This is all too much, isn't it? I hate being the center of attention, and now everyone thinks I'm an attention whore."

Callie made the mistake of taking a drink as Beth approached and once again nearly spewed the green stuff.

"Don't get your granny panties in a bunch," Will said, throwing an arm around her friend's shoulders. "They're using the term *attention slut.* Nothing to worry about."

"You do remember that my sense of humor disappeared when I started peeing every forty-two seconds, right?"

"Yes, but hope springs eternal that it'll make a reappearance before the bugger pops out of you."

"Don't hold your breath," Beth said with a snarl. Turning to Callie, she flashed a welcoming smile as if she hadn't just been hateful to one of her best friends. "Thank you so much for coming today. I'm so happy you could be here."

Blinking, Callie looked to Will for assurance that the large, round woman before her wasn't clinically insane. Will winked.

"I wouldn't have missed it for the world. I hope you like the gift I brought. It arrived just in time for the party."

"The gifts!" Beth yelled, startling Callie. "We need to open the gifts. People might want to leave, and I'm keeping them here."

Sid stuffed more cupcake into her face, presumably to avoid saying something else Will would tell her was rude, while Will once again took her friend by the shoulders. "Now would be a great time to open the presents. We've put two chairs by the gift table so you can sit right there and open while Sid takes notes for the thank-you cards."

With a mouth full of chocolate, Sid gaped, waving her fork furiously through the air.

"Head on over there and start with any pretty package you want. Sid will be right behind you." Will took the paper plate and fork from Sid, who shot her a look that could kill, and pushed her two friends across the room. Once they were moving on their own, she returned to Callie. "That was fun, wasn't it?"

"I'm sure she'll be back to normal once the baby is born," Callie said. "But I'd watch my back around Sid for a while."

"I gave Sid a really good reason not long ago to kick my ass. If she didn't do it then, I think I'm safe." Will continued to watch her friends, saying, "I bet you and Sam are going to make beautiful babies."

This time, the spew could not be stopped. Will handed Callie some napkins as she apologized to an older, dark-haired woman who'd been walking by.

"The punch packs a punch, doesn't it, Gladys?" Will said, dabbing at the older woman's sleeve.

"This is my good sweater," Gladys said, before walking away in a huff.

Will returned her attention to Callie. "Sorry about that. Not a baby person?" she asked.

"No," Callie said. "I mean, I like babies just fine, but I won't be making any with Sam. You surprised me is all."

"I can see that. I thought since you two are such an item . . ."

"An item?" Callie asked. She and Sam had made no attempt to keep their relationship a secret, but neither had they been blatant about it. The day before, at the festival and then at the Marina restaurant, had been the first time they'd even been out in public together outside of that lunch with her mother. Except for Will's dinner party, and they had not been in any way affectionate there.

"Yeah. You know. Dating. Together. A couple." Will tilted her head. "You *are* together, right?"

The crowd around them cheered, drawing their attention to the gift table before Callie could respond. Beth was holding up the cutest white bear Callie had ever seen with tears running down her cheeks.

"Looks like the hormones bounced to the other extreme again," Will said, before returning to the topic of Sam and Callie. "Surely you realize that no one sneezes on this island without half the town saying 'bless you.' I saw hints of it the night of the dinner party, but the notice that you two are together came via Helga. I think." Will tapped her chin. "Maybe it was Debbie at the real estate office."

"How do any of these people know my business?" Callie wasn't completely unaware of how gossip lines worked, but as a new arrival and only temporary resident, she had assumed no one would pay her any attention.

An obvious error on her part.

"There isn't much to do here," Will answered with a shrug. "I think that makes them all more observant. And I already told you Sam was a popular topic of speculation. You've made him look almost human, which has the locals quite impressed. They think you're good for him."

"I am good for him," Callie said without thinking. "I mean, we work well together. But this isn't like the rest of you. Sam and I are . . . Well . . ." Callie struggled to describe exactly what she and Sam were. "It's complicated."

"Love is always complicated," Will said, leaving Callie speechless for the second time in the last ten minutes. "You'd be surprised what can be overcome if you give it a try."

Checking on the gift-opening activities, Will shoved the sticky napkins she was still holding into Callie's chest. "Hold that thought. I see a pink bow on the next present. Catastrophe looms."

With that, Will walked away, leaving Callie sticky, confused, and pondering the complications of love. "You're supposed to drink the punch, not bathe in it," said Henri, who appeared out of nowhere.

"What? Where . . . ?"

"I was hanging out with Yvonne up front when I heard the ruckus back here. She figured the soiree was far enough along that no one would notice a party crasher." Henri snagged a cookie from the table beside them, popping it into her mouth without a speck of guilt on her face.

"I don't think Beth will mind, but she's a bit . . . volatile right now. So keep a low profile."

Swallowing her cookie, Henri asked, "So, what brought on the spit take?"

"The mention of babies."

"At a baby shower? How unexpected."

"It was the mention of Sam's and my babies."

Henri's face sobered. "Oh."

"Yes. Oh," Callie said. "It appears the whole town thinks we're *an item.*"

"You make it sound like you're not."

"We're . . ." She struggled again for a descriptor that would fit their situation. "I don't know what we are, but it's not an item."

"So long as you know what you're doing, who cares what people think?" Henri perused the guests around them. "They'll find something else to gossip about soon enough."

She was right, of course. Callie shouldn't care what these strangers believed, but she'd been the subject of public gossip once before and never again wanted to endure that kind of scrutiny.

"I hope they find it soon," Callie said, slipping her arm through Henri's. "But let's talk about *your* love life. You seem to have snagged the prettiest woman on the island."

Henri smiled. "She is hot, isn't she?"

"Supermodel hot. And it's not nice to gloat."

Shoving Callie off balance, she said, "Sam isn't what anyone would call ugly."

"Very true." As Callie said the words, she caught sight of Sam standing in the doorway to the room. He was watching her with a look of possession in his eyes. Her heart did a somersault against her ribs. "Very, very true."

He'd been watching her for five minutes before Callie noticed him. Other than dousing Gladys Ledbetter with punch, she seemed perfectly comfortable mingling with the locals. Natural and outgoing and his complete opposite. Not that this was a bad thing. In fact, Sam had started to think more and more about how good a thing they had.

Which had started a war in his mind. Part of him said to push her away. Put them back on firmer ground that didn't involve all-night sex sessions and him constantly thinking about her throughout the day. Then he'd picture her crawling on top of him with that determined look in her eye. Or drinking her tea by the windows, her skin kissed by the morning sun.

He was losing his grip on the situation, going well beyond a rational level of wanting her, and that was making it impossible to even think about giving her up.

"You look like a man in search of something," Callie said, once she'd crossed the room and met him by the door. He'd had to force himself not to meet her halfway. Not to kiss her in front of half the village.

"Are you interested in being found?" he asked. "I don't want to take you away from the party."

"I don't think they'll miss me," she said, glancing over her shoulder. "But for the sake of discretion, I think we need to take this somewhere else."

Sam chuckled. "I didn't plan to rip your clothes off right here on the floor."

"You don't have to." Callie nodded toward the hall, beckoning him to follow her. She didn't stop until they reached his office. "We're already the main topic of gossip these days," she said, once he'd closed the door.

"These people are always gossiping about something." Sam said.

"Well, that something is us having kids."

Sam stopped with his hand in midair. He hadn't even realized he'd been reaching for her.

"Excuse me?"

"Will called us an item," she said, dropping into his chair behind the desk. "A couple."

Sam settled into a chair on the opposite side of the desk, which felt strange since he'd only ever sat in the chair Callie currently occupied. "Where do kids come into this?"

"Will offhandedly mentioned that you and I are going to make beautiful babies."

The statement didn't scare Sam as much as it should have. An image of blonde little girls with ice-blue eyes danced at the edge of his mind. They would be beautiful, like their mother.

"Did you hear me?" Callie asked, her voice rising an octave. "They know we're sleeping together."

Sam didn't see the problem. As Callie had pointed out, they were two single, consenting adults who could do whatever they pleased, so long as they didn't do it in the village park in broad daylight.

"And that bothers you?" he asked.

"No," she said. "I mean yes." Callie spun out of the chair and marched over to the window. "I don't know."

He waited, giving her time to think. Time to make sense of whatever worries were bouncing around in that head of hers. When she continued to stare out the window in silence, Sam crossed the office and put his arms around her.

"We aren't doing anything wrong, Callie."

"I know that," she said around the thumbnail clenched between her teeth. "In my head."

"But?"

Relaxing into him, she dropped her head onto his chest. "I didn't think about how this would look to people who don't know us."

Turning her around, Sam nudged Callie's chin until she met his eye. "Did anyone in that room insult you? Let me know who it was, and I'll walk back down there and set them straight."

Toying with the button on his shirt, Callie grinned. "You'd do that for me?"

"I'd do anything for you," he said. And meant it.

Her eyes went wide, and the smile shifted into an O.

"Try not to look so surprised," Sam said, using levity to downplay the confession he'd never intended to share.

"You mean that, don't you?" Callie pulled away, and Sam had to force himself to let her go. "You can put your shining armor away," she said. "No one insulted me." With a sigh, she added, "I better get back to the party."

If Sam had needed confirmation that Callie's feelings hadn't changed, he got it in that moment.

"Callie?"

"Yes?" she said, looking back.

"Will I see you tonight?"

After studying the floor for several seconds, she said, "You know where to find me." Then she walked out.

CHAPTER 23

Callie lingered at the cottage after Sam had left on Monday morning. She needed time to think without him there, and without the chaos she was likely to find across the street. Though their night together had been like all the others, strictly physical and satisfying, what he'd said in his office still bothered her.

He *would* do anything for her.

She appreciated his willingness to fight on her behalf, but the statement had served as a blaring reminder of their inequality. The point wasn't that Sam *would* do anything for her, but that he *could*. Sam had the connections, the money, and the power to ride to her rescue at any time, in any situation.

Callie could not offer the same in return.

She'd been in this position before. Josh had been the breadwinner while Callie had stayed home, attempting to be the perfect wife. He'd controlled their finances, decided where they would vacation, and told her what car she would drive. The house they lived in had been Josh's place before they'd ever met.

Callie had brought nothing to their relationship but herself. And she hadn't been enough.

While rinsing out her mug in the sink, she reminded herself that Sam was not Josh. And since she and Sam would not be exchanging vows, the possibility of infidelity didn't exist. But for once in her life, Callie wanted to feel like an equal. Like she had something real to offer.

And then she recognized where her mind was going. Why was feeling like she was enough the hardest thing for her to master? She had survived losing everything when Josh died. Faced down the attorneys and the creditors, the abandonment by their friends, and the humiliation of having her life dragged through the papers. She'd gone back to school for her degree, changed her name, and started over.

But six years down the line, Callie still had nothing to show for her life but a mouthy bird, a box of books, and an unhealthy obsession with chocolate and peanut butter. Not exactly sparkling fodder for an online dating ad.

As she slipped on her tennis shoes, Callie dug deep to find the inner Pollyanna that Henri teased her about. She would not throw herself a pity party, and wallowing about what you didn't have did nothing to change things. This job was going to boost her résumé. Callie was going to have her pick of jobs. There would be no more begging for a chance.

She needed to turn the Sunset Harbor Inn into a sparkling boutique jewel of the mid-Atlantic in the next five weeks, and then everything would change. Which meant she'd better get to work.

With renewed determination, Callie stepped through the cottage door and almost burst into tears. The inn parking lot was dotted with cars Callie had never seen before, and people were milling about as if waiting to receive their orders. Orders that she would give them.

Callie charged through the crowd, yelling out greetings as she went, and found Jack in a panic behind his counter. "They all want to know what to do." He followed Callie into her office, practically stepping on her heels. "I told them we had to wait for you. Where were you?"

"I'm sorry I'm late," Callie said, tossing her purse into a desk drawer. "But I'm here now." She took the notepad she'd used on Saturday out of her briefcase and transcribed four names onto a Post-it before handing it to her trusty clerk. "Find these people and show them where the materials are for floor installation. Then get them working in the rooms at this end of the hall, two people per room."

Jack studied the note. "I know these people."

"I figured you might." Callie carried the notepad with her around the desk. "Is Lot here?"

"Yeah," he said. "He's helping Olaf with some furniture stuff."

Callie grinned. "Olaf is back?"

"Well, sure," Jack said. "Everyone is back. And then some."

Giving Jack a spontaneous hug, Callie could feel her Pollyanna doing a happy dance in her soul. "We're going to do this, Jack. We're going to get this project done."

After recovering from the shock of Callie's sudden embrace, Jack hugged her back. "And we don't have to do it all by ourselves!"

Callie laughed. "No, we don't. Now, you get the floors going and I'll assign rooms for painting." Dragging Jack out of the office, she added, "We'll have the upstairs ready for floors in no time."

An hour later, Callie had a dozen applications for Yvonne to process so that everyone would get paid. She considered running them over to the Anchor, but didn't want to leave in case she was needed. Instead, she would call with a warning, and then send them through the fax.

If her luck held, the ancient machine would cooperate.

"Anchor Inn. How may I help you?" Yvonne answered.

"You're not going to like me much today," Callie said by way of greeting. "I'm sending over a dozen applications for processing."

"A dozen?" Yvonne asked.

"Yes, ma'am. All but four are at the base rate. I've marked the exceptions."

"But how?"

"Never underestimate the power of making children laugh," Callie said. "Can you transfer me in to Sam? I want to tell him the good news."

"Sure," Yvonne replied, "but he has a meeting in a few minutes. He won't have much time to talk."

"No problem," Callie said. "This won't take long."

"Okay." Yvonne put her on hold, and Callie hummed along with the classical tune as she waited for Sam to pick up.

The music ended, and then Sam said, "Good morning. I hope you have good news."

"Very good news." Callie's cheeks hurt from the amount of smiling she'd done in the last hour. "Twelve," she said. "Twelve people reported for duty. I have four new floor installers and everyone else is wielding paint rollers."

"I guess I should make a spectacle of myself more often," he said, his voice not as enthusiastic as she'd expected. "I'm glad they showed up."

"You realize what this means, don't you?" Callie asked. "We're still digging out of a hole, since we were so far behind, but if we push really hard, we can get this done. By the deadline."

Sam mumbled something Callie didn't understand. "What was that?" she asked.

"I'm sorry," Sam said more clearly. "I was talking to someone else. Someone is here for a meeting. I need to go."

"Sam," Callie said, confused about why he wasn't more excited, "we're going to hit this deadline."

"Yes, I hear you. I need to go." He mumbled again, his voice muted as if he'd put his hand over the receiver; then he came back. "I'll be over soon." A click, and the line went dead.

What the hell meeting could be more important than this project? Not that she expected Sam to keep anyone waiting, but he could have sounded a bit happier that their plan had worked. These people were only saving the project. No big deal.

"Hey there," said a voice from her office doorway.

Callie glanced up to see Will Parsons sticking her head in. "Hey, yourself. I didn't expect to see you today."

"I hope I'm not bothering you," Will said. "I should have called first. This place looks crazy busy."

Beaming with excitement, Callie nodded. "Yes, it does. Thank goodness. But you're not bothering me at all. I have some documents to fax, but I can talk and do that at the same time."

Motioning for Will to have a seat, Callie rolled her chair to the long table behind her desk and laid the stack of applications beside the fax machine. Knowing the machine could be cranky when fed too much, Callie pulled four sheets and stuck them in the top.

"So what's up?" she asked Will. "Is this an official or a friendly visit?"

"Official," Will said.

A hint of nervousness settled in Callie's gut. If Will expected to see more of the hotel finished, this could go badly. "Okay. How can I help you?"

"I was wondering what you planned to do once this renovation is finished. Or rather," Will hemmed, "I *know* someone who is wondering."

"You mean where am I going to work?" Callie asked. "I don't actually know yet, but why?"

Will leaned forward in her chair. "I know I haven't technically seen what you can do here, but I did a little online search and found images of what you've done before. The decorating is fantastic."

Callie wasn't sure how she felt about being googled, but she appreciated the compliment.

"Thank you. Choosing and arranging the décor is my favorite part."

"I was hoping you'd say that." Will pulled a brochure from her bag and held it out for Callie. "This is the largest real estate business on the island. They manage most of the rental properties and are looking to give many of them a makeover. Since everything here is furnished and most of it hasn't been updated for decades, they could use your help."

"I . . ." Callie hesitated, studying the brochure in her hand. "I'm not sure what to say."

"It wouldn't be a permanent position," Will warned, "but you could stay on Anchor a bit longer. At least six months would be my guess. And you never know, something else might come open after that."

Her visitor sounded more positive than not that something else would become available. But why did Will want Callie to stay on the island? If this was about giving her a reason to stay with Sam, then the nosy islanders had seriously crossed a line.

"This does sound like something I'd enjoy," Callie said. "But I'm a little confused. Why are you going out of your way to keep me here? I hope this has nothing to do with Sam and me."

Will shook her head. "Whatever is going on between you and Sam has nothing to do with this. To be honest, I'm sort of hedging a bet."

"I don't follow."

"If my business takes off like I'm hoping it will, my life is going to get crazy busy. I've never been in charge of everything before," Will admitted. "I used to be an accountant by trade, so I can handle the numbers, but the amount of details involved in planning a wedding, especially from a distance, is more than I expected."

Callie could see where a less experienced planner could be overwhelmed, especially when dealing with a high-stress event like a wedding. "I'm not sure where I come into this."

Will motioned toward the giant hotel diagram on the wall behind Callie. "You're the detail person. I can see from here that you've thought of everything down to the trim and toilet seats."

Blinking, Callie said, "There *are* a lot of details that go into a project like this. But I'm not planning a wedding; I'm making over a building. The building doesn't have breakdowns or throw temper tantrums. And it doesn't come with an overbearing mother. Or two."

"I wouldn't make you deal with the clients," Will said. "I need someone to handle the details while *I* handle the clients. And the books. And finding more clients. I can't keep everything going here if I'm on the road, traveling to bridal shows."

This was quickly starting to sound like a job offer. In a field Callie had never considered. But it would allow her to stay on this island, which she'd love to do regardless of what happened between her and Sam. And she could put her nomad life to rest, put down roots, and maybe have a real place of her own.

"But what if your business doesn't take off?" Callie asked.

Will sighed. "Then you get to spend an extra six months here doing something you love before finding another job elsewhere. But you should probably know that I'm an independently wealthy woman." With a grin, she added, "I can afford you. What do you say?"

Callie couldn't be expected to give an answer right now. "I'd need to talk to the real estate office to see what they're offering."

"Debbie is available whenever you are."

If Will thought she wasn't good with details, she was selling herself short.

"I'm going to be busy here for the foreseeable future," Callie said. "Would she be willing to meet on a Sunday?"

"Consider it done," Will said, bouncing out of her chair. "Would next Sunday work?"

"Um . . . sure."

"I'll call you with a time." Will hefted her bag onto her shoulder. "The address is there on the brochure. I hope you'll really consider this."

Callie stood to walk Will out. "I will. And thanks for having such faith in me."

"Not a problem." Will stepped into the lobby. "I'll be calling soon."

As her new friend and unexpected benefactor made her exit, Callie returned her attention to the slip of glossy paper in her hand. As far as Mondays went, this one was turning out better than most. The project was back on track, and she might have found her own new job.

Or the job had found her. Either way, Callie felt a sense of accomplishment, and a trace of relief that she wouldn't need Sam to help her find a new position. Though she worried that he might question her motives for staying on the island. Her impending departure was the harbinger that signified the end of their relationship.

What would it mean if that departure was no longer coming? Would Sam want to keep seeing her? Would he end their affair no matter what? And could Callie handle staying on Anchor Island and not having Sam as part of her life?

They'd been sleeping together less than a week. This wasn't the great love of her life. This was great sex. Sam had been adamant that he would never marry again. And Callie wasn't taking that plunge again unless she found someone who saw her as an equal. The chances of that man being Sam were highly unlikely.

This time was about Callie and her life. Her career. Wedding planning might not have been on her radar, but that didn't mean she shouldn't consider it. Working for Will could be a fun use of her skills and talents and provide her with the stability she craved. Plus, something told Callie that Will would be a generous, respectful boss.

Independently wealthy. Wouldn't that be nice?

That settled it. If the decorating job was worth her time, then Callie would take it. And if Sam had an issue with her staying on Anchor, that would be his problem to deal with, not hers.

～

"I appreciate your seeing me on such short notice," Lucas said, taking a seat across the desk from Sam.

"You said you had good news," Sam replied. He'd been struggling not to get his hopes up since he'd listened to Lucas's message that morning. "So, you found something?"

Lucas grinned. "More like realized something that I believe means you're free to go."

Sam tensed. "You found a way to break the terms?"

"No," Lucas said, nodding. "So long as your inheritance wasn't contingent upon marriage, divorce, or a change of religion on your part, Morty's request could be enforced."

This didn't sound like good news so far. "Then how am I free to leave the island?"

"'Enforced' is the key word. The executor of the will was Walter Trindle, correct?"

"Yes," Sam answered, not sure what his uncle's oldest friend had to do with anything. "But he died a year after I took over the hotels."

"Exactly," Lucas said. "So if you leave now, who would enforce the terms of the will?"

"You're the legal expert here. Who would enforce it?"

"My guess is no one."

Sam pinched the bridge of his nose, struggling for patience. "What do you mean, you guess?" he asked.

"That's where I need a little more information," Lucas said, leaning forward in his chair. "Besides Artie, you, and me, who else knows about the terms of the will?"

Sam and Walter had been the only people present at the reading of the will, and Artie had explained at the time that the preservation society would not be notified unless Sam refused the inheritance. "As far as I know, there isn't anyone else."

"Then it's no longer a guess." Lucas sat back with a look of certainty on his face. "If you walk away now, the only way to enforce the terms of the will would be for someone to bring legal action on behalf of the estate. Since Walter is gone, there's no one left to file a challenge."

Except the preservation society. There would be nothing to stop Artie Berkowitz from spilling the beans, and Rosemary would jump at the chance to take the hotels away from Sam. Especially when she'd be getting them for less than one-tenth of what they were worth.

"You're forgetting someone," Sam said.

"Who?"

The man who'd helped complicate Sam's life three years ago. "Artie."

Lucas looked smug. "I've already talked to Artie. He's impressed with what you've done to improve the hotels. Says Morty would be proud and you deserve to have your life back."

Sam wanted to believe it. To trust that his uncle's lawyer would keep the secret if Sam decided to leave. But how could he be sure?

"And you believe him?" he asked. Lucas had known Berkowitz a lot longer than Sam had. "You take him at his word?"

"Artie has no reason to lie," Lucas replied. "Besides, he never wanted to see Rosemary get the hotels. Let's say they have a history, and it isn't a positive one. I didn't get the details out of him, but his dislike of the old busybody was clear."

What Sam wouldn't give to have known this bit of island history long before now. "All of this seems too good to be true. Ten minutes ago I was sentenced to two more years on this island, and now I'm free to go."

"Consider the gates open." Lucas rose from his chair. "But I want you to know, some of us *will* be sorry to see you leave."

Sam exited his chair as well. "I hope you know how much I appreciate your help in this. You've given me a reprieve I doubted was possible."

"Just earning my fees," Lucas said, accepting Sam's extended hand. "You've been a friend to our little speck of the world here. Thank you for helping us bring the place back to life."

It was nice to have his contributions acknowledged. "Happy to do my part," he said, feeling a weight lift off his shoulders. And he did like the island. The limitations it inflicted on his life were the real problem.

After Lucas took his leave, Sam returned to his desk, spun in his chair, and watched the boats bob in the harbor outside his window. His sentence had been revoked. He was a free man. The first thing he wanted to do was call Callie and tell her. But she didn't know he'd been bound to the island in the first place.

Better to wait until they were off the island before he gave her the full story.

And then Sam realized what he was thinking. When Callie left after Christmas, he could go with her. He could find the perfect property, and she could help him make it into something special. They could do it together. And stay together.

When had he changed his mind about their relationship? Sam struggled to pinpoint the shift, the moment he'd gone from being anticommitment to wanting more. Running the last week over in his mind, Sam landed on the answer.

The winter festival. He could still see her standing there at the side of the tent, cheering him on, giving him unconditional support. That had been pride in her eyes that day, and not only for her talking parrot. Callie didn't want him for his money, position, or power. She wanted *him*.

"How about that," Sam said, a full grin splitting his face.

CHAPTER 24

Sam walked into the Sunset Harbor Inn wearing faded blue jeans and a well-worn Clemson Tigers T-shirt under his brown suede coat as the crew collected in the dining room for lunch. Callie had been discussing the history of the inn with Elder Wonnamack when the bell over the door jingled, drawing her attention. For a split second, her heart skipped a beat.

There was something different about Sam this morning. She could see it in his face. This wasn't serious hotelier Sam, or the more casual, relaxed version who'd slept next to Callie every night for the last week.

The Sam Edwards standing before her was actually . . . happy.

"Hello there," he said, pulling off his jacket and hanging it on the already-overloaded coatrack by the door. "I see I made it in time for lunch."

Jack had ordered fried chicken from Howard's Café, and the aluminum trays were spread out along the now-faux-marble counter.

"You did," she said, still distracted by the look on Sam's face. "Are you okay?"

Flashing a smile she'd never seen before, Sam said, "I'm fine. Why do you ask?"

Callie narrowed her eyes. "You look different."

"I'm wearing work clothes. I wore the same thing all last week."

Which confused her more. "But I told you we have more people now. Why are you dressed to work?"

"You said we're still behind."

Callie hadn't thought Sam was listening when they'd talked on the phone. "We are."

"Then one more body is a good thing."

This particular body was a great thing, Callie thought, admiring the width of Sam's shoulders beneath the orange cotton shirt. Though his eyes were more distracting today. They were practically twinkling as he took in the scene around them. What the hell had happened in that meeting this morning?

"You're freaking me out a little bit here," she said, unable to ignore his new-and-improved demeanor. "Who are you, and what have you done with Sam Edwards?"

Leaning close to her, he whispered, "Can't I just be happy to see you?"

Now she knew something was up. Sam only flirted when they were alone, and even then he never said things like that.

Pulling back to look him in the eye, Callie said, "You're up to something."

"And you are being annoyingly paranoid," Sam replied, taking a step toward the counter. "Toss me a Coke, will you, Jack?" The clerk did as requested, and Sam popped the top. "What's been done so far this morning?"

Finally, business Sam was here. This one she recognized.

"We now have three two-man crews installing hardwood down here on the first floor, and four two-person crews handling the painting upstairs. I had them skip the bigger suites at the far end for now so we can knock out the standards. With four teams, we can finish at least a color block a day, applying no fewer than two coats on each wall, three when necessary."

"So the second-floor paint, minus the suites, should be wrapped up in a couple weeks?" Sam asked. "That will leave us only three weeks to install the floors and get the furniture loaded back in."

Callie shook her head. "The plan is to start installing the floors while the painting is still going on. When a block is done, the painters will move out and the floor installers will move in. Every time one step is done, the next step will move in, cycling through until we're adding the finishing touches days before the wedding guests arrive."

Sam looked pleased but skeptical. "And you have enough bodies to do that?"

This was where hope came into play. "The goal is to pick up more workers as we go. Some people I spoke to on Saturday said they couldn't help right away but would be available in a few weeks."

"Let's hope that's true," he said with an odd grin on his face. The look did funny things to Callie's brain. And other parts of her anatomy as well. "Where are we on the furniture?"

Callie had to drag her wayward mind back to the work.

"Olaf is back and working on the dining room chairs. The nightstands we were able to save are finished and ready for installation once we're ready to start setting up the rooms. The new pieces are still in boxes in the kitchen, along with all the décor and linens." Callie stepped aside to let a member of the outside crew pass by. "We're waiting on some specialty items, but those should arrive within the next two weeks."

"Good to hear." Sam pulled away from the wall and took Callie by the elbow. "Let's duck into your office for a minute."

Callie didn't have a choice but to follow, and she almost tripped over several workers as they maneuvered through the lobby. Once they were inside the office, Sam shut the door and swung Callie into his arms. The kiss he planted on her mouth took her breath away and made her weak at the knees.

When Sam finally broke the kiss to allow both of them some much-needed air, Callie slumped against him. "What was that for?"

"I held out as long as I could," he said, his voice husky. "But when you started rattling off the renovation details, the urge to kiss you got to be too much."

She couldn't help but laugh. "Renovation details turn you on?"

Lifting her chin with one finger, Sam said, "*You* turn me on."

And then he was kissing her again, stealing Callie's thoughts and making her forget there was nothing more than a two-inch door between them and a room full of people.

"I'd give you some privacy, but you're blocking the door."

Sam ended the kiss, dropping Callie to the floor with a thud.

She'd completely forgotten that Henri was working in the office.

"Hello, Henri," Sam said, still standing close enough to Callie for her to understand why he couldn't turn around.

"Heya, Sam."

Looking down at Callie, he asked, "Doesn't she have a job to get home to?"

Before Callie could answer, Henri said, "I'm a writer. I can work anywhere."

Why did she have to be such an agitator?

Callie gave Sam her most apologetic look, then slid to the side, taking Sam with her. "The door is clear now," she said, praying that Henri would make a prompt and silent exit.

Of course, Henri took her good old time. When she reached the door, she looked their way. "I'm totally using that '*you* turn me on' line," she said, giving Sam a wink before walking out.

"I don't want to know what kinds of books she writes, do I?" Sam asked.

Callie sighed. "Probably not."

"Are we completely alone now, or is your mother hiding under the desk?"

"That isn't even funny," Callie replied, an involuntary shudder running down her spine. "We're alone in *here*, but there's a hotel full of people out *there* who will probably tell their friends that we had sex during lunch unless we go back out soon."

Sam squeezed her hips. "They're jealous."

Flirtatious, making jokes, *and* shucking responsibility? This was definitely a new Sam.

"Be that as it may," she said, pushing against his chest, "we need to get out there."

Looking like a little boy who'd been told to come out of his fort and eat his broccoli, Sam stepped back. "Fine," he said, sweeping an arm toward the door. "After you."

As soon as Callie opened the door, Sam whispered in her ear, "But we're going to continue this tonight. I like having you against a wall."

Heat raced up her neck as Callie stepped into the lobby. He was going to pay for that one.

～

Sam wiped the sweat from his brow, then took a swig from his water bottle as he strolled into Olaf Hogenschmidt's territory at the back of the dining room. The man was planing what looked to be a chair leg, intent on his work and oblivious to Sam's presence. Or so Sam thought.

"You come to check my work?" the older man asked, as the whining hum of the planer died away.

Shaking his head in the negative, Sam said, "Nope." He remembered Olaf from his childhood visits. The younger version had been ready with a smile and a piece of candy for his best friend's nephew. "Just watching."

Without looking Sam's way, Olaf said, "Softening out the curves. Making it more modern, per Ms. Callie's request." He brushed shavings off the work in progress, and Sam had to agree the leg did look more modern.

"Looks good." Sam examined a newly upholstered chair to his right. The dark veneer was gone, along with the dated fabric that had once covered the seat. "This thing looks brand new."

"Supposed to," Olaf said, bumping the chair with his knee. "Took a couple extra rounds to lighten the finish, but she's sturdy and ready for another twenty years."

A memory tickled at the back of his mind. "You built it, didn't you?" He glanced around. "And several of these other pieces as well."

"You ought to know. We hauled them in here during one of your last summers here."

Sam's head jerked up. "You remember me?"

"Of course I do," Olaf scoffed. "I may be old and forgetful at times, but I'm not so far gone that I'd forget Morty's only nephew."

In his mission not to blend in with the local community, Sam had made a point to avoid Morty's friends the most. He wasn't even sure why he'd wandered into Olaf's territory, considering he'd barely done more than nod at the man in the last two years. And that was only when they passed on the street.

"Well," Sam said, not sure what to say. "It *was* a long time ago."

"Say, do you remember that time we were all fishing off the pier and Morty started acting a fool, like he often did, fell in, and nearly ended up hooked?"

Sam chuckled. "He'd been trying to push me in, but I was too fast for him."

"That's right." A semitoothless smile split Olaf's face. "Swore up and down that he'd get you back. Did he ever do it?"

"Yes, he did. Two days later, I climbed into bed to find I wasn't alone. Uncle Morty had put a big blue crab under the blankets, and that sucker was not happy to see me."

Olaf let out a loud cackle. "That sounds just like the old coot. Morty had a sick sense of humor sometimes."

"And a mean streak," Sam added, memories washing over him like a tidal wave. "When I first started visiting, he'd wait until I was out near the water, then throw a handful of bread crumbs around my feet. The gulls went nuts and scared the crap out of me."

"Holy moly, you could have lost a toe."

"If I had, Mother would have taken a chunk out of his hide." Shaking his head, Sam added, "I think that's the only thing that kept him in check sometimes."

As their laughter died down, a comfortable silence settled around them.

"He sure liked having you around," Olaf said. "We all did, truth be told."

Sam's brows shot up. "You did? I thought you guys just tolerated me for Morty's sake."

"Nah," he said, waving Sam's words away. "You were a good kid. Smart as a whip. Outgoing and always willing to help. I suppose that work ethic of yours was always there. Even though it was your summer vacation, you were always looking for something to do. Hauling in crab nets or carrying suitcases for the hotel guests."

Those summers had felt like a gift of freedom, out from under his mother's constant badgering to do or be better. Even so, Sam couldn't abide doing nothing. He needed to be moving. To have a purpose. Interesting that Olaf remembered that part but Sam hadn't.

Maybe Callie had been right about him. Maybe his ambition and drive had been in him all along, regardless of his mother's standards.

"And you haven't changed a bit," Olaf said, snapping Sam from his thoughts.

Feeling sheepish, Sam said, "Maybe not as outgoing as I used to be." Callie was right. It was better to face things head-on. He'd been unfair to slight Morty's friends, and he owed them an apology. "I can do better in that area."

"Meh." Olaf shrugged. "You're an important man now. Got things to take care of. We've kept an eye on you," he said, pointing at the ceiling above their heads. "It's what Morty would have wanted us to do."

The men exchanged a smile, and Sam felt as if Uncle Morty were standing right there with them. Nodding and flashing his big grin. Looking satisfied. And proud.

"I appreciate that," he said, extending a hand in Olaf's direction.

After wiping his own hand on the back of his overalls, Olaf took the offering. "And the same to ya," he said. "You've done good by this island, just like Morty said you would."

Sam had never entertained the idea that Morty felt the island needed Sam and not the other way around. As Olaf's words pinged around Sam's brain, Olaf returned to his task, filling the air with noise and wood chips.

And Sam returned to his painting with much to think about.

≈

By the end of the day, Callie's feet ached, her back wasn't speaking to her, and her cheeks hurt from laughter. When the locals weren't telling jokes or making fun of each other, they took aim at Sam, who played the good sport and even gave as good as he got. More than once, Callie wondered if he'd downed a bottle of liquor on his way to the inn.

But his breath was normal, his eyes clear, and his full attention on her was making her feel all the things she shouldn't be feeling about a man who would likely dump her in a matter of weeks.

Then again, maybe he wouldn't. This new Sam acted more like he couldn't get enough of her. He'd taken every opportunity to touch her. To brush by her or tuck a stray lock of hair behind her ear. And he looked at her differently. Sam rarely dropped his guard completely, outside of the moments when he was buried deep within her, and even then, Callie never felt as if he gave her everything.

Let her in all the way.

Maybe that was changing, though for the life of her, Callie couldn't figure out what had brought on the shift. Was she imagining a difference? Was the hope that Sam would be happy to know she might stay clouding her mind and making her see things that weren't there?

If that was the case, Callie needed to wake up from her dream world now, because in one afternoon Sam had knocked more holes in her defenses than she was comfortable with. She was already struggling to remember this affair had an end date, but at least if she'd lost her heart before then, there would have been distance between them to help her get over him.

Seeing him every day would make getting over Sam Edwards downright impossible. Maybe the real estate company wouldn't offer her much. Perhaps she should leave no matter what. But she really did like this island.

"You look like you're a million miles away," Sam said, sneaking up behind Callie where she stood at the stove—though, to be fair, he probably wasn't sneaking at all. She was too preoccupied trying to figure out her exit strategy for their relationship to have heard him enter the room.

"Just thinking," Callie said, sliding too easily into the comfort of Sam's arms.

Dropping a kiss on the side of her neck, he asked, "About what?"

Sharing her dilemma of living around him but without him didn't seem like a good idea. So Callie lied.

"The renovation. I keep running the timetable in my head and coming up short."

The second part was actually true. Nothing was exact, since she couldn't know how many more islanders would show up in the next few weeks, but even the best-case scenario had them running over schedule.

"You're off the clock," Sam said, pulling her tighter against his chest. "Leave that alone for tonight."

It was a good thing Sam couldn't see her face, because Callie knew she must have looked shell-shocked. "I'm starting to believe you ran into some body snatchers this morning. Seriously," she said, spinning to face him, "who the hell are you?"

The question didn't seem to faze him. "I'm the man about to give you a bath."

Callie blinked. "Uh . . . what?"

Without explanation, Sam reached around her to turn off the stove.

"Wait," she argued. "That's for the spaghetti."

"The spaghetti can wait."

Sam dragged Callie through the cottage, past the bed she'd failed to make that morning, and into the master bath. To her surprise, the giant soaker tub was filled nearly to the top, the water covered in a thick layer of bubbles. Instead of the harsh overhead lights, the scene was lit by a series of candles spread around the room.

"Where did you . . . ," she started, but then Callie noticed that the condoms had been placed conveniently near the tub faucet. "Are we both getting in there? I thought you wanted a shower."

"What I want," Sam said, "is you. Covered in bubbles and nothing else."

Her mouth went dry as Callie swallowed the knot that formed in her throat. He kicked off his shoes without taking his eyes off her. Mesmerized, she couldn't look away as he reached for the hem of his T-shirt. Slowly, he revealed his incredible abs and then his chest, with its dusting of light brown hair.

The jeans were loose and hung low enough on his hips for Callie to worry her brain might actually ooze out her ears if he kept going.

"Unless you plan to get in with your clothes on," Sam said, dropping the shirt to the floor, "I suggest you undress."

Callie would have taken the suggestion, only she'd forgotten how to use her arms. And her legs. Her eyes continued to work perfectly, thank God.

"Do you need some help?" he asked, completely relaxed, as if he were offering to open a door for her, instead of getting her naked.

Nodding up and down, Callie remained silent. Clearly, her body was focusing all its energy on making sure not to miss a single movement of the man in front of her.

"I hope you plan to participate in this at some point." His hands glided over her hips, then pulled the shirt up her torso, gracing her with his touch all the way up. "I like it when you tell me what you want."

Callie had no doubt that what she wanted was written all over her face. But just in case, she whispered, "You could go a little faster."

Sam shook his head. "Not tonight," he said, putting word to action as he lifted the shirt over her head, then stood watching her, running his fingertips over her shoulders, her breasts, and the line of skin above her waistband.

"I feel like I'm melting," she said, closing her eyes as he slowly drew the straps of her bra over her arms. "I don't know if I can endure this."

Sam nudged her chin, and Callie opened her eyes. "You can endure anything," he said, his stormy eyes locked on hers. "You're the strongest woman I've ever met."

CHAPTER 25

That wasn't a line meant to get what he wanted. Sam believed what he was saying. And that made Callie believe it, too. Once again unable to speak, she nodded her agreement, and Sam returned to admiring her body.

He lingered around her breasts, touching and testing but not tasting. She wanted his mouth on her more than Callie wanted her next breath. "Please," she mumbled, knowing he would understand.

And he did. "Not yet. Let it build."

If she let it build any more, she was going to explode. The fact that Sam clearly had a plan was the only thing that kept Callie from demanding he move things along. It wasn't as if she didn't enjoy what he was doing. She was enjoying it quite a lot.

"Can I touch you?" she asked, feeling meek and vulnerable for the first time since they'd fallen into bed together. "I want to touch you," she said more forcefully.

"You can have anything you want, Callie." Sam trailed his knuckles down her spine, then undid the clasp on her bra.

One shimmy of her arms, and the blue lace hit the floor. Callie slicked her hands over Sam's abs the moment she was free. "So hot," she said, exploring his ribs and then his chest. "Your skin is burning."

"For you," Sam replied, reaching for the button on her jeans.

Callie let him slide the jeans down her legs, sitting on the side of the tub so that Sam could remove them, along with her socks. Remaining seated, she reached for his zipper, relieved that he let her proceed without a struggle. What she hadn't expected was to find nothing else to remove.

Looking up with a smile, she said, "Now who's trying to kill whom?"

"I knew they were only going to come back off."

Helping him step out of the jeans, Callie said, "Very practical choice."

How she was even carrying on a light conversation, Callie didn't know. There was nothing light going on in that bathroom. If anything, Sam seemed darker. More determined. Like a man about to claim something he'd fight to the death to keep.

After admiring his strong thighs, Callie looked up to see fire in Sam's eyes. They'd gone beyond gray to black, and the teasing smile was gone. "Stand up, Callie," he ordered, his voice sending tremors through her limbs. "We don't want the water to get cold."

Something told her that Sam's stepping into the tub would have the water boiling in seconds. Heat radiated from his body as his mood grew more intense. For a split second, Callie felt a shiver of fear. This wasn't playful sex. Sam was giving her more, but he demanded more in return.

How much could she give him and still have something left when they were over?

"You're thinking too much," Sam said, pulling her up with one hand. Pressing her palm flat over his heart, he covered it with his own. "No thinking tonight."

His pulse beat a steady rhythm against her skin, strong and quick and full of life, and she knew what he was doing. Sam was offering her his heart. And Callie had only a split second to decide if she would take it.

~

He knew he'd gone too far by the look on her face, but Sam had no intention of turning back now. That didn't mean he couldn't retreat a little. No sense in scaring Callie away.

"You're still thinking," he said, his tone lighter. More teasing than intense.

"I'm a little curious," Callie said, confusion and concern clear in her eyes. "The bubbles. The candles. They don't seem like your style."

Sam had clearly miscalculated. Though he didn't doubt he could change her mind, Callie was still intent on keeping their relationship sex only. Admitting that he wanted more before she was ready was an amateur move, and he knew better.

Hoping to slow down that brilliant mind of hers, Sam touched all the places he knew would get a reaction. A knuckle over her nipple. A palm along her hip. A finger grazing along the band of her lace panties.

"There are sides to me you've never seen," he said. "I thought I'd reveal a new one tonight."

"Yes," she said, her eyes growing darker, more hazy, as he maintained contact. "I'm starting to see that."

Dropping kisses along her jaw, he whispered, "You're still wearing too many clothes."

Callie locked her hands on his upper arms. "I'm not wearing anything but my underwear."

"And that's too much." Sam laid his palms against her sides, slid them beneath the strip of elastic, and drove the delicate fabric down her legs in one swift movement. Without prompting, Callie stepped out of them, then pressed against him.

"Is that better?" she said, before clasping his left nipple between her teeth and taking the hardest part of him in her grasp.

Sam could only nod as the blood left his brain in a rush. He was supposed to be the seducer here, but she was taking over.

"What's that?" Callie asked. "I can't hear you."

Because he was about to say the three words that would bring this encounter to an abrupt halt, Sam jerked Callie's head up and took her mouth in a kiss that expressed everything he couldn't say. The more he demanded, the more she gave, until he thought he might die from the need to drive into her.

Breaking the kiss with a growl, Sam stepped into the tub, taking Callie with him. They sank into the water together, and she settled on top of him instantly, as mindless with desire as he was.

"Oh my God," she said, her head falling back as she lowered herself onto him. Sam lifted his hips to give her more. Callie gasped, her head popping back up and meeting his gaze. She continued to stare into his eyes as she rode him, smooth and slick, the water swirling with her movements, bubbles clinging to her breasts as they bobbed along the surface.

Wrapping her arms around his neck, Callie pressed her mouth to his, nipping his bottom lip, sucking on his tongue. She was in full control now, and all Sam could do was hold on. But he wanted to give her more. Slowing her down, he broke the kiss and took her face in his hands.

He didn't say a word, but Sam let her see what was in his eyes. See that this time was different.

Lowering his hands to her breasts, he molded them with his touch. Her eyes slid closed again, but her movements remained slow. Then his hands dropped lower still, until he was grasping her hips, thrusting with her. Finally, he pressed one finger to her clit, determined to send her soaring.

He selfishly wanted to watch her come against him. He wanted to give her pleasure, but Sam wasn't beyond taking his own. Her panting turned to moans. Her nails dug into his skin. And then they both got what they wanted, as Callie's body convulsed with a scream and Sam watched her visit the stars before he flew after her.

It wasn't until they were both breathing heavily, and Callie's face was tucked against Sam's neck, that he realized they'd forgotten about the condoms.

∽

Callie sat curled up in the blue chair, sipping her tea and watching the waves in the distance. There wasn't much moonlight, so she could barely make them out in the darkness. But she could hear them. She needed to hear them in order to block out the screaming in her head.

She'd had sex with Sam without a condom. No, strike that. She'd made love with Sam without a condom. The chances were slim that she would actually get pregnant. She and Josh had been trying for months before that fateful weekend when he and Meredith had been killed.

Which was another reason the affair had been such a blow. She'd thought they were happy. That she would give Josh the beautiful babies that he wanted and then she would feel like she'd really done something, she'd contributed in some way.

But every month her period arrived and the light in Josh's eyes dimmed that much more. He had hardly even looked at her by the time it had all ended so tragically.

Quite the ironic twist from then until now. Now Callie prayed her period would show up so she wouldn't have to deal with Sam's looking at her as if she'd trapped him. Truth be told, she felt a bit trapped herself. A baby would put a serious damper on her career aspirations.

Callie could barely take care of herself and a bird. How the hell would she take care of a baby?

"You okay?" Sam asked, dropping onto the ottoman. Callie had left him to get dressed in the bedroom.

It had taken everything she had not to ask him to go home. She needed time alone to think. After what they'd done, she felt closer to Sam than ever before, which was the reason she wanted him to leave.

This was too much for one day. The possibility of staying on Anchor. A shot at stability and the chance to do what she loved. And then there was Sam. Precious, generous, never-going-to-marry-again Sam.

Add in the baby blip, and her brain was on overload. Though her heart wasn't feeling all that great either.

"Things got a little out of hand in there," she said, keeping her eyes on the waves. If she looked at him, she might say something she'd regret.

"That's my fault," he said, drawing her attention. None of the confidence he usually displayed was there. If anything, he looked scared.

Of course he was. He could be an unwilling father in nine months.

"Don't worry," Callie said. "I won't hold you responsible."

His brows slammed together. "What?"

Callie shook her head. "Josh and I tried for months, with no luck, so I'm sure it'll be fine. But either way, you don't need to worry."

"Exactly what don't I need to worry about?" Sam's jaw was tight, as were his words.

"I mean—" she started, but he cut her off.

"Do you think I would turn my back on you if you were having our child?"

"No. I—"

"Or that I wouldn't have a problem with you shutting me out of its life?"

This wasn't going right at all. Why was he so mad? They didn't even know if there would be a baby, and he was accusing her of shutting him out?

"I wouldn't do that," Callie argued, her anger growing to match Sam's. "I don't want you to think I'd trap you like this, okay?" Storming out of the chair, she didn't even care that she was spilling tea everywhere. "I know you don't want to get married again. I knew that when we started and this was supposed to be just sex, not love and marriage and babies. Good Lord, when did this get so nuts?"

Sam followed her into the kitchen. Why wouldn't he give her some space? She needed to think, damn it.

"Are you saying you won't marry me?"

Callie tossed her mug into the sink, then waved her hands over her head. "You don't want to get married. I don't . . . want to marry a man who doesn't want to get married."

"But what if—"

"What if there's a baby?" Callie finished for him. "I don't know. If there's a baby, then I'll deal with it." She rubbed her forehead, struggling to keep the panic from taking her under. She would not have an attack. Not now. Not in front of Sam.

"*We'll* deal with it," Sam said, tugging her against him. "I have plans. It's all going to be alright."

She wanted to stay there, safe in his arms, feeling protected and cherished and as if she'd never have to worry about anything again. But then his words soaked into her muddled brain.

Pulling back, she asked, "What do you mean, you have plans? Plans for what?"

"For us," he said, with a sappy grin on his face. "I'll take care of everything."

It was happening again. Someone else trying to dictate what her life would be, and all she had to do was smile and follow along. Callie couldn't let that happen. Would *not* let that happen.

"Who asked you to take care of anything?" She bolted away from him. "I have plans of my own," she said, poking herself in the chest. "And I don't need to be taken care of."

"Calm down, please," he begged. "If you'll hear me out, you'll see that this is a good thing."

All Callie could see was her weakness being thrown in her face. Her failure to stand on her own. And then there was the fact that Sam only wanted more now that he thought she might be pregnant. *She* hadn't been enough to change his mind, but add a possible Edwards heir, and he had *plans*.

"You need to go," she said, feeling the heat crawling up her neck. Breathing was getting harder, and she could feel a cold sweat coming on. If she could get rid of him, Callie would be able to get a grip. To stop the attack before it took over.

"You can't throw me out," Sam pleaded. "Not now."

"I need time! Can't you see that?" she screamed. Her control was slipping. Pressing her hands against her temples, Callie closed her eyes. "If you care about me at all, you'll go."

For once, he didn't argue. Or push. Or demand. Callie was still standing in the kitchen with her eyes closed when she heard the front door slam.

~

Sam didn't know what to do. He sat in his car for at least twenty minutes in Callie's driveway. Then he simply pulled out and drove. The next thing he knew, he was sitting on the edge of a dock in the marina. Though there was little light from the moon, he knew where the Sunset Harbor Inn sat across the bay.

And he could practically see a light burning in Callie's cottage. Faint. Distant. Almost inconceivable. Much like the woman sitting in its glow.

The woman he loved.

How could she say those things to him? They'd made love, and yes, they'd been careless, but what did that matter now? Apparently, a great deal. To Callie, at least.

This night had been more than a miscalculation. Sam had made assumptions about their relationship that were clearly, blatantly, gut-wrenchingly wrong.

Her rejection should have made him angry, but he'd been the one to change the terms of their agreement. He'd leaped in and had expected Callie to throw her arms around him and sail off into the perfect future he'd concocted in his mind.

For the second time in his life, Sam had thought a woman loved him. And again he'd been wrong. At least Callie had been up front about her feelings. She'd never led him on. Hadn't married him and then taken off on a lovers' tryst with another man. He had to give her credit for that.

Callie wanted space, and she would have it. The inn would be finished in little more than a month. Then she would move on and so would he. Anchor Island would become nothing but a distant memory.

Unless their slip tonight did indeed turn into a baby. Callie might not want him, but Sam would never walk away from his own child. She would have to deal with that.

~

By three in the morning, Callie hadn't found much peace, but at least she'd managed to hold off the panic attack. In taking inventory of the situation, she knew some things for certain.

For one, she wasn't going to marry a man who didn't want her. Especially one ready to make decisions about her life without even consulting her. But she also knew that she'd never keep Sam away from his own child, if there was one, which Callie highly doubted there would be. Josh had been tested not long before he'd died, and that had allowed the doctors to rule him out as the reason why they couldn't get pregnant.

Callie had been scheduled for tests the week after the accident. She hadn't seen any reason to go, but it didn't take a genius to do the math and know that if Josh wasn't shooting blanks, there was only one person left who could be the problem. And really, bum ovaries would be the last element anyone needed to declare her the most disappointing human around.

Which was melodramatic and whiny, but, damn it, couldn't *one* thing go right in her life?

Not that she wanted to be pregnant right now, but someday would be nice.

Unfortunately, the issue of impending parenthood wasn't the only thing she and Sam needed to deal with. He was still her boss. They still had a hotel to renovate in the next five weeks. And there was the sticky subject of what the hell they were doing in private.

Searching for answers, Callie replayed the last seven weeks in her mind. She needed to figure out where this whole thing had gone off the rails.

And then she remembered what Sam had said. That their relationship was already complicated enough without their sleeping together again. He'd been right, but Callie had barreled ahead anyway, pushing him into an affair. Seducing him into her bed and then getting pissed when it all blew up in her face, as Sam had known it would.

That left only one thing to do. She had to end it. Now.

A quick check of the clock said *now* might need to wait a few more hours. But Callie needed to take action. So she opened her laptop. It might be cowardly to break off a sexual escapade via email, but Callie also knew if she tried doing this in person, she wouldn't survive it.

If Sam looked relieved, she might crack right open at his feet. If he tried to change her mind, she'd most likely cave and spend the rest of her life being nothing but another man's puppet.

No. Email was best. It took an hour of writing, deleting, gnashing of teeth, chugging of tea, and conferring with Cecil to get the message right. Of course, Cecil had only suggested Callie offer Sam a cracker. Not much help, but a bit of comic relief when she'd needed it.

She sat staring at the words "message sent" for a long time, fighting the urge to cancel it somehow. To change her mind, delete the message, and beg Sam to forgive her little tantrum.

And then the sun came up over the ocean and Callie realized that life hadn't stopped during the night. The world continued to spin regardless of her emotional conniption, the likes of which would put her mother's fits to shame.

She could still get a couple hours' sleep before anyone expected her at the inn. And since Sam wouldn't be sleeping over anymore, Callie could go to bed early that evening after a lonely dinner of soup for one. Maybe she'd even share her oyster crackers with Cecil and make his night. Who said she needed a man to have excitement in her life?

Callie sighed as she headed for the bedroom. Until she spotted Sam's clothes folded neatly over a chair. And there was his cologne on the dresser. Because she was an idiot, Callie spritzed a drop onto her wrist. It was as if Sam had walked into the room.

On second thought, sleep was overrated, Callie thought. She'd much rather have a shower.

CHAPTER 26

It had been a month, and Sam was still reeling from the email Callie had sent him. She'd had the nerve to tell him he'd been right all along. That they were complicated, and having any further connection outside of their professional one would only make matters worse. The message explained that he no longer needed to contribute manual labor to the renovation, since they were working with a larger crew.

And then another message, ten days later, to say he needn't worry about fatherhood. There would not be a baby in their future.

She might as well have walked into his office and taken a baseball bat to his knees.

As much as it annoyed the hell out of him, Sam agreed with her suggestion and avoided making personal appearances at the inn. But that hadn't stopped him from demanding regular status updates, delivered electronically, of course. And he continued his efforts to find a property around Charleston to invest in. Something with hidden potential that needed little more than cosmetic improvements to make it shine.

Which led to a prime opportunity that had landed in his inbox that morning. A small inn not far from Patriots Point, in close proximity to both the water and a golf course. According to his contact, the building was sound but the interior was in dire need of updating. Callie would have been the perfect person to handle the makeover, but, of course, she was no longer a part of this new endeavor. The thought caused a twinge not far from Sam's breast-bone.

He was running the numbers for viability when a knock sounded at his door.

"Come in," he said, glancing at his calendar to see if he'd forgotten about an appointment. The entire morning was open, so this was an unplanned visitor, whoever he was.

When the door opened, the gangly young man stepping through was the last person Sam expected to see.

"Is Callie alright?" he asked, concerned the young clerk would only come to see him if something bad had happened. The teen's Adam's apple bobbed as he remained near the door, his face ashen white. "Damn it, tell me what's happened to her."

"Callie is fine," he said, slamming his hands into his pockets. "Mostly."

Sam charged around the desk, and the boy looked ready to run. Struggling to remain calm, he spoke slowly. "Why are you here, Jack? Is something wrong?"

"I shouldn't have come," Jack mumbled, trying to scurry back out the door.

"Jack!" Sam yelled, then checked himself. He was already dealing with a scared rabbit. Yelling wasn't going to get him anywhere. "Tell me what's going on."

Closing the door, then leaning against it, Jack said, "It's the inn. We're not going to be done in time."

"I thought more people had signed up to work." He'd read as much in Callie's reports.

"We did, but we lost a few along the way, too." Tugging on his shirt, Jack spit out the rest. "Callie is practically killing herself, working around the clock. She won't let me stay past eight, and even if she works twenty-four-seven for the next week, we're never going to be ready before the guests show up."

"Why didn't she tell me before now?"

"I don't know," Jack said. "She's probably going to kill me for coming over here, but I had to do something. I can't let her make herself sick over a stupid hotel." Realizing he was talking to the owner of that hotel, the boy tried to backtrack. "I mean . . . Not that . . . "

"No," Sam said. "You're right. It's nothing but a stupid hotel."

Considering his options, Sam paced the small space in front of his desk. He could storm in now, demand to take over, and let Callie see herself as a failure. But Sam couldn't make ten people do the work of twenty any better than Callie could. What they needed were bodies. Able bodies willing to work overtime to get the job done.

"I know what we need to do," Sam said, grabbing his suit jacket off the coatrack in the corner. "You're going to pretend we never had this conversation."

"I can do that," Sam's new favorite employee said, tossing a shock of white hair off his forehead. "But what are you going to do?"

"Get us more bodies," Sam answered.

≈

Callie had become too dependent on Jack, as proven by the fact that she checked the clock every two minutes while he was off delivering the final invoices and packing slips to Yvonne at the Anchor. She was *not* anticipating his return because she hoped he might mention having seen Sam. Callie wasn't interested in what Sam was doing. She didn't care about him at all.

Now, if she could only convince her heart of that.

God, she missed him. Sleeping without him was awful, so Callie didn't sleep. Much. She'd set up camp on her blue chair after four days of trying to sleep in the bed. Thankfully, Yvonne had picked up the box of his things. It felt ridiculous, but she couldn't see him, and Sam clearly didn't want to see her, either.

He hadn't even answered her email, except to say he expected weekly status reports on the renovation. That was it. After all the time they'd spent together, he'd let her go without so much as a "thanks for the sex" postscript.

And then Henri had abandoned her. She'd tried to get Callie to go home for Thanksgiving, but there was no time. The inn had been behind schedule, and still was, which was proving detrimental to Callie's health. The clothes that had been tight weeks before were now falling off, and she couldn't remember the last time she'd had a good meal.

Not that it mattered. She didn't have much of an appetite these days.

The work had to be finished, and Callie wasn't ready to give up. They had eight days before the first guests arrived for the wedding. If Callie worked day and night, she could have everything in place and get the staff in at least two days before. She'd barely have time to walk across the street and feed Cecil, and maybe shower now and then, but this job would be finished on time if it killed her.

"I'm back," Jack yelled from the front door. "And I have lunch."

Callie set the paint roller on the corner of the tray and exited the dining room. "But it's only ten thirty," she said, concerned she might be so tired as to have forgotten how to read a clock.

"Since you probably haven't eaten since lunchtime yesterday, I think you're entitled to an early break."

When had Jack become so bossy? Callie was about to remind him who was in charge and how much work they had to do, when the smell of Dempsey's fish and chips hit her nose.

"Is that what I think it is?"

"Yep."

"How did you know I like fish and chips?"

Jack paused in pulling the food from the large bag. "Doesn't everyone like fish and chips?"

He had her there. "Pass it over," she said, her mouth watering already. "Is this why you took so long?"

"Sure," Jack said, stuffing a fry into his mouth as if someone might steal it from him.

"You didn't see anyone else at the Anchor?" Damn it. She was not going to ask about Sam.

"Nope." Her lunch mate stuck another fry into his mouth, and Callie took the hint to stop asking questions. It wasn't as if Jack didn't know what she was getting at. He wasn't stupid. Everyone around knew she and Sam had run aground.

Having the entire village in her business would be the one drawback to staying on the island, which she'd decided to do. Then again, Callie didn't plan to have any business for them to be in. She and Sam were over, and once this renovation was finished, they would no longer have any reason to deal with each other.

She certainly wouldn't be dating anytime soon. Her focus for the foreseeable future would be on her career only. The real estate office needed several properties updated, which would challenge her creativity to make them all different. She found the idea of decorating independent dwellings, instead of typically four-walled, boxy hotel rooms, rather exciting.

Of course, she had to finish this project first. Which had her eating faster than normal to get back to the painting.

"Are you trying to set a record?" Jack asked.

He must have woken up on the cheeky side of the bed today. "I need to get back to the dining room," Callie said, after swallowing a large bite of fish. "I still have three pillars to do, and the fireplace mantel needs a second coat."

Her young friend put a hand over her food. "Ten minutes isn't going to hurt anything." His brown eyes were filled with concern. "You need to eat like a normal person."

Ten minutes probably wouldn't be the end of the world. And devouring such good food without enjoying it was criminal.

Callie nodded. "You're right. I'll slow down."

They continued to eat in amicable silence until every crumb was gone. They were collecting their garbage into the bag the food had come in when Callie heard cars pulling up outside.

"Were we expecting another delivery?" she asked Jack. His only response was a shrug, but he also wouldn't meet her eye. "Jack? What are you up to?"

"I don't know what you're talking about," he said, slam-dunking their garbage into the can behind the desk and heading for the dining room. "I'll get back to the painting while you see who it is."

Before Callie could argue, Skinny Legs was gone and she heard footsteps on the front porch. She'd made it two steps when the door swung open and both familiar and unfamiliar faces poured in.

"What . . . ," Callie uttered, as more and more people crossed the threshold. "Will," she said, addressing the person closest to her. "What is going on?"

Glancing behind her, Will smiled. "We heard you could use some help over here."

"Well . . ." She couldn't seem to finish a thought. How did they know? "Who told you that?"

Randy helped Will pull off her coat. "A little birdie. And we're here as long as you need us."

This couldn't be happening. Besides Will and Randy, Sid and Lucas were there, as well as Beth and Joe. Struggling to process the scene, Callie grasped onto the obvious. "Beth?" she said, staring at the woman who looked ready to pop at any second.

"I'm here only for moral support," Beth said, holding up her hands. "I wish I could do more, but for obvious reasons, that's not possible right now."

"And I'm not letting her out of my sight," Joe said, removing his own coat. "Not until the little bugger arrives."

Callie couldn't hold back the tears, though she felt like an idiot crying in front of all these people. "I don't know what to say."

"You can start by telling us what you need done," Lucas said, rubbing his hands together. "I'm sure if we break into teams, we can have this place open for business in no time."

"We'd better," Will said. "I've got a nervous bride arriving in eight days."

Wiping the tears away, Callie couldn't help but laugh. "And everything will be perfect when she gets here." Taking a deep breath, she started barking orders. "I need curtains hung in all the upstairs rooms, as well as linens put on the beds."

"Kinzie and Sid, let's get to it," Will said, charging toward the stairs.

Barreling on, Callie said, "There are several pieces of furniture in the back of the dining room that need to be installed in the rooms. Each has a Post-it that will tell you where it needs to go. Who's ready to do some heavy lifting?"

Randy, Joe, Lucas, and an attractive young man stepped forward. "This is Manny," Randy said, introducing the fourth member of the group, who nodded in Callie's direction. "Looks like we're your guys."

As the muscle disappeared into the dining room, Callie spotted Bernie and some of the workers from outside lingering near the door. "You came back," she said, the tears loading up again.

"Might as well finish what we started," Bernie said in his usual gruff tone.

Though he was less than receptive, Callie threw her arms around him. A few seconds into the hug, the curmudgeon patted her on the back.

"Right," he said when she'd finally released him. "Where do you want us?"

"If we all knock out the finishing touches on the walls of the dining room, we can start loading the detail pieces in the rooms." Callie glanced around the lobby and spotted Beth looking miserable all alone at the edge of the counter. "You can't be around the paint fumes," she said, chewing her bottom lip as she considered what the woman could do. "I know."

Callie disappeared into her office, returning seconds later with a notepad and catalog.

"Have a seat right back here," she said, helping Beth lower herself into Jack's chair behind the counter. "The last task is going to be decorating this place for Christmas. We're going for festive without looking as if Santa's workshop threw up in the halls."

"You want me to pick out the decorations?" Beth asked, green eyes wide.

"Precisely," Callie replied. "This is the catalog from the Trading Post, and Floyd assured me most of this stuff is in his back room.

And if you know of anything we can get elsewhere on the island, write that down, too."

"I can do that," Beth said, looking excited to be contributing to the work.

Callie left the mom-to-be to work some Christmas magic and returned to her office. She let the tears flow freely then, relishing the sound of footsteps overhead. This was going to work. They'd needed a Christmas miracle, and here it was.

"Hey," Jack said, bounding into her office in his usual way. He froze when he saw Callie's face. "Why are you crying? I thought this was good."

"It *is* good," Callie mumbled, nodding her head up and down. Then she threw her arms around the gangly young man who had put this miracle in motion. "Thank you for doing this."

"But I didn't—"

"I know you did, so don't deny it, Jack. Now I know why you were gone so long this morning."

"It wasn't—"

"I don't know how, and right now I don't care." Pushing the stuttering teenager into the lobby, Callie added, "Back to work. We've got a hotel to finish!"

Sam enforced every ounce of self-control he had to keep from driving over to the inn and joining the others. Will had used some excuse to call him from Callie's office and give him an update. According to her estimations, with the added crew they would have the place put back together by the end of the week, providing plenty of time to bring the new staff in and have the place ready for guests before the big arrivals.

He imagined Callie trying to finish all the work on her own, not sleeping or eating. She likely would have done it, too. Her tenacity almost made up for her stubborn streak. She should have let him know weeks ago that the crew had thinned back out. That she was in the weeds and needed his help.

But that was the catch. Callie didn't need him for anything and she was determined to prove it. Even if she whittled herself down to nothing in the process.

Yes, stubborn and prideful. And beautiful and brilliant and better than anything he ever deserved.

CHAPTER 27

She did it. With the help of some of the best people she would ever meet in her life, Callie renovated and rejuvenated the Sunset Harbor Inn in less than three months. The furnishings looked amazing, the rooms were cozy and inviting, and the exterior sparkled in the sun. The gazebo still needed a paint job, but that could wait.

Callie was not going to stress over a gazebo in the dead of winter. Thanks to Beth's vision, they'd draped it in thick strands of garland with a large red bow on the front, and it made a wonderful focal point not far from the harbor. There would be many beautiful weddings staged around that gazebo, some of them maybe even planned by her.

But that was in the future. Today was about celebrating the current accomplishment. The wedding guests would arrive in two days, but first was an open house party. Everyone who'd helped with the renovation would be wined and dined, and Jack had even agreed to play DJ. Callie wasn't certain what kind of music they would get, but the air-guitar god had promised nothing too screamy—his word—and that had been good enough for her.

Standing on the front porch of the Peabody Cottage, Callie fortified herself for the test ahead. Today she would see Sam. He was the owner, after all. Not inviting him to his own open house had seemed rude, though Callie wasn't beneath considering it. Still, common sense had won out. Her pride had taken harder hits. She would survive this one.

They'd received a dusting of snow overnight, and while Callie had heard that was not a usual event here, the weather didn't seem to have scared anyone off. Many spaces in the parking lot were filled when she made the short trek that she'd made so many times before in the last twelve weeks. This one felt tougher, as if she were walking against a wall of something that was pushing back.

Stopping outside the front door, Callie took several deep breaths, then noticed movement to her left. So bundled that she could barely see their faces, Bernie and Olaf hovered around their ancient barrel, playing checkers.

The newly painted table she'd given them sat ignored in the corner.

"Why are you still using this barrel?" she asked as she stepped up beside Olaf.

"T'ain't nothin' wrong with it," Bernie said, scooting a black checker one block to the right.

Callie almost argued, then reconsidered. "Can we at least give it a coat of paint?"

"I suppose," he said, grimacing as Olaf took his checkers. "Now get inside. You're distracting me."

She considered lingering to annoy him. And to avoid what she would inevitably face inside. But then Bernie looked up for a second, an almost imperceptible smile on his lips as he winked at her. His face returned to normal so quickly, Callie wondered if she hadn't imagined the whole thing.

"The punch is good," Olaf said, ignoring the board for a moment. "And they got scallops wrapped in bacon," he added, holding up a small plate covered in exactly that.

"I'll give your regards to the chef," Callie said, walking toward the hotel entrance. She stopped once again before the door to steady herself.

Like ripping off a Band-Aid, she thought. *Get it over with.*

Charging ahead, Callie stepped into the lobby of the Sunset Harbor Inn and marveled at the difference from the first time she'd stepped inside. The first thing that hit her was the smell. Once again, Jack had been the champion. His suggestion that they pour a drop or two of vanilla into each can of paint meant the place smelled much better than it would have without the added touch.

The presence of live garland, which had also been Beth's idea, meant the scents of pine and cookies filled Callie's senses and made her feel festive and hungry at the same time. Upbeat music pulsed from the dining room, from which she could hear voices.

She hadn't seen Sam's Murano parked out front, so maybe she could have a few drinks before he arrived. Take the edge off, and then seeing him might not hit her so hard.

But before she could make her feet move, the bells chimed over the door, signaling a new arrival. Turning, she saw him and knew that no amount of alcohol would have made this easier.

Sam stood frozen in the open doorway as their eyes met. Then he looked her up and down, as if taking her in. He didn't look as haughty as she'd expected. Or as arrogant. For a second, he looked happy to see her, but then the mask was back in place, his expression flat and free of emotion.

"Hello," he said, closing the door behind him. Glancing around the lobby, his face shifted to approving. "You've done a good job with the place."

Callie knew he'd given himself a tour the day before. She'd been packing her things and spotted him through the front window of the cottage. The urge to run to him had been almost too much—until she'd reminded herself that he'd made his choice, as had she. That they were over.

"Hi," she managed to say, cursing the flutter in her voice. Clearing her throat, Callie threw her head back. "I did an outstanding job, considering the time frame I was given."

One side of his mouth hitched up. "I agree. That's what I meant to say."

She should have walked away from him. Joined the party, grabbed a drink, and ignored Sam for the rest of the night. Instead she said, "What do you think of the decorations?"

"Very festive," he said.

"But not too much," Callie added.

"No," he said. "Not too much."

This was ridiculous. "I guess we'd better join the party."

"Callie, wait." Sam took a step forward, pausing as Callie stepped back. Tucking his hands into his pockets, he said, "I wanted to tell you that I'll be moving back to Charleston in a few months. Maybe we'll run into each other."

"You're leaving Anchor?" she asked. "But what about the hotels?"

"I'll still own them," he said, tilting his head. "Someone else will be running them on-site."

All her stressing over whether to stay, and he'd been planning to leave.

"When did you decide this?"

"A while ago," he said, being vague, as usual.

"Before I came here?"

He took another step forward. This time she stood her ground.

"No. My decision came after that."

She wanted to ask more questions. To know if he'd decided to leave before or after they'd fallen apart. Was that part of the plan he'd suddenly had for them, when he'd thought they might have a child together?

Instead, she gave him some news of her own.

"Well, I'll be staying."

"What?" he said, his eyes narrowed. "Staying where?"

"Here," she said. "On Anchor." He opened his mouth to speak, but she didn't give him the chance. "Don't worry. I'll have my things out of the Peabody the day after the wedding. I've made other arrangements."

"But why?"

"Because my job here is done and the Peabody belongs to you. I have to get out."

"I don't mean that," he said, seemingly growing angry. "What will you do here? There are no more hotels for you to flip."

So, he thought that was all she could do. Of course he did. "What I do after this job is over isn't really any of your business, Mr. Edwards." Callie threw in the full name as an extra punch, proof that he was no longer more than a boss to her.

But his blue-gray eyes faded from anger to hurt, and she felt the shift like a blow.

She would not feel sorry for him. Sam was the one who'd declared he would never marry again. He'd agreed to a temporary affair. Even if he changed his mind, he would never see her as an equal, with opinions and enough strength to stand on her own. To make her own decisions.

And if she changed her mind, Callie would fall into all the old patterns she'd worked so hard to break.

They stood there for a long time, staring at each other as if neither could move. Then Sam reached for her and Callie took several steps back.

"I need to join the party," she said, willing the tears to hold off a little longer. "Thanks again for this opportunity. It taught me a lot about myself, and I'm glad I took it."

And then she charged into the dining room, where people yelled her name and put a drink in her hand and helped her pretend that her heart wasn't breaking.

～

An hour later, Sam stood in the corner of the dining room, untouched drink in hand, pretending he wasn't watching every move Callie made. He couldn't believe she was staying. Had never entertained the thought that she would want to. And to think, she'd chosen to do so when she'd believed Sam would still be on the island.

Having to see him around the village wouldn't have bothered her at all. Un-fucking-believable.

"You should tell her," said a female voice from beside him. Sam looked down to find a very pregnant Beth Dempsey near his elbow. A glass he assumed held water rested on the top of her stomach. Smiling up at him, she added, "Makes a good table."

"I'm sure it does," he said, not sure how to converse with a pregnant woman. Especially one he didn't know very well.

"What's holding you back?" she asked.

"I'm not sure what you mean." He knew exactly what she meant, but telling a woman in her condition to mind her own business seemed . . . precarious.

Beth took a sip of water, then said, "You love her. That much is obvious."

"That's the hormones talking," Sam said.

"Possibly." Another sip of water. "But I doubt it."

They stood in silence, Beth humming along with the music Jack was playing from the other side of the room. "I don't know what this is," she said, "but I like the tune." A young male was singing about being weightless. Sam could see how the concept would appeal to a woman roughly the size of a planet.

"I would ask you to dance," he said, " but I don't think it's wise in your condition."

She started bouncing up and down. "I don't know. Maybe dancing would jar this kid loose. The bugger needs to come out."

"Please don't do that." She was making him nervous. "I think you should sit down."

But before he could get her a chair, Beth's eyes went wide as she latched a hand onto his arm like a vise grip. "Too late," she said. "Get Joe. Get him now."

Since Sam couldn't walk away without his arm and Beth wasn't letting go, the only option he had was to yell across the room. On the third try, Joe finally heard him. He turned with a smile, until he noticed Beth's face. Then he looked ready to kill.

"What is it?" Joe said, crouching under Beth's nose. She was breathing heavily, making heeing and hawing sounds.

"Water," she said. *Hee hee haw haw.* "Broke."

Sam looked down at the same time Joe did and spotted the puddle between Beth's feet.

"Lucas, get your car!" Joe yelled, lifting Beth into his arms.

"What?" his brother said. "It's a BMW!"

"Get the fucking car."

Lucas did as he was ordered, charging out of the room. The rest of the crowd swarmed behind the couple as they followed, Will and Sid flanking Joe while Randy collected coats. In a whirl, the entire party moved to the porch, watching Joe slide a panting Beth gently into the backseat of a silver BMW, then climbing in with her. Sid jumped into the passenger seat, and through the window Sam could see her on her knees, holding Beth's hand in her own.

"We'll meet you there," Will yelled, as she and Randy ran toward a Malibu.

Seconds later, the snow-covered lot was filled with tire tracks, and what partygoers remained were taking bets on the sex of the impending bundle of joy.

As people filed back into the hotel, Sam spotted Callie farther down the porch, watching the baby parade disappear into the distance. As if she could feel him watching her, she turned to meet his gaze in time for him to see the tear slide down her cheek.

He'd taken a step toward her when a woman Sam didn't know stepped through the door.

"Callie, I need to call Tom and Patty Dempsey to let them know what's going on. Can I use the phone in your office?"

Blotting her face, Callie nodded. "Sure, Kinzie. Go ahead." She shook her head, as if she could shake the tears away, then headed back into the hotel. Sam touched her elbow, but she jerked her arm away. "Leave me alone, Sam. Please, leave me alone."

Henri arrived the morning of the wedding. Callie tried not to be offended that her cousin stopped to see Yvonne before driving over to the cottage. Most of Callie's meager belongings were stacked near her front door, though she had to remind herself the door wasn't *hers*. If the cottage had belonged to anyone else, she would have paid any price to stay.

But she wouldn't rent a place from Sam. She needed to sever all connections with him, and after today, she would. Callie was still technically on Sam's payroll, representing the Sunset Harbor Inn to the wedding guests, making sure they were happy and the wedding went off without any mistakes or issues.

She was also observing the event from Will's point of view, seeing how her future boss operated, and learning what would be expected of her when the time came. Will's nerves were evident to anyone who knew her, but she hid them well when the bridal party was around. The Sunset had borrowed one of Dempsey's cooks to prepare the reception meal, which looked to be a success.

And Opal had supplied the cake, of course, which was a work of art that tasted as good as it looked. All of the traditions had been completed, including the bouquet and garter tosses, as well as the father-daughter dance, when Callie found Will hovering at the back of the dining room.

"You did it," she whispered into the taller woman's ear, which was only possible because Callie was wearing heels, while Will wore flats.

"*We* did it," Will replied, nudging Callie's shoulder. "This place is gorgeous. The bride's mother can't stop raving about the rooms, and the bride has already said they intend to come back here every year on their anniversary."

Pride swelled in Callie's chest. "That's good to hear," she said. "Sam will be pleased to have the return business."

"I almost wish this place had been an option for Beth's wedding last spring."

"Speaking of," Callie said, "how are mom and baby?"

"Disgustingly happy," Will said, but her eyes lit up when she said it. "Mary Ann is beautiful, as to be expected. Hard to tell on the hair yet, but I think she's going to have her daddy's blue eyes."

Watching the bride do the twist with her ring bearer and flower girl, Callie couldn't help but smile. "There's a lot of happiness going on around here," she said. "It's nice to see."

Her voice soft, Will said, "But you're not happy."

Callie considered lying but didn't see the point. "No, but I will be. Eventually."

"Are you sure you two can't make it work?" Will asked. "I happen to know Sam is absolutely miserable."

"And how would you know that?"

"Randy told me," she said. "Sam has a tendency to work out when he's upset about something. He's been in the gym every night since the party."

What Sam did or didn't do was none of Callie's concern. "Maybe he's feeling out of shape."

"You were doing so well with the truth there for a minute," Will said, dragging Callie out of the dining room. "I get that it's your life and I need to butt out, but I hate to see two stubborn people screw up a good thing."

"You don't—"

"Let me finish. I left Randy once, and it was the dumbest thing I've ever done in my life." Will crossed her arms. "I was smart enough to come back, but when I think of what I could have missed, it scares the hell out of me."

"Sam and I are not the same as you and Randy. We're . . . complicated," Callie said, rubbing a hand across her forehead. "There's too much between us. Too much history. We're not a good fit."

Will raised a brow. "You don't really believe that."

"It doesn't matter anyway," Callie said. "Sam is leaving, and I'm staying, and we'll both get on with our lives."

"Wait, what did you say?"

It hadn't occurred to Callie that Sam's imminent departure from the island would be a secret. He hadn't asked her not to mention it, so it wasn't as if she was breaking a confidence.

"He told me at the party that he's moving back to Charleston. He'll bring people in to run the hotels here, and I assume he has another property in mind over there."

And then she remembered what else Sam had said. He hoped they might see each other in Charleston. Why would he have said that? She was right here, practically a stone's throw away right now, and he didn't want to see her. Hadn't made any effort to change her mind.

Except he'd reached for her. And she'd brushed him off.

"Doesn't make sense," Will was saying, but Callie hadn't been paying attention.

"If you don't mind," she said, laying a hand on Will's arm, "I have something I need to do."

Will glanced back to the dining room. "I suppose we can handle things from here."

"Thanks," Callie said, grabbing her coat from the back of her office door. "I owe you one, Will," she tossed over her shoulder, before pulling the hotel door closed behind her.

Callie nearly wiped out twice, thanks to running in heels on snowy gravel, before she reached the cottage. Once inside, she switched to tennis shoes and grabbed her keys.

CHAPTER 28

This was probably the dumbest idea Sam had ever had. And he would undoubtedly regret what he was about to do, but if he'd learned anything from Callie, it was that sometimes you had to be willing to look like a fool to get what you needed.

He'd spent more than an hour packing his clothes. Putting the dress pants in, then taking them out. Finding his oldest jeans and putting them in instead. Sam didn't own a lot of T-shirts, but he would fix that later. If necessary. For now, the five he could find would have to suffice.

Once he had finished packing, he'd paced his tiny living room, rehearsing what he would say. His first instinct had been to make demands. To say how it was going to be and brook no argument. Then common sense had smacked him upside the head. If he wanted this to work, making demands was the last way to go about it.

So he tried for reasonable. Stating the facts in a practical way. But that wasn't right either. In the end, he knew exactly what to do. He'd be honest.

And if that failed, he wasn't above begging.

By five o'clock, he'd practically paced a hole into the floor. Desperate for something to do while he waited, Sam carried his suitcase outside. He could throw it in the trunk now and be ready when the time came.

He reached the Murano only to realize he'd forgotten his keys. Leaving the suitcase in the driveway, he climbed onto his tiny porch but stopped when he heard a car come down his narrow lane. Turning, he saw her. And he saw the moment Callie noticed the suitcase. Pulling into a drive two cabins up, she turned her car around and sped off in the direction she'd come.

She'd been on her way to see him. That had to be a good sign.

Dashing into the house, Sam grabbed his keys and raced back outside, renewed hope sending his heart slamming against his ribs.

∼

How many times could Callie be an idiot before the lesson finally sank in? *Sam did not want her.* He was leaving the island without even saying good-bye, and she'd been crazy to think that anything could work for them.

If only he hadn't seen her. That was the worst part. He knew she'd caved. Sam would always know that she'd been ready to come crawling back, when all he wanted was to be rid of her.

Gah! She was such a complete and total idiot.

"Whoa," Henri said, as Callie nearly barreled her over, stomping into the kitchen. "What the hell is wrong with you?"

"Nothing," Callie growled. "Nothing is wrong with me." Dropping onto a kitchen chair, she dropped her head into her hands. "Nothing except I'm a worthless, pathetic idiot."

Henri didn't respond right away, which felt like confirmation and only made Callie feel worse until she groaned into her hands.

"Let's take a step back here." Henri pulled out the chair beside her and took a seat. "First off, you are not worthless or pathetic."

"Yes, I am," Callie said quickly.

"No, you're not. And if you say either of those things again, I'm going to give you one of Aunt Melba's pinches."

Jerking her head up, Callie covered her upper arm closest to her cousin. "You wouldn't."

"If you don't get a grip, I will."

Callie wanted to argue, but Aunt Melba did that twist thing when she pinched, and it hurt like hell. And Callie knew Henri wasn't bluffing.

"Now," Henri said, "tell me what's going on. Why did you race in and out of here a little while ago?"

How could she explain that she'd suffered a temporary bout of delusion and thought Sam might actually care for her? Believed, like the idiot that she was, that he might love her?

"Would you buy a temporary-insanity plea?"

"Knowing who raised you, I normally would." Henri leaned back in her chair. "But not this time."

Callie ran her hands over her face. "I was afraid of that."

"You went to find Sam, didn't you?" *Why* did her cousin have to be so damned astute? As if she'd heard the question, Henri added, "I write romance novels for a living. I could see this coming from a mile away."

"Then why didn't you stop me?" Callie asked. "My life isn't a book. Real life doesn't come with happy endings all wrapped up pretty and neat."

"First of all, not all happy endings are pretty." Henri tapped a finger on the table as she spoke. "And no, your life isn't a book. But there's nothing wrong with fighting for what you want. If you ask me, you should have fought for him a long time ago."

"No one asked you," Callie said, pushing out of her seat. "And it doesn't matter now. He's leaving."

"In a few months."

"No. Today. I saw him putting suitcases in his car."

Henri followed Callie to the sink. "You realize Christmas is in four days. He's probably going home to visit and then coming back."

Callie hadn't thought of that. But that didn't change the facts. "Doesn't matter."

"It does matter. You still have a chance to fix this."

Jerking open the jar of tea bags, Callie dropped one into a mug. "There's nothing to fix," she said, turning on the faucet at the same time a knock sounded at her front door.

Both women froze, looking at each other as if there might be an ax murderer knocking politely to come in and kill them.

"Who is that?"

"I don't know," said Henri. "I left my X-ray vision glasses at home."

Callie set the mug in the sink. "It must be Will," she said, shuffling toward the door. "They must need me for something across the . . ." But the words fell away as she opened the door to find Sam standing on her porch, holding a suitcase.

Her ability to speak deserted her. All she could do was stare at him, half expecting to blink and find that this was all in her imagination.

"Hi," Sam said, holding the suitcase in a white-knuckled grip.

"Hi." If her heart beat any faster, Callie worried Henri might have to call 911.

"This looks like a good time to pay Yvonne a visit," Henri said, easing past Callie, then around Sam, who didn't move or look away from Callie's face.

"I saw you," Sam said. "By my cabin."

Humiliation washed over her. "Yes, that was me."

Sam shifted. "Why were you there?"

She couldn't admit the truth. Not yet. "Why were you putting that suitcase in your car?"

Looking down, as if he'd forgotten he was holding something, Sam said, "I planned to go somewhere."

"Oh." Of course he was going somewhere. That didn't answer her question at all.

"Can I come in?" Sam asked. "I'd like to tell you where I was going."

If she let him in, it was going to be more difficult to watch him leave again. But her manners kicked in and Callie stepped back. "Sure."

Stepping into the foyer, Sam set the suitcase down next to the boxes she had stacked along the wall. "I see you're going somewhere, too."

"I told you I would be out after the wedding. Henri is here to help me move to another cottage in the village."

"Oh. About that," he said, taking Callie by the hands and pulling her into the living room. He dropped onto her blue chair, tugging until Callie took a seat on the ottoman. "You like this chair a lot, don't you?"

The question took her by surprise. "Yes, I do. It's my favorite piece in the cottage."

"Then you should have it," he said, as if suggesting she pack the chair into her purse.

"But it belongs here."

"Yes, it does." He was talking in circles. Confusing her. "The chair belongs here, and so do you."

Callie hopped to her feet. "I don't understand any of this. You were supposed to tell me where you were going."

"Here," Sam said, rising to his feet. Standing too close for Callie to think. "I was coming here, because this is where you are and I want to be wherever you are, Callie."

"But you said you were leaving Anchor. You're moving back to Charleston." Desperate for space, she put the couch between them. "And I don't want to move back to Charleston."

"Then we won't move."

"What?" *Why did he say "we"?*

"If you want to live on Anchor, then we'll live on Anchor. I've come to realize this place means as much to me as it ever did, with or without Uncle Morty here." Sam circled the couch, catching Callie's hands before she could run again. "I shouldn't have planned a future for us without giving you a say. Without asking what you wanted."

Something warm was spreading through Callie's chest, but her brain still felt muddled.

"You planned a future for us?"

"I was an ass," he said, squeezing her fingers. "I thought I could buy a hotel and we would renovate it together. Make it ours. But I never stopped to ask if that's what you wanted."

"When . . ."

"I tried to tell you the night we made love in the bathtub. I'd started looking for properties earlier that day."

That meant his plan hadn't been because of a baby. He'd wanted her before. He'd wanted *her*.

"No," Callie said, pulling her hands free and pacing into the kitchen. "I don't have anything to give you. I haven't done enough yet. It's not enough."

"What are you talking about?" Sam asked.

"You have everything," Callie said, her voice hitching as she tried not to cry. "You own things. You have money and power." Pounding on her chest, she tried to make him see. "I don't have anything. I married Josh and I had nothing and I tried so hard to be enough, but I couldn't do it. I couldn't make him happy."

"Callie, you're wrong. You're more than enough." Sam took her by the shoulders, forcing her to look at him. "You're the most organized person I've ever met, and an incredible decorator. You see a problem and you solve it before anyone else could even break it apart. You understand people. You see the good and the possibilities in everything."

Cradling her face in his hands, he added, "But more than that, you're beautiful and intelligent. Sexy and determined. And you're the woman I love. The only woman who has ever given me peace and made me feel alive. If anything, I'm not enough for you."

Callie clung to Sam's shirt, desperate to believe him. "Someday you'll change your mind," she said. "And I won't survive it when you do."

Pressing his forehead to hers, Sam said, "I will never, ever change my mind. And I intend to spend the rest of my life making you see how special you are. Callie, you have more to give than I could ever deserve. I love you." He pulled away to look into her eyes. "I *love* you."

Callie wrapped her arms around Sam's waist, holding on for dear life to the man she'd thought she could never have.

"I love you, too, Sam. I love you so much."

Rich laughter rumbled through his chest beneath her ear. "Does that mean I can stay?"

Pulling back, Callie said, "If you make one move for that door, I'll sic Cecil on you."

"Darling," he said, "neither of us is going near that door for several hours." A familiar storm appeared in his eyes. "Maybe not for days."

"I intend to hold you to that promise, Mr. Edwards," Callie said, leading him toward the bedroom. "We have several weeks to make up for."

Stopping in the hall, Sam waited until Callie turned to face him. "I love you, Callie."

"Good," she said, stepping into his arms. "Because I love you, too." After a too-short embrace, Callie jerked back. "But what about that property in Charleston? Are you giving that up for me?"

"I'd give up anything for you," he said, tugging her back. "But in this case, I simply won't be overseeing the renovation in person. It's still a great investment, and I was hoping you might consult on the design."

Callie's face lit up before a sly grin took over. "I don't know," she said. "I've just finished this huge project within a very tight time frame. My stock is higher now, so my services are much more expensive."

He loved hearing the confidence in her voice. "And you're worth every penny. But I assure you, we'll meet any price."

"Then I'll have my people call your people."

Sliding his hands around to the small of her back, he said, "Good. But right now, I believe we were heading somewhere down this hallway."

"Yes, we were." Callie took Sam's hand and led him to the bedroom. They were breathless from kissing before she spoke again. "Are you sure you can be happy here?"

"I can be happy anywhere so long as you're with me. But let's just say that Morty found a way to remind me how much I once loved this island." Sam tucked Callie's hair behind her ear. "That doesn't mean we have to stay here forever, but whatever we decide, we'll do it together."

"As equals?" she asked, a trace of doubt etched around her eyes.

"Not sure I can say that." Callie's face fell, before Sam pressed on. "But I'll do my best to rise to your level, if you'll be patient with me."

His words took several seconds to sink in, but he could see when understanding dawned.

"Now you're just playing with me."

Sam nuzzled her neck. "I'm trying to, but you keep talking."

Callie took his face in her hands, forcing him to meet her gaze. "I want you to be sure. I need to know that you really want this. That you understand what you're getting."

"I'm getting you," he said, touching her nose with his. "What more is there to understand?"

She tilted her head. "That means you get my mother, too."

He hadn't thought of that. Good thing he loved Callie more than anything. "Can we limit how often she visits?"

Ice-blue eyes rolled heavenward. "We can try, but I can't guarantee we'll be successful."

"Are you prepared to meet the great and powerful Eugenia Edwards?" he asked, knowing his mother wasn't such a bargain either.

Callie's nose crinkled. "She isn't going to think I'm good enough for you."

"Then it's a good thing I don't care what she thinks."

With a nod, Callie agreed. "That *is* a good thing."

"But she might surprise you. When I let her know I wouldn't be home for Christmas, she barely made a fuss." Sam rubbed a thumb along Callie's bottom lip. "She might be mellowing in her old age."

Stepping backward, Callie reached the bed and pulled Sam down next to her. "I could turn on my spectacular people skills and win her over," she said, her eyes on Sam's mouth, which made it difficult to focus on what she was saying. "Eventually, she might think of me as the daughter she always wanted."

Sam's body hardened as Callie dropped onto her back. "Can we stop talking about my mother now?" he asked, his body and brain warring over whether to be turned on or utterly disturbed.

Callie laid a hand on his cheek, and her eyes darkened. "How about we stop talking altogether?"

With that, she took his mouth, ending the war with one hot stroke of her tongue. And, as Sam had promised, they spent the next several hours showing each other how much they had to give. Which was more than he'd ever imagined.

EPILOGUE

B loody hell. The little bugger is off again."

Jude Sykes pinched the bridge of his nose as Joe Dempsey chased his rambunctious daughter around the gazebo. As the flower girl, Mary Ann was required to stand still and look pretty for the wedding pictures. Looking pretty, she could do in her sleep. Standing still was another matter altogether for a one-year-old who'd only recently found her legs.

In direct contrast with the runaway pixie, Jacob Littleton, a somber and serious-looking three-year-old, perched calmly on the bottom step of the gazebo, his ring-bearer pillow hugged tight against his chest. Jacob took his duties very seriously, as he did all things. Mary Ann had made him drop the pillow twice already. He was not about to let her do so again.

"Come on, pumpkin," Joe said, settling his daughter next to Jacob, who had to swipe her wayward curls out of his eyes. "Sit pretty for Daddy. Don't you want your picture taken in your fancy dress?"

"Cake!" Mary Ann exclaimed, trying to make a break for it again. This time her daddy kept her in place with one hand on her knee.

"If you sit, you get cake," Joe said, resorting to bribery. "If you get up, no cake."

Mary Ann stuck out a mutinous bottom lip but crossed her arms and stayed put. Joe backed away slowly while the photographer dropped to one knee.

"This is why I don't do weddings," Jude mumbled. "I should charge Will double my wages for this one."

"We signed a contract, Picture Boy," Will Parsons said, stepping up between Callie and the photographer. She made a goofy face at the pouting children, making them both laugh and allowing Jude to land the shot.

"I need the bride and groom," he yelled, as he rose to his feet, examining the kiddie shot. "You didn't tell me there would be children, love."

"It's a wedding," Will said, as Callie waved over her groom. "Kids were a given."

"Not in my world," the Brit mumbled.

"I can't believe how perfect the weather turned out," Callie said, holding a hand over her eyes to dull the glare of sunlight off the harbor. "Last year at this time, there was snow on the ground."

The bride wore a white faux-fur wrap over a stunning, sequined mermaid gown that showed off her figure to perfection and had every man in attendance exceedingly envious of the groom. Not that the groom noticed anyone but the woman taking his hand.

Sam Edwards was a changed man. He'd become a cynic about love, and with good reason, until he'd fallen headlong in love with Calliope Henderson. There were disagreements. Differences of opinion. But Sam had vowed exactly one year ago to show Callie every day that she was more than any man deserved.

And he'd kept that promise. Callie ended many a day with sore cheeks from constant smiling and laughter. If anyone had told her that the stuffy, uptight hotelier who'd tried to terminate her employment before he'd even hired her would become as lighthearted as a child, Callie never would have believed it. But then, Sam was full of surprises.

He'd vowed to give Callie the wedding of her dreams, which was why the event had taken a year to plan. And though planning weddings had become Callie's new profession, Sam had insisted she surrender all the planning to him. Which she'd done, but only once he'd agreed to allow Will, Callie's new boss, to consult.

According to Will, Sam had informed her of his intentions and choices, but she wasn't sure the man understood the meaning of the word *consult*.

As Callie stood in the center of the gazebo she'd helped design, with the sun dancing off the water behind her and all her new friends enjoying the perfect day her new husband had given her, she wouldn't have changed one single thing about the moment.

"Are you happy, Mrs. Edwards?" Sam asked, his smoky gray eyes shining as he held her close against him.

Pretending to straighten his pristine bow tie, she said, "Happier than I ever thought possible." Looking up, Callie couldn't believe this man was her husband. Hers. Forevermore. "There's a latent wedding planner hidden deep inside you, my dear. Maybe you should work with Will and *I* should run the hotels."

Dropping a kiss on her nose, Sam said, "I have no doubt you could run my hotels with little effort, but this is the only wedding I'm ever planning."

"Ever?" Callie said, struggling to hide her smile.

"Ever," Sam said, taking her mouth for a less innocent kiss.

"These are wedding photos," Jude yelled, "not boudoir shots."

The groom reluctantly ended the kiss, but he refused to let so much as a breath of air pass between him and his bride.

"Let's bring in the rest of the wedding party, please," Jude directed, as Will herded her husband, Randy, as well as the flower girl's parents, Joe and Beth Dempsey, onto the gazebo stairs. "Where's the maid of honor?" she asked, looking around for the slender woman with the shock of white-blonde hair.

"Right here," Henri answered, dropping Yvonne's hand and hiking up the hem of her long gown. As she took her place beside her cousin, there was still one person missing.

"We need Lucas." Will scanned the crowd.

"He was with Sid at the dessert table last time I saw them," Beth said.

"I still feel bad that Sid couldn't be in the wedding," Callie mumbled, searching the crowd along with everyone else.

"She was fine with it," Beth said. "I doubt we would have found a dress to cover her belly at this stage of things anyway."

Watching the tiny boat mechanic waddle their way, Callie sighed. "She looks so miserable."

"She is," Beth replied. "But little Pilar will be here any day now, and Sid won't remember any of the misery."

Callie cut her eyes to the curly-haired bridesmaid. "You don't really expect us to believe that."

Keeping her green eyes on Sid, Beth said, "That's my story and I'm sticking with it."

"For fuck's sake," Sid yelled, "I'm fine. Get your scrawny ass up there so they can take the damn picture." With one hand braced on her lower back, Sid shoved her husband toward the gazebo with the other.

"But you said—"

"Don't ruin this for Blondie." Sid shoved again. "Get in the picture."

Seconds later, the party was in place and Jude snapped off a round of shots before a loud wail echoed from the pregnant woman. Bending at the waist, Sid kept a hand on her lower back.

"Not again," Sam said, charging down the steps with the rest of the party. "The limo is waiting out front. It can hold six of you."

"But that's for you guys!" Beth said.

"It's the best option." Sam helped Randy clear a path through the crowd as Lucas fussed around his wife, who was cursing and panting in tandem. "We'll call the hospital to let them know you're on the way."

The Anchor Health Clinic had been upgraded to the Edwards Medical Center, which served as a small but well-equipped hospital, including a full birthing ward, six months before.

Eugenia Edwards approached her son as the pregnancy posse circled the end of the Sunset Harbor Inn. "I say, what in the world is all the commotion?"

"Sid Dempsey has gone into labor," Sam said.

"Right here at your wedding?" Evelyn Henderson asked, a hand pressed to her chest in horror. "How rude to steal my daughter's day."

"Don't be a ninny, Evelyn," Eugenia said. "Babies come when they're ready, not when it's convenient."

Sufficiently silenced, Callie's mother slithered back to her table, and, with a twinkle in her eye, Sam's mother returned to her relatives.

"That's going to be an interesting dynamic," Callie said, leaning against her husband's side.

"I suggest we not put them in the same room too often." As they stood arm in arm on the fringe of the crowd, Sam squeezed his bride. "You want to go, don't you?"

"Would that be a terrible thing to do?" Callie asked, debating whether she could abandon her guests.

"It's our wedding," he said, shuffling Callie toward the end of the building. "They can eat and be merry without us just as well as they can while we're here."

"Have I told you how much I love you?" Callie asked, giggling as she hopped through the damp grass in her ivory pumps.

Sam swept her up into his arms and continued to jog toward the parking lot. "Not in the last five minutes. You can make it up to me by repeating those words for the next sixty years."

"You've got a deal." Callie held on to her veil as Sam dropped her on the passenger seat of his Murano. Minutes later, they pulled into the Edwards Medical Center parking lot, Callie's veil draped across the backseat and Sam's bow tie hung over the rearview mirror.

Less than two hours later, they celebrated the new arrival as Lucas passed out pink bubblegum cigars with a mixture of fear and pride in his eyes.

"That look on his face is killing me," Sam whispered in Callie's ear. "The unflappable lawyer looks scared out of his mind."

"You don't think you'd be scared in his situation?"

Her husband pulled her close. "I'd be the happiest man on Earth," he said, with complete confidence.

"Good," Callie said, dropping a kiss on his cheek. "Because you'll be the one passing out cigars in about seven and a half months."

Tension filled the arms wrapped around her as Sam froze. He didn't look like the happiest man on the planet. In fact, he looked ready to pass out.

"Are you . . . ," he started.

Callie nodded, worried this might not have been the best way to tell her brand-new husband that he was going to be a father.

Sam continued to stare, wide-eyed, as if she'd confessed herself to be from another planet, instead of pregnant. When he did finally react, Sam took Callie completely by surprise.

With one swift movement, he lifted her off her ivory toes and twirled them both in a giant circle. Plopping her back down, he said, "Are you sure?"

"Of course I'm sure," she said, laughing as she caught her breath. "The doctor confirmed it two days ago. I've just been waiting for the right time to tell you."

"We're going to have a baby," he whispered, with awe in his voice. And then, more loudly, "We're going to have a baby!"

Lucas jammed two cigars between Sam's lips as backs were slapped and hugs exchanged. Callie hadn't doubted that Sam would be happy about their impending life change, though she doubted he understood the realities to come. Truth be told, Callie wasn't sure she understood them either, but she had friends who would help her through it.

And the most wonderful husband any woman could ever ask for. Callie sighed as the celebration died down, wondering how she'd ever gotten so lucky, but something told her that all the happiness in this tiny waiting room could be attributed to the ground beneath their feet.

There was something special about Anchor Island, and Callie felt extremely lucky to have landed on her shores.

ACKNOWLEDGMENTS

Writing this book has been both wonderful and bittersweet. I have lived on Anchor Island, at least in my mind, every day since early 2010. I have grown to love all of the characters who inhabit her shores, and I will miss them dearly as I move with enthusiasm and excitement on to new worlds and meet new characters.

As I've mentioned before, Anchor Island is fully and affectionately based on the very real Ocracoke Island, North Carolina. I could never have brought this magical place so clearly to life without the *Ocracoke Island Journal* (http://villagecraftsmen.blogspot.com/), as well as the Village Craftsmen Newsletter (link found on the blog site.) Thank you to Phillip (Mr. Craftsman himself) for sharing everything from current events to personal histories of islanders throughout the years. You brought Ocracoke to life for me, which brought Anchor to life on the page.

Also, thank you to the SeaSide Inn at Hatteras, which was the inspiration for the Sunset Harbor Inn. There's a great photo gallery on the inn's website (www.coverealty.com/seasideinnrates.asp), in which you'll recognize the lovely little hotel that brought Callie and Sam together.

Thank you to Katrina Bunn for the Eton Mess dessert idea, which added a fun layer to Callie's character. I never would have imagined a Brit food–loving heroine without your help. My ever-reliable writing support group—Fran, Marnee, Maureen, Jessica, and Sabrina—pulled me through yet again. I don't know what I would do without them. This book is better for the love and input of the amazing editor Kelli Martin, and none of this would be happening without my agent, Nalini Akolekar.

I must give a special shout-out to all the readers who have visited and returned over and over to Anchor Island. A simple thank-you isn't remotely sufficient to express my gratitude for your willingness to take a chance on a new author, for loving this little island as much as I do, and for making my dreams come true. You have changed and enhanced my life in beautiful ways, and I will never forget that it is you, dear readers, who truly bring these books to life.